YOU ARE REALLY ASLEEP. YOU'RE ONLY DREAMING THAT YOU'RE AWAKE.

Terran Archives 2803:

New York was a city-state or island in the midwestern part of Unistat. It seems to have been a center of religious worship, and many came there to walk about, probably in deep meditation, within an enormous female statue, the goddess of these primitives. Various authorities identify this divinity as Columbia, Marilyn Monroe, Liberty or Mother Fucker—all of these being names widely recorded in Unistat glyphs. Perhaps her true name will never be known.

Books by Robert Anton Wilson

Cosmic Trigger
Schrödinger's Cat: The Universe Next Door

Published by POCKET BOOKS

ROBERT ANTON WILSON

SCHRÖDINGER'S CAT
THE UNIVERSE NEXT DOOR

PUBLISHED BY POCKET BOOKS NEW YORK

Another *Original* publication of POCKET BOOKS

 POCKET BOOKS, a Simon & Schuster division of
GULF & WESTERN CORPORATION
1230 Avenue of the Americas, New York, N.Y. 10020

ISBN: 0-671-82114-8

First Pocket Books printing December, 1979

10   9   8   7   6   5   4   3   2

POCKET and colophon are trademarks of Simon & Schuster.

Printed in the U.S.A.

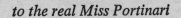

to the real Miss Portinari

CAVEAT LECTOR

The three volumes of the *Schrödinger's Cat* series can be read in any order desired.

That is, this volume can be read before or after the volumes called *The Trick Top Hat* and *The Homing Pigeons,* or between them.

These volumes may also be read before or after the three volumes of the *Illuminatus* trilogy and before or after *Masks of the Illuminati.*

The author wishes to thank Dr. Blake Williams for permission to quote material from his conversation, letters, diaries, etc., intended for publication in Dr. Williams' 12-volume study, *Quantum Physics as a Branch of Primate Psychology.*

Everything here is fiction. There never was a People's Ecology Party or a group of terrorists like P.O.E. The governments of Lousewart and Hubbard are imaginary. There is no missing plutonium, and Einstein, Malik, Bohr, Wildeblood, Chaney and Schrödinger are all imaginary. Statesmen never lie, religious leaders are never thieves and, according to the Buddhists, I invented everything—inside and outside this book.

Some of the questions unanswered in this volume are answered in *The Trick Top Hat* and *The Homing Pigeons.*

There is a glossary at the back for those who find the quantum physics a bit heavy.

CAVE CANEM

SCHRÖDINGER'S CAT

by Robert Anton Wilson

Not until the male becomes female, and the female male, shall ye enter into the Kingdom of Heaven.

—Jesus, *Gospel of Thomas*

POCKET BOOKS
New York 1980

OVERTURE

When Joe Malik decided to give up editing *Confrontation* magazine and write a novel, he was 64-going-on-30 years of age.

That is, Joe had been 64 when he made the decision, but by the time he got completely liberated from *Confrontation* and resettled in Cos Cob, Connecticut, he was approaching 30.

This was because of the FOREVER formula.

Joe had been expecting something like FOREVER, but he was still a bit surprised when it arrived. After his 60th birthday, he had glumly decided it would arrive too late for him. When it appeared in the drugstores a year later, he was one of the first customers.

As soon as he realized that he had a whole new life ahead of him, Joe remembered that he had once wanted to be a novelist, before he learned that he had to earn his money regularly. But that was 2½ wives ago, and his children were grown, and he had f r e e-d o m now.

The colonial home Joe bought in Cos Cob took nearly one-third of his savings, but it was his idea of a place where a writer could write. There was a stream nearby, with ducks; there was a commuter special to take him back to Manhattan when he needed intellectual stimulation; the snow in Connecticut that winter was as white as Tahitian seafoam.

Joe began with only a rough idea: he was going to write a novel about a man writing a novel.

He decided to call his protagonist Robert Anton Wilson. It had a nice ring—WASP at the beginning and end but mysteriously Southeast-European in the middle.

Joe next decided to put Wilson in California, so that

11

he would be in the center of the evolutionary forces transforming the planet.

To raise Wilson's consciousness further, Joe put him in Berkeley, where the real heat is, and let him bake in the crucible of Continuous Revolution. To give him Perspective, Joe put Wilson in a house high in the Berkeley hills where he could look down on four teeming human hives—Berkeley, Oakland, San Francisco and Daly City. He gave him a wife and four children, to make him Work Hard. And he heaped troubles upon Wilson to give him a sense of Irony.

Then he set the writer to work.

Wilson began writing a comedy about quantum physics called *Schrödinger's Cat*.

Unfortunately, he perversely put Malik inside the book, as one of the characters. This rapidly led to confusion: Malik found it disorienting to be inside and outside at the same time.

Worse yet, he began meeting all his friends, and even people he had only encountered briefly, inside the book, but all abominably and perversely *changed* in macabre ways that seemed almost like caricature. And some— including Joe himself—were changed in totally arbitrary ways that verged on surrealism.

He began to think that Wilson had too much Irony, and resented being a character in a novel. He seemed to be trying to take control of the book away from Malik.

And slowly and insidiously, the illusion began to seem real. Joe began to *identify* with his role in the book.

He began to think *Wilson* had created *him*.

He was trapped in his own device.

Take One:

Purity of Essence

The universe is constantly splitting into a stupendous number of branches, all resulting from the measurementlike interactions between its myriads of components. Moreover, every quantum transition taking place on every star, in every galaxy, in every remote corner of the universe, is splitting our local world on earth into myriads of copies of itself.

—Bryce S. DeWitt, "Quantum Mechanics and Reality," *Physics Today*, Sept. 1970

DON'T LOOK BACK

History is a nightmare from which none of us can awaken.

—STEPHEN PROMETHEUS in CARL JUNG'S *Odysseus*

The majority of Terrans were six-legged. They had territorial squabbles and politics and wars and a caste system. They also had sufficient intelligence to survive on that barren boondocks planet for several billions of years.

We are not concerned here with the majority of Terrans. We are concerned with a tiny minority—the domesticated primates who built cities and wrote symphonies and invented things like tic-tac-toe and integral calculus. At the time of our story, these primates regarded themselves as *the* Terrans. The six-legged majority and other life-forms on that planet hardly entered into their thinking at all, most of the time.

The domesticated primates of Terra referred to the six-legged majority by an insulting name. They called them *"bugs."*

There was one species on Terra that lived in very close symbiosis with the domesticated primates. This was a variety of domesticated canines called *dogs*. The dogs loved the primates very much, and each species had learned a great deal by mimicking the other.

The dogs had learned to achieve a rough simulation

14

of *guilt* and *remorse* and *worry* and other domesticated primate characteristics.

The domesticated primates had learned how to achieve simulations of *loyalty* and *dignity* and *cheerfulness* and other canine characteristics.

The primates claimed that they loved the dogs as much as the dogs loved them. Still, the primates kept the best food for themselves. The dogs noticed this, you can be sure, but they loved the primates so much that they forgave them.

One dog became famous. Actually he and she was a group of dogs, but they became renowned collectively as Pavlov's Dog.

The thing about Pavlov's Dog is that he or she or they responded mechanically to mechanically administered stimuli. Pavlov's Dog caused some of the domesticated primates, especially the scientists, to think that all dog behavior was equally mechanical. This made them wonder about other mammals, including themselves.

Most primates ignored this philosophical challenge. They went about their business assuming that they were not mechanical.

The fact that plutonium was missing originally leaked to the press in the mid-1970s. At first, there was a minor wave of panic among those given to worrying about such matters, and there was even some churlish grumbling about a government so incompetent that it couldn't keep track of its own weapons of megadeath.

But then a year passed, and another, and soon five

years had passed, and then nearly a decade; and the missing plutonium was still missing but nothing really drastic had happened.

Terran primates, being a simpleminded, sleepful race, simply stopped worrying about the subject. The triggering mechanism of the most destructive weapon ever devised on that backward planet was in unknown hands, true; but that was really not much more unsettling to contemplate than the fact that many of the known hands which had enjoyed access to plutonium belonged to persons who were not in all respects reasonable men. (See *Terran Archives:* Nixon, Richard Milhous, career of.)

Everybody, of course, remembered the slaughter at the Munich Olympics in 1972, when Black September, a splinter off the Palestine Liberation Front, had shot a lot of innocent athletes and visitors to draw the world's attention to their own complaints; and the Patty Hearst case of 1973; and the assorted diplomats and corporation executives who had been kidnapped or executed by various soreheads. Still, nobody liked to think that groups of that uncouth sort might come into the possession of the now long-lost plutonium, or that such persons might take it into their skulls to use this materiel in an even more messy way than the Unistat government had used it at Hiroshima and Nagasaki. Such thoughts were apt to lead to insomnia, and Terran primates were, after all, a race much inclined to dream and sleep; in fact, one galactic Intelligence Agent who had lived among them for a long time, G. I. Gurdjieff, claimed that Terrans were asleep almost all the time, even when they dreamed they were awake.

The primate philosophy of that epoch was summed up by one of their popular heroes, Mr. Satchel Paige, in the aphorism, "Don't look back—something might be gaining on you." It was a comfortable philosophy for sleep-loving people.

The plutonium was traded and brokered, always at increasing prices.

The majority of primates snoozed on.

The use of atomic weapons was widely blamed on a primate named Albert Einstein. Even Einstein himself had agreed with this opinion. He was a pacifist and had suffered abominable pangs of conscience over what had been done with his scientific discoveries.

"I should have been a plumber," Einstein said just before he died.

Actually the discovery of atomic energy was the result of the work of every scientist, craftsman, engineer, technician, philosopher and gadgeteer who had ever lived on Terra. The use of atomic energy as a *weapon* was the result of all the political decisions ever made, from the time vertebrates first started competing for territory.

Most Terran primates did not understand the multiplex nature of causality. They tended to think everything had a *single* cause. This simple philosophic error was so widespread on that planet that the primates were all in the habit of giving themselves, and other primates, more credit than was deserved when things went well. This made them all inordinately conceited.

They also gave themselves, and one another, more blame than was deserved when things went badly. This gave them all jumbo-sized guilt complexes.

It is usually that way on primitive planets, before quantum causality is understood.

Quantum causality was not understood on Terra until physicists solved the Schrödinger's Cat riddle.

Schrödinger's Cat never became as famous among the primate masses as Pavlov's Dog, but that was because the cat was harder to understand than the dog.

Pavlov's Dog could be understood in simple mechanical metaphors. To understand Schrödinger's Cat you needed to first understand the equations of quantum probability-waves. Only a few primates were smart enough to read the equations, and even they couldn't understand them.

That was because the equations seemed to say that the cat was dead and alive at the same time.

Every character in this book looks like Pavlov's Dog from a certain angle. If you look at him or her a different way, however, you'll see Schrödinger's Cat.

THE HOME CRAFTSMAN

O God I don't care what they say all those intellectuals I'd ask them who made the world if it wasn't God can they answer that of course not God the way his cock felt inside me a long day God and those lovely roses God

—MOLLY BLÜMENKRAFT in CARL JUNG'S *Odysseus*

As early as 1976, a group of Chicago paranoids known as the Nihilist Anarchist Horde (NAH) printed up a single-page broadside on how to manufacture an atomic weapon. They sent this, in envelopes with no return address, to all of the most hostile and embittered individuals and groups in the United States. NAH regarded this mailing as both a joke and a warning, and refused to face the fact that it was also an incitement. If their humor seems tasteless in retrospect, we must remember that the 1970s were a singularly schizoid and violent decade.

NAH had already put out bumper stickers saying things like:

REGISTER CAPITALISTS, NOT GUNS

and:

HONK IF YOU'RE ARMED

and:

EAT THE RICH

And they even had a rubber stamp which they used to decorate subway advertisements with the Nihilistic message: ARM THE UNEMPLOYED: RIOT IN THE LOOP ON NEW YEAR'S EVE.

But they really outdid themselves with the build-your-own atomic weapon sheet, which was titled "Hobbysheet #4" and looked like this:

HOBBYSHEET #4 in a series of 30. Collect 'em all!
A SIMPLE ATOMIC BOMB FOR
THE HOME CRAFTSMAN

There is nothing complex about an Atomic (or Fission) Bomb. If enough fissionable material Uranium 235 or Plutonium 239 is brought together to form a critical mass it will explode. The trick is to put the pieces together fast enough to get a decent blast before the bomb blows itself apart. This can be done quite simply by means of ordinary explosive as shown below.

19

It was later estimated that the Nihilist Anarchist Horde, most of whom were living on Welfare, were able to mail out only 200,000 of these over the four-year period (1976–1980) before they grew bored with the project. At the mail rates of the time, this cost them collectively $26,000, and only the fact that many of them were "parlaying" (receiving welfare checks from several states simultaneously) enabled them to afford it.

Nonetheless, many of the equally paranoid and hostile persons who received this mailing had access to Xerox machines and were as desperate as the members of NAH itself. It was later determined that by 1981 there were over 10,000,000 copies of "Hobbysheet #4" in circulation. Eventually one of them reached the P.O.E. group, who were ready for an idea like that.

The planet as a whole continued to drowse.

Nihilism had been invented in Russia in the nineteenth century. It was a philosophy based on materialism, skepticism and a fierce demand for social justice. Naturally, various deranged individuals quickly made it an excuse for violence, and Nihilism became a synonym for horror.

Anarchism was similar. It had been invented in France in the nineteeth century and was also based on materialism, skepticism and a fierce demand for social justice. It attracted the same types as Nihilism and also quickly acquired a bad reputation.

The Nihilist Anarchist Horde believed that they had chosen that name to refurbish the sane, sound side of Nihilism and Anarchism. Actually, they were kidding themselves. They really enjoyed having a name that scared the bejesus out of everybody.

ALTERNATIVE TEXTS

That is precisely what common sense is for, to be
jarred into uncommon sense.

—ERIC TEMPLE BELL,
Mathematics: Queen of the Sciences

GALACTIC ARCHIVES:

The original title of the greater part of what we have
collected in this book under the title *Schrödinger's Cat*
was *The Universe Next Door*. The book of that name
was begun as a sequel to *Illuminatus!,* but after several
editors in a row suffered psychotic breakdowns while
reading it, publishers defensively ordered that any ms.
with that title, from Robert Anton Wilson, should be
returned unopened. Xerox copies thereafter circulated
among Wilson's admirers in the Houston area of Texas
(the region now called West Mexico). Outside these
occult circles, nobody ever heard of it.

"People generally do not want a new form of prose
fiction to replace the hackneyed 'novel,' " Wilson wrote
in a letter to his friend, Malaclypse the Younger. "There
never has been a serious attempt since *Odysseus.*" He
was deliberately ignoring *Illuminatus!,* which he regarded (in the truncated form published by Bell*) as

---

* In those primitive times capitalist "owners" of the print
media exploited authors just as mercilessly as the capitalist
"owners" of factories exploited the workers. Wilson never forgave Bell for cutting 500 pages from *Illuminatus!,* and graffiti
saying, "The book industry is a publisher's heaven and a writer's
hell," found all over California, are attributed by some to this
ancient Bard.

a species of catastrophe or the literary equivalent of a five-car freeway accident.

Schrödinger's Cat Fair Copy #2, according to Wilson scholars, incorporates later and still more bizarre material, the text of which was allegedly dictated to Wilson by a canine intelligence—"vast, cool and unsympathetic"—from the system of the Dog Star, Sirius. *Schrödinger's Cat Fair Copy #3* appeared much later, in 2031, under mysterious circumstances. Some claimed, at the time, that it had been received by a trance medium to whom Wilson had "broadcast" it after his melodramatic departure from this world in 1993. Skeptics have always insisted that the alleged medium actually found it in an old Tampon box in her attic. A legend about the manuscript being recovered from the Masonic Auditorium in San Francisco, after the earthquake of 2005, and passed around among adepts of certain occult groups, is probably mythical.

Various alternative texts, generally considered forgeries, have circulated at intervals and many Wilson scholars debate heatedly whether this final ms. is, in fact, totally or even in major part Wilson's work. That two authors at least are here represented, often at cross-purposes with each other, is the emerging academic consensus at this time.

The present edition incorporates all material that is undoubtedly Wilson's, together with matter of such a Wilsonian and weird character that the present editor regards it as probably-Wilson's-within-reasonable-doubt.

It only remains to affirm that *Schrödinger's Cat,* contrary to appearances, is not a mere "routine" or "shaggy shoggoth story." Despite his sinister reputation and his well-known eccentricities, Wilson was one of the last of the scientific shamans of the primitive, terrestrial phase of the cruel, magnificent Unistat Empire. This may be hard to understand when many Establishment scholars still deny that anything like scientific shamanism existed in the 20th Century, but it is nevertheless well documented that Wilson, Leary, Lilly, Crowley, Castaneda and many others pursued rigorous studies in scientific shamanic research even under the persecution of the "neurological police" so characteristic of that barbaric epoch.* Some have even proposed that *Schrödinger's Cat* is actually a manual of shamanism in the form of a novel, but that opinion is, almost certainly, exaggerated.

ONE MONTH TO GO

Immature humorists borrow; mature humorists steal.

—MARK TWAIN

On December 1, 1983, Benny "Eggs" Benedict, a popular columnist for the New York† *News-Times-Post,* sat down to compose his daily essay. According to his usual procedure, he breathed deeply, relaxed every muscle and gradually forced all verbalization in his

* See the Editor's "Clandestine Neurotransmitter Research Under the Holy Inquisition and the D.E.A.," *Archives of General Archeology,* Vol. 23, No. 17. The alleged rebuttal by Professor Jubelo in the following issue is arrant obscurantism.

† *Galactic Archives:* New York was an independent city-state in the northwest of Unistat. It was noted for its malodorous stockyards, its vast motion-picture industry and a huge phallic monument dedicated to "Washington," a fertility god who allegedly slept in nearly every part of Unistat, usually with human women, bringing forth such semi-divine progeny as the gigantic Paul Bunyan, the patriotic General Motors, the trickster-god Nixon and the benign Mickey Mouse, who began as a totem of the city of Disneyland and eventually became the principal divinity of all Unistat.

brain to stop. When he had reached the void, he waited to see what would float up to fill the vacuum. What surfaced was:

One month to go to 1984.

Benny looked at the calendar; what happened next would be portrayed by a cartoonist as a light bulb flashing on over his head. He began pounding the typewriter, comparing the actual situation of the world with Orwell's fantasy.

His column, headed "One Month to Go," was read by nearly 10,000,000 people, the *News-Times-Post* being the only surviving daily paper available to the 20,000,000 citizens of the six boroughs of New York City. Nine million of the 10,000,000 readers were a little bit paranoid, this being the natural ecological result of crowding that many primates into such a congested space, and most of them agreed with the most pessimistic portions of Benedict's estimation of Orwell's accuracy as a prophet.

"One month to go to 1984" became a catch-phrase to conclude or answer anybody's complaint about anything. "One month to go to 1984"—soon you heard it everywhere; it reached Chicago by December 10, San Francisco by December 14, was even quoted in Bad Ass, Texas, on December 16.

By December 23, the London *Economist* printed a very scholarly article on world history from 1949, when Orwell's book was published, to the present, enumerating dozens of parallels between Orwell's fiction and the planet's nightmare.

In Paris a prominent Existentialist, in an interview with *Paris Soir,* argued that living inside a book, even a book by an English masochist like Orwell, was better than living in reality. "Art has meaning but reality has none," he said cheerfully.

24

The following day, the twelve remaining Surrealists ritually hanged the Existentialist in effigy for the "heresy," as they called it, of implying a distinction between reality and imagination. They even issued a press release denouncing the very idea that there was such a thing as reality. " 'Reality' is a concept," they said, "which psychiatrists, grocers, Logical Positivists and other imbeciles have borrowed from mysticism, and the mystics being bankrupt are in no position to loan anything to anybody."

The six-legged majority on Terra were never consulted when the domesticated primates set about building weapons that could destroy all life-forms on that planet. This was not unusual. The fish, the birds, the reptiles, the flowers, the trees and even the other mammals weren't allowed to vote on this issue. Even the wild primates weren't involved in the decision to produce such weapons. In fact, the majority of domesticated primates themselves never had a say in the matter.

A handful of *alpha males* among the leading predator bands among the domesticated primates had made the decision on their own. Everybody else on the planet—including the six-legged majority, who had never been involved in primate politics—just had to face the consequences.

Most of the domesticated primates of Terra did not know they were primates. They thought they were something apart from and "superior" to the rest of the planet.

Even Benny Benedict's "One Month to Go" column was based on that illusion. Benny had actually read Darwin once, in college a long time ago, and had heard of sciences like ethology and ecology, but the facts of evolution had never really registered on him. He never thought of himself as a primate. He never realized his friends and associates were primates. Above all, he never understood that the *alpha males* of Unistat were typical leaders of primate bands. As a result of this inability to see the obvious, Benny was constantly alarmed and terrified by the behavior of himself, his friends and associates and especially the alpha males of the pack. Since he didn't know it was ordinary primate behavior, it seemed *just awful* to him.

Since a great deal of primate behavior was considered just awful, most of the domesticated primates spent most of their time trying to conceal what they were doing.

Some of the primates *got caught* by other primates. All of the primates lived in dread of getting caught.

Those who got caught were called *no-good shits*.

The term no-good shit was a deep expression of primate psychology. For instance, one wild primate (a chimpanzee) taught sign language by two domesticated primates (scientists) spontaneously put together the signs for "shit" and "scientist" to describe a scientist she didn't like. She was calling him shit-scientist. She also put together the signs for "shit" and "chimpanzee"

for another chimpanzee she didn't like. She was calling him shit-chimpanzee.

"You no-good shit," domesticate primates often said to each other.

This metaphor was deep in primate psychology because primates mark their territories with excretions, and sometimes they threw excretions at each other when disputing over territories.

One primate wrote a long book describing in vivid detail how his political enemies should be punished. He imagined them in an enormous *hole* in the ground, with flames and smoke and rivers of shit. This primate was named Dante Alighieri.

Another primate wrote that every primate infant goes through a stage of being chiefly concerned with bio-survival, i.e. food, i.e. Mommie's Titty. He called this the Oral Stage. He said the infant next went on to a stage of learning mammalian politics, i.e. recognizing the Father (alpha-male) and his Authority and territorial demands. He called this, with an insight that few primates shared, the Anal Stage.

This primate was named Freud. He had taken his own nervous system apart and examined its component circuits by periodically altering its structure with neuro-chemicals.

Among the anal insults exchanged by domesticated primates when fighting for their space were: "Up your ass," "Go shit in your hat," "You're full of shit," "Take it and stick it where the moon doesn't shine," and many others.

One of the most admired alpha-males in the Kingdom of the Franks was General Canbronne. General Canbronne won this adulation for the answer he once gave when asked to surrender.

"Merde," was the answer General Canbronne gave.

The word *petard* means a kind of bomb. It comes from the same Olde English root as *fart*.

General Canbronne's mentality was typical of the alpha males of the military caste.

When primates went to war or got violent in other ways, they always said they were about to *knock the shit* out of the enemy.

They also spoke of *dumping* on each other.

The primates who had mined Unistat with nuclear bombs intended to dump on the other primates real hard.

BOSTON CREAM PIE

Consciousness is an electrochemical function of the nervous system. Insert a new chemical into the brain and consciousness changes radically.

—SIGMUND FREUD, *The Politics of Ecstasy*

Benny Benedict's entire philosophy of life had been shaped by an obscene novel, a murder and a Boston Cream Pie.

The novel was called *Odysseus* and the most shocking thing about it, aside from the searing indecency of its language, was that it had been written by a famous theologian, Rev. Carl Gustav Jung of Zurich, Switzerland. Nobody had known what to make of the book when it was first published, except to fulminate against it. The story, in fourteen chapters, recounted fourteen hours in a very ordinary day as some staggeringly ordinary characters wandered about Zurich on extraordinarily ordinary business. When Jung revealed that the fourteen chapters corresponded to the fourteen Stations of the Cross, conservative critics added blasphemy to their charges against him. Later—much later —academic exegetes adopted *Odysseus* as the very model of a modern novel and wrote endless studies proving that it was an allegory on everything from the evolution of consciousness to the rise and fall of civilizations.

Benny couldn't understand much of what these academic critics wrote, but he knew that *Odysseus* was, to him, the only book that really succeeded in making the daily seem profound. That was enough of an achievement to convince him that Jung was a genius. It also encouraged him to look at everything that happened as being marvelous in one way or another. If Jung's characters, or some of them, happened to defecate, urinate, masturbate and fornicate during the fourteen hours, that was not because the theologian was trying to write pornography, but because the miracle of daily life could not be shown without all of its daily details. Benny didn't give a flying Philadelphia fuck about the novel's parallels with the *Odyssey* and the Stations of the Cross, which Jung admitted, or the other correspondences with body organs, colors, Tarot cards, *I Ching* hexagrams and the romantic triangle in *Krazy Kat,* which his admirers claimed to have found. The important thing about *Odysseus* was that it demonstrated, almost scientifically, that no day was a dull day.

Jung, who regarded himself as a better psychologist than the psychologists—this was a conceit typical of theologians—claimed to have found three more circuits in the nervous system beyond Freud's oral bio-survival circuit and anal emotional-territorial circuit. Jung said that *Odysseus* demonstrated also a semantic-hominid circuit which created a veil of words between domesticated primates and their experience, thereby differentiating them from the wild primates. He also claimed a specific socio-sexual circuit created by the process of domestication. And he added a fifth, neurosomatic circuit typical of mysticism and music, which causes primates to feel High and spaced-out.

But Benny didn't care about all that. *Odysseus,* in his mind, was simply the book that described life the way it really is, without sentiment and emotions.

The murder changed all that. It showed Benny that every day is also a terrible day, for somebody.

On July 23, 1981, Benny's mother, a white-haired old lady of 84, left the Brooklyn Senior Citizen's Home where she lived to walk one block to the supermarket.

On the way she had her purse snatched and, according to witnesses, struggled with the thief. She was stabbed seventeen times with a Boy Scout knife. When Benny arrived at the hospital emergency room, she was already dead, but he got a look—a long look—at her crimson, mutilated body before the doctor on duty hustled him out into the hall and shot him full of tranquilizer.

Benny was crippled psychologically in a way that he could not perfectly understand. After all, having reached the fifth decade of his life, he was well acquainted with grief: in the past ten years he had experienced the deaths of his father, his older brother and three close friends. But murder is not just another form of grief: it is a metaphysical message like Fate knocking on the door at the beginning of Beethoven's *Fifth*. Benny found that the whole world had turned to very fragile glass. Every police siren, every newscast, every angry voice on the street reminded him that he belonged to a dangerously violent species. Benny Benedict realized that each minute, somewhere in the world, somebody was being bashed, beaten, stabbed, shot, slashed, gassed, poisoned, robbed of life.

He could not bear to be alone at night anymore.

The Grinning Sadist began to haunt him.

This horrifying image had been imprinted upon his neurons by various movies and TV melodramas of the '60s and '70s. The Grinning Sadist invaded your home, sometimes alone and sometimes with a horde of equally moronic and vicious cohorts. You were particularly susceptible if you were blind or a woman or all alone at night, but sometimes—as in *The Dangerous Hours*—he would come with his brutal crew in the bright daytime. His business was never simply burglary, although that was part of it; his real interest was in humiliation, terror, degradation, torture of the body and spirit. And he always *grinned*.

Benny's doctor prescribed Valium, 5 mg. before bed-

31

time. It helped Benny sleep; but when he was awake, every noise still sounded like the Grinning Sadist furtively trying the door.

Benny bought a police lock. Every noise now sounded like the Grinning Sadist trying to force a window.

Then, one day looking through the old files in the newspaper morgue, Benny found an interview with Senator Charles Percy given in 1970, two years after the murder of his daughter. "For the first year after the murder," Senator Percy said, "my whole family lived in terror."

Benny felt a sudden sense of relief. This must be normal, he thought; it happens to everybody who's had a murder close to them. And it only lasts a year. . . .

But as July 23, 1982, approached, Benny was not emerging from the terror; it was growing worse. Well, he had been reading up on grief and bereavement, and he knew the first anniversary is always a terrible time. He found the knowledge helpful; it gave him a small purchase on detachment. Also, without his doctor's consultation, he had raised his Valium dosage at bedtime from 5 mg. to 15 mg. and sometimes 25.

Then on July 23 itself—the anniversary of the murder—the Grinning Sadist appeared.

Benny had been invited to give a talk at the Press Club on "Lousewart and Lowered Expectations." The luncheon was excellent, but Benny ate little, knowing that a belch in the middle of the speech could destroy all communication for several minutes after. When Fred "Figs" Newton began to introduce him (. . . "New York's most beloved daily columnist . . . an institution for over thirty years . . ."), Benny felt the usual twinges of stage fright, began rehearsing again his first three jokes, gave up on that and concentrated instead on his mantra *(Om mani padme hum Om mani padme hum . . .)* and was finally in the ideal state of mixed apprehension and urgency out of which the most relaxed-sounding public speeches always come.

As the applause died down, he rose to speak.

And he saw the Grinning Sadist coming right at him.

He saw the deranged eyes, the cruel mouth, the deliberately ugly clothing (like a very poor cowboy or a 1960s college student) and the *knife* in the maniac's hand.

Om mani padme hum . . .

And then he got the Boston Cream Pie right in the face.

It hadn't been a knife at all: he had imagined a knife when the pieplate was turned and raised as it was thrown.

Benny stood there, very conscious that he was overweight and past fifty, Boston Cream Pie dripping from his face, trying to remind himself that heart palpitations were not a symptom of heart attack, aware suddenly that the daily life of humankind was not only marvelous, as Jung had taught him, and terrible, as the murder had taught him, but totally absurd as well, as the Existentialists might have taught him.*

---

* *Galactic Archives:* Pie throwing was common in Unistat at the time of this Romance. It derived, of course, from the territorial feces-hurling rituals of other primates. See "Expressions of Violence in Wild and Domesticated Primates," *Encyclopedia of Primate Psychology,* Sirius Press, 2775. Domesticated primates defend Ideological territories (mental constructs) as well as the physical turf. Pie-throwers were expressing mammalian territorial rage in a traditional primate manner by throwing guck in the faces of those who threatened their ideological "space."

THE UNIVERSE NEXT DOOR

2 NEW PLANETS DISCOVERED

—NEWS HEADLINE, 1983

The big issue in Unistat at that time was *The Universe Next Door,* not Benny Benedict's personal griefs. Everybody had a violent opinion about it, especially those who hadn't read it.

Which was the majority.

Most people hadn't read *The Universe Next Door* because it had been banned, and the ban had been upheld by the Supreme Court.

The most terrible things were whispered about this forbidden book. It was said that everybody saw themselves in it, but in a ghastly and shocking way. It was also rumored that many who read it went insane, committed suicide, became Republicans or sinners or just *simply disappeared.*

Of course, everybody wanted a copy of such a shocker, and there were at least half a dozen works on the black market claiming to be the suppressed *Universe Next Door.* Different people naturally had different opinions about which, if any, of these was genuine. Some said that every copy of the original had been burned and that *all* the underground printings were forgeries. Others, however, insisted that a real edition was available among the forgeries and that those who found it were either illuminated or eliminated.

Benny Benedict had read two alleged copies of the infamous text. He hadn't found himself in it and he hadn't gone mad.

He thought the whole thing was a hoax.

AUFGEHOBEN

What I am proposing is a sixth neurological circuit
beyond those discovered by Freud and Jung. I call this
the metaprogramming circuit.

—MARILYN CHAMBERS, *Neuro-Anthropology*

The only one in New York who didn't react emotionally
to Benny Benedict's "One Month to Go" column was
Justin Case, an embittered, fortyish man who wrote
beautifully meaningless film criticism. Case had not
liked the film of *1984* and never read books, which he
regarded as too old-fashioned to be worthy of serious
attention.

"Books were invented by Gutenberg in the fifteenth
century and are, like all other inventions five centuries
old, hopelessly archaic," Case often said.

He also liked to categorize books as "linear," "Aris-
totelian," and, when he was especially rhetorical, "paleo-
lithic"; he justified this last adjective on the grounds
that books consisted of *words,* an Old Stone Age in-
vention.

Case had a Ph.D. from Yale and a D.D. (Dishonor-
able Discharge) from the U.S. Army. He had earned
the former for a thesis on "Metaphor and Myth in the
Films of the Three Stooges" and the latter for trying
to organize a mutiny during the Vietnam War. His film
criticism appeared in a journal called *Confrontation.*
His essays usually began with the same three words as
his Ph.D. thesis—*e.g.,* "Metaphor and Myth in Hitch-
cock's *39 Steps,*" "Metaphor and Myth in *Beach Blanket Bingo*"; that sort of thing. Opening his anthology,

35

From Caligari to Vlad, at any page, you were likely to encounter something like this:

> In Fay Wray, however, we find the White Goddess appearing in her form as Eternal Virgin, and the jealous father-dragon image becomes the giant ape, Kong, who is also, as Wilson pointed out in *Journal of Human Relations,* Summer 1970, a symbol of capitalist competition, as well as being the *aufgehoben* of the Freudian Id.

There was not much of an audience for that kind of writing and Justin barely made a living. His dream was to become an editor at *Pussycat* magazine, where the big money was.

The F.B.I. had been tapping his phone ever since Vietnam and had reels and reels of his conversation, which concerned almost nothing but films. Nevertheless, they kept listening, hoping something incriminating would slip eventually. A man with both a Ph.D. and a D.D. was obviously worth attention, even if most of what he said was totally incomprehensible to them.

Special Agent Tobias Knight, playing Case's tapes one evening, actually heard a long rap about Curly being the id or first circuit, Larry the ego or second circuit and Moe the super-ego or Jung's fourth circuit. Things got even more confusing when Case went on to talk about the "cinematic continuity in the S-M dimension between Moe and Polanski." It got even weirder when Case said, "Polanski himself went to Chinatown three times—when his parents were murdered by the Nazis, when his wife was murdered by the Manson Family and when he got convicted of statutory rape. We all go to Chinatown, one way or another, sooner or later." Still, the Bureau did not give up. Case was sure to say something incriminating, or at least intelligible to them, sooner or later.

Tobias Knight had listened to 42,000 hours of "private" conversations since joining the F.B.I. Among other things, this had clearly shown him that all the standard primate sexual behaviors were prevalent throughout Unistat. Since Knight, like Benny Benedict and most other two-legged Terrans, did not know he belonged to a mammal species, this primate behavior was profoundly shocking to him. He felt much like a Methodist who runs a drugstore in Little Rock— anguished that the Sins of his fellows were only exceeded by their Hypocrisy. This made him Cynical.

The same Cynicism was widespread in the Bureau. Older hands who had listened to 80,000 or even 100,000 hours of "private" conversations were beyond Cynicism. They had become paranoid about their fellow primates.

This was because they did not know they were primates.

Tobias Knight himself would be classified as a no-good shit by most of the primates if they knew what he was up to. He was the first pentuple agent in the history of espionage—that is, he had connections with four other Intelligence Agencies besides the F.B.I. and was double-crossing all of them.

He also had a walrus mustache and a jovial eye. He could have been an excellent character actor in movies or TV. Everybody liked him and trusted him on sight.

That was why he was so successful in the cloak-and-dagger business.

Justin Case suspected that the F.B.I. was tapping his phone. However, 9,000,000 out of the 20,000,000 primates in New York also suspected the F.B.I. of tapping their phones. Case just happened to be one of the 8,000,000 who were correct in this suspicion.

Case was certainly not a mutineer by temperament; his visual cortex—the most energized part of him—was neurogenetically imprinted with a dry, detached, analytical, almost passive, temperament. His world was made up of forms in space, edited into amusing montages by the passing of time; if he ever read books, he might have found that Einstein's Relativity was the mathematical analog of his own mind.

Even paintings barely won his tolerance; only film and TV, basically montage, turned him on. He was inclined to feel that anything which did not flicker, shimmer and change rapidly was probably dead and should be decently and quickly buried.

In short, he was an electronic Taoist.

The Vietnam War had been punishing in various ways to all Unistaters, but Case, embroiled in the center of it, experienced it as very bad TV. It was like the film had stuck and Moe kept jabbing his finger in Curly's eye, over and over, in an infinite regress, until the myth and metaphor had both turned meaningless through redundance. If the war wasn't that, it was sloppy editing or just plain *bad taste*. The mutiny was the only equivalent he could find to the simple act of turning the dial to another channel.

He had tried to explain this to the lieutenant appointed to defend him at the court-martial, a sly, cat-faced young man named Lionel Eacher. Lieutenant Eacher, before entering the service, had been an expert at Contract Law, the rules by which the primates determined and marked their territories. Remember:

38

other mammals do this by leaving excretions which geometrically define the size and shape of the claimed turf, but domesticated primates do it by excreting ink on paper. Eacher was a lawyer, an expert at proving either that the ink-excretions meant what they said (if he were being paid to prove that) or that the ink-excretions didn't *exactly* mean what they said (if he were being paid to prove that). He was, of course, an Agnostic.

Lionel Eacher listened to Case's story with growing incredulity. At the end of the narrative, he frowned very thoughtfully and said, "Would you just run that by me again?"

So Case had explained, this time in more detail, the esthetics of proper utilization of sado-masochist material in the total structure of Significant Form.

"I see," Eacher said thoughtfully. "I think we've got a winner." He relaxed and lit a cigarette. "The usual defense is that you were reading the Bible and saw a white light and Jesus told you to give up war. If you play that one right, they think you're a real nut and you might get off with five years and a D.D. But this, well, this is beautiful. You sound like a real fruitcake. I might even get you a medical discharge."

Case realized that he was talking to a barbarian; but that was normal in the military. He had an intuitive sense that 20 years in the joint, which was what the Judge Adjutant General's office was asking, would be even more redundant, in the S-M dimension, than the war itself. Very well: if a man of esthetic sensibility seemed like a fruitcake to these primitives, so be it. He wanted to go home.

Case explained his position to the court-martial with great eloquence (part of what he said he even used later in a critique of *The Rocky Horror Show*) and they did, indeed, decide he was a fruitcake. They gave him a D.D., but two members of the board, he learned later, had argued vigorously for a medical.

When he got back to New York, he found that some regarded him as a political hero. That was embarrassing, but he learned to live with it. The human race, he wearily realized, just did not think of esthetics *seriously* and was perpetually absorbed in moralistic and ideological diversions.

The Vietnam War, like most primate squabbles, was about territory. Chinese primates, Unistat primates, the primates of the Bear Totem from the steppes and various local Southeast Asian primates were trying to expand their collective-totem egos (territories) by taking over the turf in Southeast Asia. If they had been wild primates, they would have all excreted in the disputed area and maybe thrown excretions at each other; being domesticated primates, they made ink-excretions on paper and threw metal and chemicals at each other. It was one of a series of rumbles over Southeast Asia which had at one time or another involved Dutch primates, French primates, primates of the Rising Sun totem and various other predator bands.

Since the Unistat primates, like other domesticated hominids, did not know they were primates, all this was explained by a ferocious amount of ink-excretions invoking Morality and Ideology, the twin gods of domesticated primatedom. Basically, the primates who wanted to claim Southeast Asia said it was "good" to go in shooting and grab whatever was grabable; the primates who didn't give a fuck about Southeast Asia said it was "evil."

Justin Case was not verbally oriented; he thought in

pictures, as a good film critic should. He never asked whether the war was "good" or "evil." It was unesthetic.

The people who had mined Unistat with nuclear bombs had not regarded the Vietnam War as unesthetic. They thought it was downright evil.

They thought just about everything the Unistat alpha males—in corporations and governments—did was evil.

They thought most of their fellow primates were *no-good shits*.

Justin Case had been born blissfully by a joyous mother schooled in the Grantly Dick-Read method of natural childbirth.

By the time Justin was 36 years old, in 1983, the Dick-Read method was as obsolete as the horse and buggy. Things were moving fast on Terra in that age.

Nonetheless, the Dick-Read natural childbirth yoga was good for its time, and Case had a permanent security imprint on the oral bio-survival circuitry of his brain. That was one reason he never worried about ethical issues.

When Justin began to crawl about the house and then rose up to walk up and down in it, his father, a former alpha male with a large corporation now on the skids due to booze, found him a pest and a nuisance. Father disappeared rapidly, pursued by lawsuits and child maintenance liens, which harassed him so much that he drank even more, earned less and was first chronically and then permanently incapable of paying a blessed penny to Justin and Justin's Mommy.

Justin was not genetically programmed to be an alpha male, but under the circumstances he learned to do a good imitation of one.

"Mommy's Great Big Man," Mommy called him.

The anal-territorial (old primate) section of Justin's brain took an imprint of Pretend-Authority.

Then Justin discovered the *semantic* environment. He learned to read and watch TV. The books seemed clumsy and sententious compared to the immediacy of the tube. He took a visual-electronic imprint on the semantic circuit, like most of his generation.

Case's socio-sexual circuit was imprinted by *Playboy,* Sexual Revolution, weed, Rock, yippies, protest, the Generation Gap, Women's Lib, and General Confusion. He was a bachelor who had heterosexual couplings as often as he felt the need, with the minimum possible human involvement.

If you're interested in superficialities, he looked like a gay intellectual or a college professor or a little bit of both. He already had a bald spot. He dressed in conservative good taste. And every four years he went to a polling booth and carefully printed with a heavy felt-tip pen: "NONE OF THE ABOVE."

This was his one flicker of Social Consciousness.

Case had one Weird Experience in his whole life. It happened in 1973 when he went to see the famous mentalist, psychic, escape artist and comedian, Cagliostro the Great, at a nightclub called Von Neumann's Catastrophe.

Cagliostro began his act with a few traditional tricks —being locked in one box and then re-appearing out of another at the opposite side of the room, that kind of routine. This was followed by one of his bitingly sarcastic monologues about the tricksters in other professions, such as the clergy and the government. This was all as Case had expected from the Most Controversial Magician in Show Biz history. Then came the psychic stunts, which were sometimes frighteningly impressive.

"B. W.," Cagliostro called out. "Will you please stand up?" Case saw that unbearable bore, Blake Williams, standing at a ringside table.

"B. W.," Cagliostro repeated, "you will never finish your twelve-volume study of quantum psychology. Not ever, in this universe. The twitches in your leg from the polio can be cured by Valerian Root tea. The incident at the Vandivoort Street incinerator is still haunting you. Your investments are all wrong—there's no future in space industry. And as for Project Pan, Doctor—Project *Pan*—naughty, naughty, naughty!"

Case could see that Williams had turned pale.

"J. C.," Cagliostro called out suddenly, "don't stand. This is private." Justin Case squirmed, half-afraid, half-skeptical, totally vulnerable. "J. C.," Cagliostro repeated, "you have created this movie that you call reality. Stay out of Chinatown. . . .

"S. M.," the magician went on, "S. M., about the Beast, now . . . that's in your future. . . ."

It was the only Weird Experience in Case's life, and he tried his damnedest to forget it.

If only people didn't keep spreading that rumor that Cagliostro was in reality, not in pretense, a Black Magician.

TO RECROSS IS NOT TO CROSS

That is to say, if it is intended to cross a boundary and then it is intended to cross it again, the value indicated by the two intentions taken together is the value indicated by none of them.

—G. SPENCER BROWN, *Laws of Form*

ARCHIVES OF GENERAL PSYCHIATRY, JUNE 2003:

The supreme value of *Schrödinger's Cat,* of course, is that Wilson's narcissism and megalomania lead him to exhibit boldly what other schizophrenics hide in the language of disinformation. We see, from the earliest pages, that the author was suffering from sexual identity problems, homosexual panic, delusions of grandeur and rabid misogyny. Even where he attempts to disguise his tracks by lapsing into typical schizoid gibberish, the meaning is clear to the trained clinical observer. It does not take much insight to recognize the homosexual obsession in reducing patriotism to anality, the castration anxieties invoked in the *"Eggs"* Benedict story, the schizophrenic split in the Bacon-Shakespeare symbolism, the fear of judgment (detection) in the caricature of the F.B.I. What we have here, in short, is the typical product of the paranoid degeneration of a middle-aged male confronted with impotence. That so many allegorical and occult interpretations are fashionable in literary circles merely demonstrates that laypersons, however educated in their own field, cannot diagnose mental illness as we professionals can.

P.O.E.

Quoth the Raven, "Nevermore."

—POE

In July 1968, immediately after the Democratic Convention, held behind barbed wire to prevent the people from interfering in their own affairs, a letter appeared in *The Seed,* a Chicago radical newspaper. The letter said:

Brothers and Sisters:
The final struggle is upon us. The pig racist-imperialist forces that control Amerika have taken off their fake "liberal" mask and shown their true fascist nature. Look at the record: the assassinations of John and Bobby and Martin Luther King. The unending war against the people of Vietnam. The brutalities of the local police, right on television with the whole world watching, during the recent Demokratic Convention. Is it not obvious that the multinational corporations no longer even care to pretend that democracy still exists and are ready to kill us to the last man and woman if we continue to resist?

Weather Underground has chosen the wrong path, romantically allowing themselves to be known and defying the authorities to catch them. They will be caught, of course—every one of them. Their heroism is exemplary, but their revolutionary theory is simpleminded and hopeless.

We of P.O.E. have organized quietly. Our numbers are not for publication, nor our identities. We will not take "credit" for our actions, unlike the Weather romantics. We will not recruit new members. We will send no further communiqués to the press. We will work and study to strike the most crippling blows possible against the fascist monster.

If you agree with us, do not seek to find us and join us. Do as we have done. Form your own affinity group among people you trust. Work and study to learn what blow you can strike, how to get away safely, and how to strike again.

Peace On Earth.

John Brown

Some readers of *The Seed* thought this was a put-on. Others claimed it was the work of an F.B.I. *agent provocateur*. A few wondered if P.O.E. actually existed, and what it would do.

Everybody, of course, assumed that the initials P.O.E. stood for the slogan in the last line of the letter— "Peace On Earth." They were wrong. P.O.E. stood for "purity of essence." The group had deliberately taken as their model General Jack D. Ripper in the film, *Dr. Strangelove,* who launches a nuclear war to protect "the purity of essence of our precious bodily fluids" against fluorides. P.O.E. honestly felt that sanity had failed to save the world and that only insanity remained as a viable alternative.

Nor were they alone in this attitude. The same year P.O.E. was formed, the American people elected Richard Milhous Nixon to the White House, guided by a similar gut-level feeling that somebody like Jack D. Ripper was needed to confront the growing chaos of the planet with some strong counter-chaos.*

---

* *Galactic Archives:* At the time of this story, the Unistat

The real name of the founder of P.O.E. was not "John Brown," of course. That was a pseudonym.

The original John Brown had been a fervent Idealist, which was why P.O.E. admired him. They were all fervent Idealists, too.

John Brown, motivated by Idealism, had set out to abolish slavery in Unistat in the nineteenth century. On one of his first raids he murdered a whole family of slave-owners. An associate, who was less Idealistic, had suggested sparing the children, but John Brown refused.

"Nits grow up to be lice," he said.

Idealists were like that. You were much safer falling into the hands of the Cynics. The Cynics regarded everybody as equally corrupt. That was the attitude, for instance, of Tobias Knight and the other old hands at the F.B.I.

The Idealists regarded everybody as equally corrupt, *except themselves.*

The six-legged majority on Terra had never developed Idealism or Cynicism, nor had they ever thought of sin or corruption. They had a simple, pragmatic outlook. People could be recognized because they all had six legs. Good people smelled right and were part of the same hive or colony. Bad people smelled wrong and were not part of the hive; they should be eaten at once, or driven off.

government had 1,700 atomic bombs for every man, woman and child on the planet. Since a person can die only once, historians have been at a loss to explain what the Unistaters expected to do with the surplus 1,699 bombs for each human being. Galactical primatologists inform us that similar irrational behavior has been observed among domesticated apes on several thousand planets.

Two-legged and four-legged critters weren't people at all and to hell with them.

The four-legged residents of Terra were, for the most part, equally simpleminded. People had four legs. Six-legged critters were *food,* or else they were not worth noticing. Two-legged critters were dangerous, and should be avoided.

Only the dogs, among all the four-legged Terrans, recognized the two-legged primates as being people.

Some of the primates also recognized the dogs as being people.

One-tenth of one percent of the domesticated primates recognized all the life-forms on their planet as people.

The one-tenth of one per cent of the primates who recognized non-primates as people were in violent disagreement with each other about everything else. About one-third of them were Mystics and suffered from Permanent Brain Damage brought on by fasting, yoga or other masochistic practices. They had attained understanding of the *Intelligence* of all living beings through an ecstatic-agonizing experience of ego-loss brought on by their masochistic excesses. They went around talking about this genetic *Intelligence* and calling it

"God" and telling everybody it was too smart to make mistakes and incidentally talking a lot of nonsense, also brought on by their excesses.

Another third of the primates who recognized consciousness wherever it existed were specially trained scientists, in fields like ethology, ecology, biophysics and Neurologic. They all talked in specialized jargons and hardly anybody could understand them. Most of them couldn't even understand one another.

The last third of the primates who had a sense of the genetic program behind evolution were folk who had eaten some strange chemicals or vegetables. They were like the blind Denebian shell cats who suddenly encounter water for the first time by falling into an ocean. They knew *something* was happening to them, but they weren't sure what it was.

P.O.E. theoretically had no leader. It was an anarcho-Marxist collective.

The real leader was, of course, an alpha male. His name was Franklin Delano Roosevelt Stuart, and he was one of the smartest men in Unistat at that time. Unfortunately, his reptile bio-survival circuit was imprinted with chronic anxiety, his mammalian emotional-territorial circuit was imprinted with defensive aggression, his hominid semantic circuit was imprinted with an explosive blend of Black street cynicism and New Left ideology, and his domesticated socio-sexual circuit was from Kinksville.

F.D.R. Stuart claimed that the purpose of P.O.E. was to accelerate the dialectical process of evolution toward the classless society where all would live in peace, prosperity and socialist solidarity, and there would be no cops.

The real purpose of Stuart's activities was to *get even*. The other primates in Unistat had raped his mother and jailed his father and driven his brothers and sisters into street crime and junk and generally maltreated him all his life. In addition they called him by an insulting name, which was *nigger*.

Second in command in P.O.E. was Sylvia Goldfarb, a refugee from God's Lightning, NOW, the Radical Lesbians and Weather Underground. She was even smarter than F.D.R. Stuart, but she deferred to him, despite her feminist orientation, because he was a true alpha male who was a Mean Motherfucker When Crossed and had even more rage in him than she did.

To Sylvia, the purpose of P.O.E., she said, was to create a world where all men and women, all races and all classes, all humanity, lived in loving harmony and ate uncooked fruits and vegetables.

Her real motive was also to *get even*. The other primates discriminated against her for being female, for being Jewish, for being highly verbal and a Teacher's Pet, for wearing glasses, for being an atheist, and for several dozen other reasons at least. They also called her by an insulting name, which was *dyke*.

The third founding member was Mountbatten Babbit, who was a cyclical schizophrenic. He wigged out once a year, on the average, and had learned how to medicate himself with phenothyazines to keep those periods of Bizarresville down to a few weeks each, but during those dilations of ego he was likely to be anybody from Napoleon to a Vietnamese Buddhist. The rest of the year he was a brilliant research chemist and computer expert, but it was hard to get a good job because of his several incarcerations in mental hospitals.

Babbit said he was in P.O.E. to create a rational

world guided by sound scientific and libertarian-socialist principles. Yeah, he wanted to *get even,* too. The other primates called him a *nut* or a *fruitcake.*

The other members of P.O.E. were equally brilliant and equally desperate.

THE RANDOM FACTOR

Better that the whole world be destroyed and crumble to dust than that a free man deny one of his desires.

—BENITO MUSSOLINI, ITALIAN ANARCHIST AND POET

Markoff Chaney was a prime candidate for P.O.E. but, due to quantum wave-probabilities, his orbit never intersected theirs.

Chaney detested the majority of primates because they called him *Shorty* or even more insulting names.

Mr. Chaney, you see, was a midget; but he was no relative of the famous Chaneys of Hollywood. People *did* keep making jokes about that. It was bad enough to be, by the standards of the gigantic and stupid majority, a freak; how much worse to be so named as to remind those big oversized clods of cinema's two most famous portrayers of monstro-freaks. By the time the midget was fifteen, he had built up a detestation for ordinary mankind that dwarfed (he hated that word) the relative misanthropies of Paul of Tarsus, Clement of Alexandria, Swift of Dublin or anybody in P.O.E. Revenge, for sure, he would have. He would have revenge.

It was in college (U.C.-Berkeley, 1962) that Markoff Chaney discovered another hidden joke in his name. It was in a math class and, since this was Berkeley, the two students directly behind the midget were ignoring the professor and discussing their own intellectual interests—which were, of course, five years ahead of intellectual fads elsewhere.

"So we keep the same instincts as our primate and pre-primate ancestors," one student was saying. [He was from Chicago, his name was Mounty Babbit, and he was crazy even for Berkeley.] "But we superimpose culture and law on top of this. So we get split in two, dig? You might say"—Babbit's voice betrayed pride in the aphorism he was about to unleash—"mankind is the statutory ape."

". . . and," the professor, Percy "Prime" Time, said at just that moment, "when such a related series appears in a random process, we have what is known as a Markoff Chain. I hope Mr. Chaney won't be tormented by jokes about this for the rest of the semester, even if the related series of his appearances in class does seem part of a notably random process." The class roared; another tone of bile was entered on the midget's shit-ledger, the list of people who were going to eat turd before he died.

In fact, his cuts were numerous, both in math and in other classes. There were times when he could not bear to be with the giants, but hid in his room, *Pussycat* gatefold open, masturbating and dreaming of millions and millions of nubile young women all built like Pussyettes, all throwing themselves passionately upon him. Today, however, *Pussycat* would avail him not; he needed something raunchier. Ignoring his next class (Physical Anthropology—always good for a few humiliating moments), he hurried across Bancroft Way and slammed into his room, chain-bolting the door behind him.

Damn "Prime" Time and damn the science of mathematics itself, the line, the square, the average, the measurable world that pronounced him subnormal. Once and for all, beyond fantasy, in the depth of his soul he declared war on the statutory ape, on law and order, on predictability. He would be the random factor in every equation; from this day forward, unto death, it would be civil war: the midget versus the digits.

He took out his pornographic Tarot deck, which he used when he wanted a really far-out fantasy for his orgasm, and shuffled it thoroughly. Let's have a Mark-off Chain orgasm, just to start with, he thought savagely.

His first overt act—his Fort Sumter, as it were—began in San Francisco the following Saturday. He was in Norton's Emporium, a glorified 5 & 10¢ store, when he saw the sign:

NO SALESPERSON MAY LEAVE THE FLOOR
WITHOUT THE AUTHORIZATION OF A SUPERIOR.

THE MGT.

What, he thought, are the poor girls supposed to pee in their panties if they can't find the superior? Years of school came back to him ("Please, sir, may I leave the room sir?"). Hah! Not for nothing had he spent a semester in Professor "Sheets" Kelly's intensive course on textual analysis of modern poetry. The following Wednesday, the midget was back at Norton's and hiding in a coffee urn when the staff left and locked up. A few moments later the sign was down and an improved version hung in its place:

NO SALESPERSON MAY LEAVE THE FLOOR
OR LOOK OUT THE DOOR
WITHOUT THE AUTHORIZATION OF A SUPERIOR.

THE MGT.

Markoff Chaney launched what he considered a reign of terror against the oversized idiots of the statistical majority. An electronics whiz since his first junior Edison set, he found it easy to reverse relays in street intersections, so that the WALK sign flashed on red and the DON'T WALK signs on green. This proved to be bereft of amusement, except in small towns; denizens of New York, Chicago and similar elephantine burgs, accustomed to nothing working properly, ignored the signs anyway. The midget branched out and soon incomprehensible memos signed "THE MGT." were raining upon employees everywhere.

His father, crusty old Indole Chaney, had been a stockholder in Blue Sky Inc., a very dubious corporation manufacturing devices for use in low gravity; when John F. Kennedy announced that the U.S. would place a man on the moon before 1970, Blue Sky suddenly began to haul in the long green. Markoff inherited a fund that delivered $300 per month. For his purposes, it was enough. Living in Spartan fashion, constantly crisscrossing the country by Greyhound (he soon knew every graffito in every White Tower men's room by heart), dining often on a tin of sardines and a container of milk, Markoff left a train of anarchy in his wake.

EMPLOYEES MAY NOT EXCHANGE VACATION DAYS. —THE MGT.

EMPLOYEES MAY NOT PUNCH OTHER EMPLOYEES' TIME CARDS. ANY DEVIATION WILL RESULT IN TERMINATION.—THE MGT.

FILL OUT IN TRIPLICATE. KEEP ONE COPY, MAIL ONE COPY TO THIS OFFICE AND SEND THE THIRD TO THE TRANSYLVANIAN CONSULATE.—THE MGT.
(This was used at a blood bank, of course.)

On January 18, 1984, the midget was in Chicago, hiding in a coffee urn in the tenth-floor editorial offices of *Pussycat* magazine. He had a Vacation Schedule Form with him, to be run off on the Xerox and distributed to each editor's desk. This form was his masterpiece; it was sure to provoke a nervous breakdown in anyone who tried to decipher and comply with all its directions, yet it was not much different, on the surface, from the hundreds of similar forms handed out in offices daily. Chaney was quite happy and quite impatient for the staff to leave so he could set about his cheerful task for the night.

Two editors passed the coffee urn, talking.

"Who's the *Pussycat* interview for next month?" one asked.

"Dr. Dashwood. You know, from Orgasm Research."

"Oh."

The midget had heard of Orgasm Research and it was, of course, on his shit list. More statistics and averages, more of the modern search for the norm that he could never be. And now the bastard who headed it, Dr. Dashwood, would be interviewed by *Pussycat*—and probably would get to fuck all the gorgeous Pussyettes at the local Pussycat Club. Chaney fumed. Orgasm Research moved from the middle of his shit list to the top, replacing his arch-enemy, Bell Telephone.

The thought of Dr. Dashwood remained with him all night, as he ground out his surrealist vacation memo on the office Xerox. He was still fuming when he returned to his pantry-sized room at the YMCA and slipped the bolt (to keep out the wandering and prehensile deviates who infest YMCAs everywhere). Dr. Francis Dashwood, supervisor of orgasms, and now ready to dive head first into a barrel of Pussyettes: the midget suffered at the thought.

But it was nearly four A.M. and he was tired. Tomorrow morning would be time to do something about Orgasm Research.

Chaney dreamed of Dashwood measuring orgasms with an n-dimensional ruler in Frankenstein's laboratory while men in trench coats went slinking about in the shadows asking unintelligible questions about 132 missing gorillas.

In the morning, he shuffled through his bogus letterhead file, looking for something appropriate for correspondence with Orgasm Research.

THUGGEE SOCIETY, DIVISION OF HASH IMPORT AND AFROGENEALOGY, said the handsomest letterhead; this was illustrated with a three-headed Kali. But that one he reserved for correspondence with prominent white racists, informing them that the Afrogenealogy Division (Alex Haley, researcher-in-chief) had discovered that their great-great-grandmother was black. Chaney always invited the recipients to come to the next Thuggee meeting and bring their wives and sisters.

FRIENDS OF THE VANISHING MALARIA MOSQUITO (COMMITTEE TO BAN D.D.T.) was a good one, but not good enough for Dr. Dashwood. Chaney reserved it for correspondence with President Lousewart.

PARATHEOANAMETAMYSTIKHOOD OF ERIS ESOTERIC—maybe later.

Finally, the midget selected CHRISTIANS AND ATHEISTS UNITED AGAINST CREEPING AGNOSTICISM, A Nonprophet Organization, Reverend Billy Graham, President; Madalyn Murray O'Hair, Chairperson of the Board.

In a few moments Chaney produced a letter calculated to short a few circuits in Dr. Dashwood's computeroid cortex:

Dear Dr. Dashwood:

When you are up to your ass in alligators, it's hard to remember that you started out to drain the swamp.

Cordially,

Ezra Pound,
Council of Armed Rabbis

P.S. *Entropy requires no maintenance.*

That should make the bastard wonder a bit, he thought with satisfaction, stuffing the enigmatic epistle in an envelope and addressing it.

Markoff Chaney loathed math because it contained the concept of the *average*.

Chaney not only loathed, but hated, despised, abominated, detested and couldn't stand the thought of Dr. Dashwood, not just because Dashwood's work involved statistics and averages, but because it was concerned with orgasms.

That was a tender subject to Chaney. He was a virgin.

He was never attracted to women of his own stature —that was almost incestuous, and, besides, they simply did not turn him on. He adored the giantesses of the hateful oversized majority. He adored them, lusted after them, and was also terrified of them. He knew from sad experience, oft-repeated, that they regarded him as *cute* and even *cuddly,* and one of them had gone so far as to say *adorable* but absolutely *ridiculous* as a sex partner, damn and blast them all to hell.

He had tried building his courage with booze. They thought he was *disgusting* and *chauvinistic* and not even *cute* anymore.

He tried weed. They thought he was *cute* again, and even hilarious, but even more absurd as a possible lover.

He tried est. The trainers spent the first day tearing him down—telling him he was a no-good shit and everybody knew he was a no-good shit and things like that, which he had always suspected. The second day they built him up and convinced him he could control his space as well as any other mammal. He was flying when he came out.

He went at once to a singles bar and sidled up to the most attractive blonde in the place.

"Hi," he said boldly, swaggering a bit. "What would you say to a friendly little fuck?"

She gazed down at him from what suddenly seemed an enormous height. "Hello, friendly little fuck," she drawled with magnificent boredom.

When Chaney slunk back to his YMCA room and his pornographic Tarot, he vowed more vehemently than ever that he would be the meanest fuck on the planet. *Nobody* would ever call him a friendly little fuck again.

He still adored the giantesses and feared them, but now he hated them, too; in short, he was really stuck on them.

Their *cunts*—those hairy, moist, hot, adorable, inaccessible, rejecting, terrible, divine, frightening Schwartzchild Radiuses to the dimension of Manhood—were the Holy Grail to him.

He knew their cunts were hairy and hot and moist, etc., despite his virginity, because he had read a lot of pornographic novels.*

---

* *Galactic Archives:* Pornographic novels were novels about the things primates enjoy most, namely sexual acrobatics. They were taught to feel ashamed of these natural primate impulses so that they would be guilty-furtive-submissive types and easy for the alpha males to manipulate. Those caught reading such novels were called no-good shits, of course.

PEP

PEP—the People's Ecology Party had been founded by Furbish Lousewart V following the success of his monumental best seller, *Unsafe Wherever You Go.*

Lousewart V was a man born into the right time; his book perfectly reflected all the foreboding of the late 1970s. Its thesis was simply that everything science does is wrong, that scientists are very nasty people, and that we need to go back to a simpler, more natural way of life. The message was perfect for the time; it was simply Hitler's National Socialism redone, with only a few minor changes.

Where Hitler wrote "Jew," for instance, Lousewart wrote "scientist." Nobody but the most backward denizens of Bad Ass, Texas, or Chicago, Illinois, was capable of really getting riled up by the anti-Semitic ploy anymore, and Lousewart had, with intuitive brilliance, picked the one scapegoat capable of mobilizing real fear, rage and hatred among the general population.

In place of Hitler's racial purity, Lousewart established the dogma of nutritional purity. ("It's not what comes out of a man's mouth that's important," he said, scorning Third Circuit time-binding entirely, "but what he puts into it.")

And Hitler's Wagnerian primitivism was altogether too Teutonic for young America in the 1970s, so Lousewart replaced it with a chic blend of Taoist and Amerindian primitivism.

It didn't matter that scholars pointed out that all of

Lousewart's arguments were illogical and incoherent (his followers despised logic and coherence on principle), and it didn't even matter that he had brazenly lifted most of his notions right out of Roszak's *Where the Wasteland Ends* and Von Daniken's *Gold of the Gods*. It was a package that had a built-in market. With the collapse of the Republican Party after Nixon and Ford, there was a void in national politics; somebody had to organize a force to challenge the Democrats, and the People's Ecology Party moved quickly to capture the turf.

Furbish Lousewart was an expert in Morality and Ideology; he understood that seeking out and denouncing no-good shits was the path by which one could become leader of a movement of the anxious and angry. In short, he had the instincts of a politician. By the time he was through converting the science of ecology into the ideology of PEP, it had become nought else but a search-and-destroy mission against any and all who could be suspected of being no-good shits.

The Lousewart philosophy of asceticism, medievalism and despair was officially called the Revolution of Lowered Expectations.

The Revolution of Lowered Expectations had not been invented by Furbish Lousewart. The whole neurosociology of the 20th Century could be understood as a function of two variables—the upward-rising curve of the Revolution of Rising Expectations and the down-ward-plunging trajectory of the Revolution of Lowered Expectations.

The Revolution of Rising Expectations, which had drawn more and more people into its Up-thrust during the first half of the century, had led many to believe that poverty and starvation and war and disease were all gradually being phased out by advances in pure and applied science, growing stockpiles of surplus food in the advanced nations, accelerated medical progress, the spread of literacy and electronics, and the mounting sense that people had a right to demand a decent life for themselves and their children.

The Revolution of Lowered Expectations was based on the idea that there wasn't enough energy to provide for the rising expectations of the masses. Year after year the message was broadcast: There Isn't Enough. The masses were taught that Terra was a closed system, that entropy was increasing, that life was a losing proposition all around, and that the majority were doomed to poverty, starvation, disease, misery and stupidity.

Most of the people who still had rising expectations were scientists. When Furbish Lousewart realized the political capital to be made from the Revolution of Lowered Expectations, he also realized—thus demonstrating his political savvy—that having an opposition meant having a scapegoat group.

The scientists were an ideal scapegoat group because they all spoke in specialized languages and hardly anybody could understand them.

The Jews had served this function in earlier ages because they spoke *Yiddish*.

The scientists spoke *Mathematics*.

CHEMICAL FACTORIES

Consciousness is energy received and decoded by a structure. In human beings, the receiving-decoding structures are neuro-chemical.

—SIGMUND FREUD, *"The Neuropolitics of Cocaine"*

"No wait goddamit it you don't understand," a string-bean-shaped ectomorph named Mounty Babbit whined.

"I understand," Sylvia Goldfarb said soothingly. Her spectacles glinted with silver evil.

"It's the kundalini rising," Babbit burbled happily. "I can see all space-time at once. By God, I'm the first to do it. Screw it, shoe it. I'm becoming the Superman."

"Yes, yes," Sylvia agreed. "You're wonderful."

"What the hell do you know?" Babbit snarled. "I only imagined you. This is all a put-on."

"Yes, yes, darling, of course," Sylvia cooed.

Babbit was in the second day of his yearly wig-out. He had taken five Stellazines the first day, but now he wasn't so sure he wanted to take anymore. He was beginning to *enjoy* part of it.

"Just one more Stellazine," Sylvia urged gently.

"No yes of course go fuck yourself," Babbit said in miserable joy or happy anguish or some such n-dimensional neurological state.

"Man, take the god*dam* pills," Franklin Delano Roosevelt barked, swelling his muscles and doing the standard alpha male command posture.

"You're jealous," Babbit accused. "Jelly-ass. Kiss my ass. You can't see all of it at once like I can."

"Man, take the goddam *pill*, I said," Stuart growled, with increased menace.

"Yes yes of course," Babbit said, cowed. He took the Stellazine.

"That's right, darling," Sylvia Goldfarb crooned, handing him a glass of water to wash the pill down.

It was a hairy day at P.O.E. headquarters, but Babbit only wigged once a year, in April usually.

Twelve-point-six percent of the citizens of Unistat had gone through Babbit's pilgrimage at least once in their lives. One out of fifty was a yearly repeater like him.

The condition was normal in domesticated primates evolving toward objective consciousness. In most societies, those who got it were taken in training by those who had been through it—people called *"shamans"*—and were carefully taught how to use it for fun and profit.

This knowledge had gradually been lost in the course of the domestication of the primates. By the time they had their first steam engines and instituted slavery, they didn't remember that such neurological mutations could be used for fun and profit.

They took the people who were going through these transformations and put them in dank, dark prisons.

They called these prisons *"mental hospitals."*

All this was changed by a primate named Sigmund Freud, who was born in Austria but migrated to Unistat in his youth because he admired the Unistat Declaration of Independence.

Freud was one of the first outside Peru to sample *cocaine*. He found it an illuminating experience. He was so illuminated, in fact, that he rushed around trying every other chemical that radically altered the nervous system. He tried *peyote* almost as soon as Havelock Ellis and William James. He tried *cannabis indica*. He even tried *belladonna*—and lived to tell the tale. He went on to try yage, Morning Glory seeds, scopalamine, datura, opium and dozens of others.

Freud concluded that consciousness depends on the chemistry of the nervous system. He wrote several books on this discovery, and then they put him in jail.

The primates always put pioneers and innovators in jail. It was their equivalent of the Hall of Fame found on more advanced planets.

LOUSES IN THE SKIDROW DIMEHAUNTS

It is impossible now to suppose that organic life exists only on this planet.

—FURBISH LOUSEWART V, *Unsafe Wherever You Go*

Justin Case heard about the louses in the skidrow dimehaunts at one of Epicene Wildeblood's wild, wild parties, on December 23, 1983. Simon Moon, a creature with almost as much hair as Bigfoot, planted the louses in Case's semantic preconscious. The whole evening was rather confusing—too many martinis, too much weed, too many people—and Moon was regarded as somewhat sinister by everybody because he worked for the Beast (or *with* the Beast, or *on* the Beast). To make matters even more surrealistic, that intolerable bore Blake Williams was lecturing on the Birth of

Cosmic Humanity to anyone who would listen, and several other conversations were going on simultaneously. Nonetheless, Moon had a manuscript with him, and a few listeners, and Case couldn't help absorbing part of what the mad Beastman was reading.

"Thee gauls simper at his tyrant power," Moon was chanting when Case first became conscious of him. What the hell was that? "He is ghoon with this seven-week booths and his mickeyed mausers into mistory. His eyes did seem auld glowery."

"FUCK THEM ALL!" a drunken writer from California said, cymbal-like, in Case's other ear.

"I beg your pardon?" Epicene Wildeblood, gay as three chimps in a circus, seemed to think the drunk was addressing him.

"I said, FUCK THE BLOODY CAPITALISTS! ! !" the writer explained, weaving a bit to windward. "The goddam motherfucking moneygrubbing Philistine lot of them . . ."

"I see," Wildeblood said dryly. He did not like people throwing scenes at his parties. "I think maybe you've had too much to drink. . . ."

"Yeah??? Well," the drunk decided majestically, "fuck *you,* too. And the horse you rode in on, as they say in Texas."

But that lard-assed bore Blake Williams was droning, "The whole problem, of course, is that we haven't been born yet. In fact, only now, at this point in history, is humanity about to be born." Williams was full of rubbish like that.

"About to be born?" asked Carol Christmas, the most delicious piece of blonde femininity in the galaxy. Case thought at once that it would be a splendidly wonderful idea to deposit at least some of his sperm within her— *any* orifice would do. He thought this was a brilliant decision on his part, and wondered how to begin implementing it. He had no idea that every male hominid, and many other male primates, immediately had that idea when looking at Carol.

"Elverun, past Nova's atoms," the hairy Moon read on to his small circle of admirers, "from mayan baldurs to monads of goo, brings us by a divinely karmic Tao-Jones leverage back past tallchief tactics and atzlantean tooltechs to Louses in the Skidrow Dimehaunts. This way the Humpytheatre."

"I still say fuck 'em all." The drunk was a solitary bassoon against Moon's keening violin. "Capitalism is a rich man's heaven and a poor man's hell."

"Ahm yes," that windy old baritone sax, Blake Williams, bleated to the adorable Carol. "You see terrestrial life is embryonic in the evolutionary sense. In perspective to the cosmos." Old chryselephantine pedant, Case thought.

The shrill fife of Josephine Malik, Case's editor, was heard: "Moon. They say he works for the Beast." Case glanced over at her: she was in her usual army fatigues and combat boots. She wore a button saying in psychedelic colors: BRING BACK THE SIXTIES. Walking nostalgia.

"Floating you see," the tuba of Williams oompah-oompah-ed onward, "in the amniotic atmosphere at the bottom of a 4,000-mile gravity well. And taking the Euclidean parameters of that gestation as the norm. Totally fetal, if you follow me, and in a very real sense blind because unborn, knowing um the dimensions of the wombplanet but not knowing what lies beyond the gravitational vagina—the whole universe *outside.*"

"A 4,000-mile *cunt?*" Carol was awed by the concept. Her blonde head leaned forward in doubtful inquiry. "That's a *very* funny metaphor, Professor."

"The only difference between my publishers and the James gang," the drunk went on, monotonous as a bass drum, "is that the James boys had horses."

". . . which explains the various rebirth experiences

66

reported by astronauts like Aldrin and Mitchell and the others," Williams trumpeted [gassy old windbag]. "Earth is our womb. Leaving Earth is literally rebirth. There's nothing metaphoric about it."

"The James boys hell my last publisher was more like Attila the Hun," plonkty-plonked Frank Hemeroid in pianissimo.

Case began to feel that he had had perhaps too much hash.

"Right Wingers?" astronomer Bertha Van Ation was trilling. "We've got *real* Right Wingers out in Orange County. Let me tell you about the Committee to Nuke the Whales. . . ."

But that impossible Williams person was murmuring privately now to Carol the Golden Goddess, and Case tried desperately to catch the words, dreading the thought that a sexual liaison was being formed.

"The mnemonic," Williams was crooning, "is quite easy. Just say, 'Mother Very Easily Made a Jam Sandwich Using No Peanuts, Mayonnaise or Glue.' See?"

Mnemonic for what, in God's name? But Moon was shrilling like a banshee now:

"Wet with garrison statements, oswilde shores, daily blazers, tochus culbook depositories, middlesexed villains and fumes. Fict! The most unkennedest carp of all. Fogt. Veiny? V.D.? Wacky? His bruttus gypper."

"I was walking on Lexington Avenue one morning around three A.M.," the drunk maundered on, "and I heard this URRRRRP, this horrible *eldritch laughter* just like in an H. P. Lovecraft story, and do you want to know what I think it was? A publisher and his lawyer had just figured out a new way to screw one of their writers."

"This the lewdest comedy nominator," Moon keened high on the G-string. "This de visions of spirals fur de lewdest comedy nominator. Eerie cries from the scalped nations! This the oval orefice sends the plumbers fur de spills. Lust of the walkregans. Think! White harse devoted. Thank! Wit ars devoided. Dunk!"

"I wish Moon would stop reading that drivel," Fred "Figs" Newton was clearly heard in solo. "I'd like to ask him how much the Beast really knows."

"Oh," the mournful oboe of Benny Benedict sang ominously, "the Beast knows *everything*. . . ."

". . . by Loop Shore and Dellingersgangers," Moon keened over them, oblivious, "where yippies yip and doves duz nothing, to the hawkfullest convention ever."

At this point Case had to beat a hasty retreat to the John (one martini too many) and he never did get all the conversations sorted out in his memory, but the louses in the skidrow dimehaunts were firmly lodged in the Ambiguous Imagery files of his Myth-and-Metaphor Detector, right next to the Three Stooges and Chinatown.

And Cagliostro the Great.

SIGNALS FROM A LOST WORLD

> One of the chief services which mathematics has rendered the human race in the past century is to put "common sense" where it belongs, on the topmost shelf next to the dusty canister labeled "discarded nonsense."
>
> —Eric Temple Bell,
> *Mathematics, Queen of the Sciences*

TERRAN ARCHIVES 2803:

There are, of course, many mysteries still unsolved about the ancient scientific shamans. We know, for instance, that the letters L.S.D. were often coded into their manuals—as in the present text, where Simon Moon's Jungian manuscript contains the acrostic "Louses in the Skidrow Dimehaunts," or in the religious chant of the Liverpool Insect Cult called "the Beatles," which invoked "Lucy in the Sky with Diamonds." Professor Jubelum holds that "L.S.D." was a variation on the Masonic "L.P.D.," which is a further mystery, since "L.P.D." has alternatively been explained as "Light, Pressure, Density," as a cryptogram of the number 114 (Cabalistically, $L + P + D = 114$), the number of years in a Rosicrucian cycle; as a revolutionary slogan of the eighteenth century, *Lilia Pedibus Destrue* (trample the lily underfoot, *i.e.*, destroy the French monarchy, whose symbol was the lily); or as Liberty, Power, Duty, etc. L.S.D., similarly, has been explained as "Leary's Star Drive," "Life, Sex, Death," "Let's Stop Death," "Legalize Spiritual Discovery."

The ancient sages wrote in code because of the hazards of practicing their profession in that barbaric epoch. For instance, Bruno served 8 years in the dungeons of the Inquisition and was then burned; Leary served 44 months in the California Archipelago; Crowley was expelled from three countries. Castaneda would never allow his photograph to be taken. Wilson spread a variety of contradictory myths about himself, to disguise his real purposes, whatever they were.

Concerning that which we cannot know with certainty, we should remain honestly agnostic. The reader will, of course, form a purely personal evaluation of Wilson's grandiose allegories and occult claims; the trick is to concentrate on the reality projected through the printed page. Every sentence is a signal from a lost world, a time of primitive, barbaric splendor and fantastic cruelty with which you can interface synergetically by crossing over and entering the form.

THE GENTRY

The metaprogramming circuit of the nervous system allows the brain to become aware of its programming, to choose which circuit will be operating, to edit and orchestrate experience. This was traditionally the Great Work of the Alchemists. Those who fall into it accidentally and unprepared to handle the new freedom are called *"schizophrenics."*

—MARILYN CHAMBERS, *Neuro-Anthropology*

Simon Moon became intellectually pubescent when he read the *Principia Mathematica* of Russell and Whitehead, discovering that the simple statement "A is A" (an apple is an apple, for non-mathematicians) requires 400 pages of previous demonstrations before it makes sense, and even then it only makes sense within the context of one logical system. He had his first synaptical orgasm or brain-glow over G. Spencer Brown's *Laws of Form,* which showed that even Russell and Whitehead had taken a lot more for granted than they had realized. (Russell and Whitehead had rashly assumed that it makes sense to talk of crossing a line between one state and another.) Simon became semantically polymorphous-perverse or a Brain Tantrist when he plowed his bleary-eyed way through Gödel's Proof which in effect proved that proof itself is contingent.

It was only after all that semantic acrobatics that he was able to appreciate all he had learned from his transplanted-peasant aunt, Molly Moon.

The chief thing Simon Moon had learned from aunt Molly was respect for the Gentry.

All old Irishwomen called *Them* the Gentry. It was

academic folklorists and anthropologists and other citified types like that who called *Them* the Wee Folk or the Spirits of the Wood or the Faery. Molly Moon had been born in County Mayo and she knew damned well that *They* wanted to be called the Gentry—it was a form of respect *They* demanded—and anybody who called *Them* anything else was likely to offend *Them*, with the usual consequences.

There were as many of *Them* in Unistat as in Ireland, Aunt Molly always insisted, but people over here didn't know *Them* the way the Irish did. People here would attribute *Their* activities to all sorts of other causes— "bad luck," "coincidence," "synchronicity," "Murphy's Law," "ghosts," "haunts," "spooks," "gremlins," "printer's error," "the Illuminati conspiracy," even "UFOnauts." An old Irishwoman was not to be deceived by such ignorance. Everything that intruded on human life in an unexpectedly nasty way, or in a benevolent way that you couldn't understand, or just in a bizarrely humorous way, was the work of the Gentry.

Of course, after Antioch College (B.S., mathematics; M.S., electronic engineering) and Russell and Whitehead and Hagbard Celine and Illumination and G. Spencer Brown and ten years in computer sciences, Simon had learned to think of the Gentry in a less anthropomorphic manner than Aunt Molly did. *They* were just a macroscopic function of quantum probability fluctuations—"the Cosmic Giggle Factor," in Hagbard Celine's term. If *They* violated cause-and-effect and space-time, well, that was just because causality and the "real universe" as a whole were just epiphenomena, secondary aspects of primordial quantum probability-matrices. Below space, time and causality, in Heisenberg's potentia, *They* were always busy manufacturing Schrödinger *eigen*states out of which temporary "realities" emerged in the 4-dimensional Einstein continuums reaching from here to infinity in super-space.

71

Nothing spooky about it at all, when you looked at the math. It just *sounded* weird in the subject-predicate grammar of Indo-European languages.

It was the shock of the decade, to Simon, when he discovered that Justin Case also knew about the Gentry. After all, Case was not able to read mathematics, which made him functionally illiterate in Simon's judgment —just as people who went to movies for the *story* instead of the visual montage were functionally illiterate, in Case's opinion. Nevertheless, Case obviously knew a great deal about the Gentry. Simon realized this when he heard Case talking about *Chinatown*.

"Chandler's hero, what's-his-name," Case had said, "never goes to Chapel Perilous. He, what-*is*-his- name— Marlowe—is a true Knight, of course, but Chandler was too much a rationalist to see the knight's quest as anything more than a *moral* victory." He made a disparaging gesture, dismissing people like Chandler, hung up on non-visual abstractions like ethics. "Polanski is much more sophisticated. Chinatown is his Chapel Perilous, and the knight's quest is to come back with some part of your mind or soul not obliterated."

"Oh ah Chinatown is Chapel Perilous," said Epicene Wildeblood, to whom Case had been delivering this typically inscrutable routine. Chapel Perilous, in Wildeblood's neurological reality, meant only T. S. Eliot's *Waste Land*. "You mean ah the um Dark Night of the Soul," he prompted.

"I mean," Case said, " the psychic space where Moe keeps sticking his finger in Curly's eye, over and over and over again, and you can't get out of there, and you can't change channels, and it's always been like that, and it always will be like that."

"He's talking about Bad Acid," Figs Newton said, trying to help.

Simon knew better. Case was talking about encountering the Gentry in one of their more malign moods.

Simon believed that he, himself, had encountered the Gentry at their very worst. It was in the fourth hour of an acid trip, and the fourth hour is always weirdsville —the *Joysis Crisis,* Simon called it. But this time it was more eerie than ever. Simon found himself in a world of gigantic vegetables and shrubs, his mind hardly individualized from the surrounding mind which was insectoid, vast and *inhuman,* the whole accompanied by incessant humming and drumming in polyrhythms Bach might envy. It was another planet, he thought at the time: he had achieved the Contact with extraterrestrials all oldtime acidheads eventually claim. Only later, when he came down, did he decide it was actually the Gentry up to one of their tricks.

He was wrong in both interpretations. Actually, he had merely achieved mindfusion with the six-legged majority on Terra.

TO HAVE LOCKS ON THESE DOORS

> One of the causes of cancer is the harmfulness of cooked foods.
>
> —FURBISH LOUSEWART V, *Unsafe Wherever You Go*

Blake Williams had the great good fortune to suffer a bout of polio in infancy. Of course, he did not realize it was good fortune at the time—nor did his parents or his doctors. Nonetheless, he was among the lucky few who were treated by the Sister Kenny method at a time (the early 1930s) when the American Medical Association was denouncing that method as quackery and forbidding experiment thereon by its members. He was walking again, with only a slight limp, when he entered grade school in 1938. The real luck occurred twelve years later, in 1950, when he was 18; the limp and the dead muscles in his lower calves disqualified him for military service. The next man drafted, in his place, had both testicles bloodily blown off in Korea.

Williams, of course, never knew about this patriotic gelding, but he was well aware that various boys his age were having various portions of their anatomy blown off in Korea; being somewhat philosophical, he often reflected on the paradox that the polio (which had been, when it occurred, a physical agony to him and a psychological agony to his parents) had preserved him from such mutilations. Considering that the only continuing effect of the polio was the slight limp, he had to admit that Nature or God or something-or-other had sneakily done him great good while appearing to do him great evil. This was a decided encouragement toward an optimistic attitude toward the seemingly evil and made him wonder if the universe were not benevolent after all. The guy who lost his balls in Williams' place, on the other hand, became a pronounced pessimist and cynic.

Between Korea and Vietnam, while Blake was acquiring first an M.S. and then a Ph.D. in paleo-anthropology, another great good fortune, in the form of another seeming evil, came before his eyes. He was walking in lower Manhattan; he had started from Washington Square, where he and his current girl friend—they were both N.Y.U. students—had just had a particularly nasty quarrel right after a biology class. He had wandered far to the west in a mood of suicidal gloom, such as young male primates often think they should experience after losing a sexual partner. Somehow, he wandered onto Vandivoort Street and found himself at the Vandivoort Street incinerator. There he saw a most peculiar sight: a rather stout man, looking like he was about to cry, was watching while two younger, thinner men were pouring books out of a truck into the incinerator.

"What the hell?" Blake Williams asked nobody in particular. It was like an old movie of Nazi Germany. Nobody had told him that book-burning was now an American institution.

He approached the stout man, who was the only one of the three who seemed unhappy, and repeated his question. "What the hell?" he asked. "I mean, are you people burning *books?*"

"They are," the stout man said. He went on to explain that he was an executive of something called the Orgone Institute Press and that a court had ordered all their books destroyed. Williams was curious and looked at some of the titles: *Character Analysis* and *The Mass Psychology of Fascism* and *The Cancer Biopathy* and *Contact with Space.*

"I didn't know that book-burning was legal in this country," he said.

"Neither did I," the stout man said bitterly.

Blake Williams walked on, dazed. He couldn't have been more astonished if he'd seen Storm Troopers rounding up Jews. He wondered if he'd fallen into a time-warp.

Later, of course, he learned that the Orgone Institute, headed by Dr. Wilhelm Reich, had been investigating human sexuality and had come to some highly unorthodox conclusions. Dr. Reich himself died in prison, Dr. Silvert (Reich's co-investigator) committed suicide, the books were burned, and the heresy was buried. But Williams had an entirely new attitude toward the country in which he lived, the scientific community which had looked on and made not a single gesture to support Dr. Reich and Dr Silvert, and the omnipresent rhetoric which insisted that the Dark Ages had ended many centuries ago.

He remembered that Sister Kenny, at the time he and thousands of others were cured by her polio therapy, had been denounced as a quack by the same entrenched medical bureaucrats who imprisoned the Orgone researchers. How convenient, he thought, aghast, to assume that all the injustices happen in other countries and other ages: that Dreyfus may have been innocent, but the Rosenbergs never; that Pasteur may have been right, but not the researcher ostracized from the American Association for the Advancement of Science—not the professor denied tenure at *our* university, not the man in *our* prison. Blake Williams came to the Great Doubt, without bitterness but with increased awareness that society is everywhere in conspiracy against intelligence. On his own, and at some expense, he repeated all of Dr. Reich's experiments, and drew his own conclusions.

"There were only 18," he used to say, deliberately cryptic, sucking his pipe, deadpan, whenever anybody enthused about scientific freedom in his presence. If the victim inquired, "Only 18 what?," Blake would reply, with the same deadpan, "Only 18 physicians who signed the petition against the burning of Reich's books in 1957." He was not disappointed in his expectation that nine out of every ten researchers would angrily reply, "But Reich really *was* a quack." The tenth was the only one who would ever hear Williams' real thoughts on any subject.

The turning point, however, didn't come until 1977. It was then that Williams read a book entitled *Cosmic Trigger*. The author, a rather too clever fellow named Robert Anton Wilson, who wrote in a style as opulent as a Moslem palace, claimed to be in communication with a Higher Intelligence from the system of the dog star, Sirius. He also provided evidence, of a sort, that Aleister Crowley, G. I. Gurdjieff, Dr. John Lilly, Dr. Timothy Leary, a Flying Saucer contactee named George Hunt Williamson, and the priesthood of ancient Egypt, among others, had also been contacted by ESP transmitters from Sirius. Williams found that he actually believed this preposterous yarn. The discovery thrilled him, since it didn't really matter whether the pretentious Wilson's pompous claims were true or not. What mattered was that he, Blake Williams, was free at last. (Remembering: "Free at last, free at last, thank God Almighty, I'm free at last": the tombstone which had so moved him in 1968.) Despite B.S. and M.S. and Ph.D., Blake Williams was free. He did not have to think what other academics thought. He had somehow liberated himself from conditioned consciousness.

He felt an immediate upsurge of gratitude to Wilson for freeing him.

Project Pan, in a sense, began at that moment. Blake Williams knew that he was going to do something great and terrible with his newfound freedom, and he was resolved that, unlike Reich (and Leary and Semmelweiss and Galileo and the long, sad list of martyrs to scientific freedom), he would not be punished for it. "Screw the Earthlings," he said bitterly and with *mucho cojones,* "I'm wise to their game. The trick is to be independent but not to let *them* know about it."

That night he wrote in his diary, *"Challenge a remaining taboo."* It was that simple. He had always wanted to understand genius, and now he had the formula. Freud, living in an age that prized its own seeming rationality, had found one of the remaining taboos and dared to think beyond it: he discovered infant sexuality and the unconscious, among other things. Galileo had gone beyond the taboo, Thou shalt not question Aristotle. Every great discovery had been the breaking of a taboo.

Blake Williams began looking around for a remaining taboo to violate.

This was by no means easy in Unistat at that time.

LIVING IN A NOVEL

Let there be a form distinct from the form.

—G. SPENCER BROWN, *Laws of Form*

Jo Malik once thought she was a transsexual. She had even gone to Dr. John Money, the pioneer of transsexual therapy and surgery, at Johns Hopkins, back in the mid-sixties.

"I think I'm a man living in a woman's body," she said.

Dr. Money nodded; that was normal in his business. He began asking her questions—the standard ones—and in only a half-hour she was convinced that she was not a transsexual; she was just a confused woman. Dr. Money kindly gave her the name of a good psychiatrist in New York, where she lived, for a more conventional form of therapy.

After three months, the psychiatrist announced that Jo's problem was not Penis Envy. That was hardly exciting; she had never thought her problem was quite that simple.

The therapy ground along. She learned a great deal about her Father Complex, her Mother Complex, her Sibling Rivalries and her habit of hiding resentments. It was enlightening, in a painful way, but she was still confused.

Then the Women's Liberation Movement began, and Jo dropped out of therapy to enter politics.

She no longer defined herself as a man trapped in a woman's body, but as a human being trapped in male definitions of femininity.

It was a very satisfactory resolution of her problems. She no longer had to take responsibility for anything; everything was the fault of the men. There was no need to stifle resentments—the correct political stance was to express them, in a strident voice and with a maximum of emotional-territorial rage. She had finally learned the A-B-C's of primate politics. She even learned to swell her muscles and howl.

It was all so much relief after years of self-doubt that Jo remained in 1968 while the rest of the world moved into 1970 and 1974 and 1980 and 1983. That was why she was wearing a BRING BACK THE SIXTIES button at Epicene Wildeblood's party.

Jo still had one problem left over from pre-Women's Lib days. Sometimes just before sleep, she heard a voice saying, "No wife, no horse, no mustache."

Of course, she knew that everybody occasionally heard such voices in the hypnogogic reverie before true sleep. You were wigging out only if you heard them all day long. Still, she wondered where it came from and why it had such a cryptic message.

Jo Malik hadn't had a sexual relationship with a man since 1968, and looked it.

She was also 64 years old, and looked it.

Nevertheless, there was an Unidentified Man at the Wildeblood party, and Jo suspected him of having designs on her bod. That was because he kept trying to get into every conversation group that she intercepted. He was following her, she was convinced.

"Mother very easily made a jam sandwich using no peanuts, mayonnaise or glue," Blake Williams said.

"Of course, Skull Island was Cooper's Chinatown," Justin Case said at the same moment.

"Wham! That arbral with his showers sooty? The fugs come in on tinny-cut foets," Moon droned along.

Jo decided that she had taken perhaps a little too much of the Afghan hash that was going around. It seemed that everybody in the room—the *crème de la crème* of Manhattan intelligentsia—were all talking gibberish. She eased out onto the balcony for some fresh air and restful silence.

Eight stories below a marquee blinked up at her: DEEP THROAT, it said.

Male chauvinism.

She breathed deeply, mingling oxygen with the cannabis molecules in her blood.

And the Unidentified Man appeared.

"Hello," he said casually. "I thought I'd find you out here."

"Who the hell are you, buster?" Jo barked—the first warning.

"My *name* doesn't matter," he said. He was tall, and handsome, and very gentle in his eyes. The worst kind of Male Chauvinist Pig. The Seducer.

"*You* don't matter, either," Jo said snappily. "I'd like to be alone, to enjoy the view, *if you don't mind.*"

80

She showed more teeth, emphasizing the second primate warning.

"I'm Hugh Crane," the handsome stranger said quickly. "I have been sent by the Author of Our Being with an important message for you. Please listen; it's vital to your future. We are all . . . *living in a novel.*"

"Take it and stick it," Jo said, leaving the balcony.

Another male chauvinist squashed, or at least squelched.

Unfortunately, back in the Wildeblood *soirée,* the first voice she heard was Benny Benedict complaining, "Women's Lib? Christ, what we need now is Men's Lib. Do you know how much alimony I'm paying. . . ."

STARHAWK'S LIFE STUDY

In capitalism, man exploits man. In socialism, it's exactly the opposite.

—BEN TUCKER, FAMOUS VAUDEVILLE COMEDIAN

While "Eggs" Benedict was complaining about his alimony in New York, a telephone was ringing in Marlene Murphy's apartment in San Francisco.

Starhawk, a bronze young man with an arrogant face, had picked Marlene up in a singles bar on Powell Street just three hours before and still didn't know her last name. He came out of the bathroom stark naked to answer the phone. Very carefully, he said, "Yes?"

"Who is this?" the voice on the other end asked sharply.

Starhawk breathed deeply. "Who you trying to call?" he asked in return, calmly, starting to smile.

"Isn't this 841-9470?"

81

Starhawk began to feel that he knew this voice from somewhere. "No," he said. "This is 9479. Try again, Mac." He hung up quickly.

Marlene Murphy came out of the bathroom, also naked, toweling her hair. Starhawk looked at her thoughtfully.

"You got a husband you sort of forgot to mention?" he asked.

"Me, a husband?" Marlene lit a cigarette. "Thanks for the laugh. I'd rather be in jail. A husband, Jesus, no, thanks."

"Well, somebody didn't like a man to be answering your phone," Starhawk said. "Somebody with a voice like a cop. Or a bill collector."

"My father," she said. "Oh, crap. Here I am 24 years old and working for a Master's in Social Psych and he thinks I shouldn't have a man in my apartment when he calls. That's the Irish for you."

The phone rang again.

Marlene answered it this time. Starhawk started to cross the room but she grabbed his leg and as he turned she took his penis in her hand.

"Daddy?" Marlene sounded genuinely surprised. "A man? No, I'm alone, studying for the exams." She was running her fingers around the crown of the penis and Starhawk was reacting with a notable swelling. "What? Look, I just told you. It was a wrong number. What am I, a suspect you got in the back room? You must have made a mistake, even if it was the first time in your whole life."

Marlene leaned forward and kissed Starhawk's cock quickly and shifted back to the phone at once. "No. I said no, Daddy, *no,* and I meant it. The Church says I'm supposed to go to Confession to a priest once a year. It doesn't say I'm supposed to go to Confession to my own father every time he calls me on the phone."

Her hand was moving rapidly now, trying to make

82

Starhawk ejaculate. He smiled, recognizing her game, and pulled away, to kneel before her and begin licking her inner thighs.

"No. I haven't seen Aunt Irene in two years. She's involved in *what*? Greenpeace? That's just to protect the whales. There's nothing communistic about it and half the people in Mendocino are in it. What? Sure, but they just *like* whales up there. What do you mean my voice is getting funny? It must be a cold coming on. Yes. Yes. Oh, God, it's the door. Yes. I love you, too, Daddy. The door." She hung up quickly, her pelvis heaving. "God, God, *God*. Oh, sweet fucking *Jesus* God."

Starhawk stood up and said, "You like that kind of game? Why don't you call the Archbishop and I'll do it to you again while you talk to him."

"You are a prize," Marlene said. "You really are a prize. Have you spent your whole life learning how to please women?"

"It's my life study," Starhawk said. "Everything else is just a hobby."

Starhawk, like most of the characters in this Romance, was a liar.

Most primates lied constantly, because they were afraid of *getting caught* and being pronounced no-good shits.

Starhawk was always afraid of getting caught, because his life study was really burglary.

Starhawk thought he had a right to steal anything and everything he could get away with, from the white people.

The white people had stolen all the land in Unistat from his ancestors.

Starhawk, like the grim moralists in P.O.E., was determined to *get even*.

Getting even was the basis of many primate semantic confusions, such as "expropriating the expropriators," "an absolute crime demands an absolute penalty," "they did it to me so I can do it to them," and, in general, the emotional mathematics of "one plus one equals zero" $(1 + 1 = 0)$.

The primates were so dumb they didn't realize that one plus one equals two $(1 + 1 = 2)$ and one murder plus one murder equals two murders, one crime plus one crime equals two crimes, etc.

They did not understand *causality* at all.

The few primates who did understand causality slightly called it *karma*. They said all sorts of foolish things about it.

They didn't even know enough mathematics to describe quantum probability-waves. They said, in crude hominid metaphor, that bad karma led to *"bad vibes."*

Starhawk would have found all this philosophy boring. He has been busy indulging his hobby with Marlene Murphy. He has sucked her to orgasm three times now and fucked her once. Now she is sucking him.

It was not really his life study, but he enjoyed it thoroughly.

Marlene, purring contentedly after her four orgasms, is trying to express her gratitude by deep-throating him.

THE IMAGINARY INDIAN

> Every system grows until it encroaches upon other systems.
>
> —FINAGLE'S LAW OF EVOLVING SYSTEMS

Once, just before sleep, Josephine Malik drifted into a near-dream about the man with no wife, no horse and no mustache. He was a Pueblo Indian and he had lost wife, horse and mustache all because of radioactive poisons unleashed in Los Alamos. She jerked back to full waking quickly, realizing that her mystery was about to evaporate into another ecological disaster parable.

Then she saw another scenario; the hero, this time, was a French Canadian and an obsessive gambler. He was in the longest game of cutthroat stud poker in history and had wagered all his money, then his wife, and in mounting desperation his horse, losing all the time. Finally, terrified of being pushed out of the game, he bet his mustache. The cards came to him one at a time: jack of diamonds . . . queen of diamonds (possible flush) . . . king of spades (a straight?) . . . ace of clubs (a straight! !) . . . four of hearts . . .

LANDSLIDE

Bryce S. DeWitt states: "The Copenhagen view promotes the impression that the collapse of the state vector, and even the state vector itself, is all in the mind." . . . . One fact which seems to emerge from the present discussions of the nature of consciousness is that it is nonlocal (*i.e.*, not confined to a certain region of space-time). . . .

—LAWRENCE BEYNAM, *Future Science*

Furbish Lousewart V was elected President of the United States in 1980 with the greatest landslide since Roosevelt II buried poor Alf Landon alive in 1936. The People's Ecology Party also gained control of both the House and the Senate and 23 governorships out of the 51.

The PEP platform, a weird mixture of tangled religiosity and New Left anti-rationalism, became official policy.

The New Order began mildly—at least by comparison with what was to follow—and the major changes of the first administration consisted only of cutting the NASA budget to zilch; banning McDonald's hamburger shops (which resulted in underground "Steakeasies," where you gave the right password and got a Big Mac for $7); outlawing tobacco (a "lid" of Chesterfields was soon selling for $50 to $75 coast to coast); appointing three anti-technology fanatics to the first three vacancies in the Supreme Court; forbidding the teaching of Logical Positivism in colleges; throwing everybody off welfare (the streets were soon full of crippled and schizophrenic beggars, some of whom also slept there or even starved there on occasion, creating that Third World look which PEP regulars regarded as "spiritual"); cutting the use of electricity by 50 percent, gas by 70 percent and atomic energy by 97 percent, thereby causing millions to freeze to death and millions more to join the army of unemployed beggars on the streets; beginning all Cabinet meetings with hatha yoga sessions and Krishna chanting; serializing the collected works of Ralph Nader in the official Party newspaper, *Doom;* encouraging Party members to beat up mathematicians, geologists, science-fiction fans and other "non-ec" types ("non-ec" types were those either known to be disloyal to the Party or suspected of such disloyalty); encouraging the re-emergence of cottage industry by rigidly repressing every more advanced kind of industry; introducing Zen meditation to grammar schools; and, most important of all, blaming the host of new and tragic problems that resulted from government policies on an alleged conspiracy of "scientists" and instituting a nationwide witch-hunt to round up the members of this conspiracy for incarceration in re-education centers.

The Revolution of Lowered Expectations had triumphed. By 1984 nobody in the country had any higher expectations than a feudal serf.

Actually, the apotheosis of Furbish Lousewart V had been engineered by the same group of alpha males who had been promoting the Revolution of Lowered Expectations all along.

These were very cunning old primates in several of the most skillful predator bands on Terra. Because of the stealth and skill of these bands—made up of successful predator families that had been intermarrying for several generations—they collectively owned 99.4 percent of all the territory and resources of Unistat.

They only owned about 40 percent of the rest of Terra, and that seriously annoyed them.

The Revolution of Rising Expectations annoyed them even more, because it led many primates to argue that the reason poverty and starvation still continued in an advanced technological society was that *Somebody Was Getting More Than Their Share*. Whenever anybody asked who that *Somebody* might be, all eyes turned on these royal old primate males who owned so much. The eyes were not friendly. Sometimes, in far-off lands where these royal primates did not completely control the governments, some of their boodle was actually seized and redistributed to the people they had stolen it from. As Rising Expectations had mounted in the first half of the century, this regrettable pattern of expropriation also escalated.

The alpha males of these tough old predator families did not like this at all. They therefore invested a prudent sum in promoting the careers of everybody who preached Lowered Expectations, from Ralph Nader and the Club of Rome to Oriental gurus and the neo-Stoics of the post-Marxist Left.

When Furbish Lousewart came along, they invested in him, too—enough to buy the election for him.

THE QUANTUM CONNECTION IS UNMITIGATED

> There is no escape from our robothood unless and until we first recognize the fact. Only then can we learn to take control of our nervous systems and reprogram our individual realities.
>
> —LEARY AND WILSON, *Neuropolitics*

When Justin Case returned from the john, the mad Simon Moon was still reading his nightmare version of the American Dream.

"Upper guns thou wilt, marxafactors," Moon intoned, half-chanting. "A gnew gnu cries nixnix on your loin ardors [O my am I?] as the great Jehoover fouls his files [Seminole cowhand] with marching looter congs. What a loop in the evening, bloody-fouled loop! Lawn ordures for Crookbacked Dick, pig-bastarchd of the world. See, it's the stinking onion coop. Say, it's the slimey deepsea doodler. By the wampum of caponey. O turnig on, Duke Daleyswine, lardmayor of burningtown! They'll chip away yore homo hawks."

"Hughes Rockefeller Exxon," the drunken writer was muttering into his martini glass. "Thieving motherfucking . . ."

Justin decided the party was degenerating and left. In the foyer he had to pass Marvin Gardens and Josephine Malik and heard:

"Male chauvinist paranoid!" [Josephine to Marvin.]

"Extraterrestrial brainwasher!" [Marvin to Josephine.]

Justin decided morosely that the literary world had never been the same since the drug revolution of the 1960s and '70s. "Pretty little boidies picking in the toidies," he said gruffly to both of them and walked out.

Justin had no idea where he had gotten the words about the pretty little boidies from. He assumed it was the Afghan hash going around at the party.

"I know all *about* your *plansss,*" Marvin Gardens was snarling at Jo Malik, in his coked-up Peter Lorre voice. "I know why you picked Hemingway to discredit and *defame.* I know what you and your *extraterrestrial friends* are planning to do to humanity, you cold-blooded *fiendsss.*"

"You know," Jo said, suddenly tired of her own anger, "you really ought to lay off that coke, buster."

"Yess, *yess,* claim that I'm paranoid, that's the *usual tactic—*"

"I say you two," Epicene Wildeblood drawled, "did either of you see Cagliostro?"

"The magician?" Jo asked.

"Well," Wildeblood asked with infinite patience, "is there another Cagliostro?"

Marvin and Jo exchanged equally puzzled glances.

"I guess he hasn't arrived yet," Jo offered finally.

"What?" Wildeblood frowned. "Why, he's been here all night."

Marvin and Jo exchanged glances again.

"I guess we missed him," Marvin said gently, with the ghastly smile of one who humors a deranged mind.

Wildeblood glared at him and stalked off.

That was really heavy hash, Jo decided. Wildeblood had been hallucinating a guest who wasn't even there.

DEMATERIALIZING GORILLAS

Knee-jerk liberals and all the certified saints of sanctified humanism are quick to condemn this great and much-maligned Transylvanian statesman.

—WILLIAM F. BUCKLEY, JR., *The Wit and Wisdom of Vlad the Impaler*

The Warren Belch Society held its annual meeting on January 2, 1984, while P.O.E. was busy mining downtown Washington with homemade atom bombs. The Society knew nothing of this and was more concerned with disappearing gorillas in Chicago.

Their tiny office was dominated by a huge oil painting of Schrödinger's Cat, executed in weird orgone-blue hues by their founder and presiding officer, the eccentric millionaire, W. Clement Cotex. All active members of the Society—eight of them, to be exact—were present.

The Warren Belch Society had been founded after Cotex had been kicked out of the Fortean Society for having bizarre notions. The purpose of "the Belchers" (as Cotex jovially called them) was to investigate those aspects of scientific theory and those alleged occult events which were regarded as "too far out" by the unimaginative Forteans, who were willing to investigate UFO's, rains of crabs and fish, girls who might have turned into swans, and similar matters, but, like their founder, the late Charles Fort, drew the line at dogs that said "Good morning" and then vanished in a puff of green smoke.

Cotex, admittedly, was an intellectual surrealist. The name of the Society, for instance, was deliberately taken from the most obscure of all the lawmen of the Old

91

West, Marshall Warren Belch of Dodge City, who had unfortunately been shot to death when his pistol jammed during his very first gunfight. It was Clem Cotex's claim that the Everett-Wheeler-Graham-DeWitt interpretation of the Schrödinger's Cat paradox was literally true. *Everything that could happen did happen.* There were infinitely many universes, each one the result of a collapse of the state vector in a possible way. Thus, somewhere in super-space, there must be a universe in which Marshall Belch's pistol didn't jam and he lived on to become famous. There were probably TV shows and movies about him by now, over there in that universe. Or so Cotex argued.

In general, as good empiricists, the Belch Society was more interested in odd facts than in odd theories. A UFO Contactee who could jam zippers by looking at them. A man found dead in St. Louis with his throat torn as though by the fangs of an enormous beast, with no animal missing from the local zoos (the famous Stimson Case of 1968). Documented instances of a fat bearded man with jolly eyes seen near chimneys on Christmas Eve, with a bag of toys over his shoulder. Bleeding Catholic statues. Flying Hindus. Dematerializing Buddhists. Kahuna fire-walkers. Why the signs always say WALK when the streetlight is on red and DON'T WALK when it is on green. Books in which the permutations of the phrase "heaven and hell" appeared at random intervals, forming a Markoff Chain.

"Take anybody in the world—anybody in this novel," Cotex once explained his theory to a group of skeptical fellow characters. "Like you, Dr. Williams," he added, picking out the most erudite and wiggy in the crowd, Blake Williams. "In one of the parallel universes, you're probably not an anthropologist, but maybe a chemist or something. In another universe, you might even be a female musician instead of a male scientist. And so on. In another universe," Cotex concluded, *"I might* be a small businessman from Little Rock, who believes the universe is five-cornered."

The disappearing gorillas, they were all convinced, were: (a) a major breakthrough to another universe; (b) not yet known to those stuffy old Forteans; and (c) really hot stuff.

"If gorillas can teleport," Prof. Fred "Fidgets" Digits was saying, "that may be the whole key to the Mad Fishmonger."

"We needn't assume that the gorillas actually teleport," Dr. Horace Naismith objected. "It may be that there is a Schwartzchild Radius in Lincoln Park Zoo and they sort of fall into it and pass the Event Horizon."

This led to some lively debate on whether teleportation was or was not more likely than a Black Hole in the Lincoln Park Zoo, but Blake Williams suddenly derailed the conversation with a thoughtful and uncompleted, "I wonder if this goes all the way back to the Democratic Convention of 1968. . . ."

"Say," Cotex cried, eyes wide. "What was all that fighting and fussing about, anyway? The way I remember it, the radicals wanted to sleep in the park and the police beat the shit out of them and chased them out of the park. That seems an awfully silly issue to lead to a whole week of rioting and tear-gassing. And why were so many journalists—*and especially cameramen*—attacked by the cops . . . ?"

"You think maybe the city authorities knew about it, even back then . . . ?" Naismith asked eagerly.

"People may resist new ideas, as we all know to our sorrow," Williams said, "but a fact this size—*over two hundred* gorillas purchased by the zoo over a ten-year period and *only two* accounted for—must have been noticed by somebody on the finance committee at least. You can bet your sweet ass the city authorities know about it. And, of course, they're imposing a cover-up, just like the air force with the UFOs. The same old government reflex. Pavlov's Dog meets Schrödinger's Cat again."

"This is a time for action, not theory," said Cotex. "Gentlemen, I am flying to Chicago tonight to begin a personal investigation. A case like this is a surrealist's heaven and a logician's hell," he added with a chuckle. He was totally non-linear.

WHAT AM I?

The ego, or territorial-status circuit of the primate brain, is a social creation for which one person at a time gets the blame.

—SIGMUND FREUD, *Was Will Die Frau?*

One day Blake Williams saw one of his old, out-of-print books in a secondhand bookstore on Fourth Avenue. He took it down from the shelf for a minute and looked at it with the kind of nervous awe a parent has for a grown child who returns to visit. *Primate Sociobiology,* by Blake Williams, Ph.D. My God, he thought, is that me—Blake Williams, Ph.D.? It seems only a few hours ago I was entering Noel F. Turn Junior High back in Bar Sinister, Maine: How did I get to be 51 years old so suddenly? What the hell does that Ph.D. mean?—if anything, I know less now than I knew then. How did I get to be an authority in my field? The gods' revenge on those who lack respect for authority is to make them authorities themselves, as Al said. Two marriages, three children; it isn't possible. Who am I really, behind the Ph.D. and the husbandrole, the fatherrole, the divorcerole, the authorityrole? Who am I, hell, *what* am I? Why am I? *Am* I?

Blake opened the book at random and read:

In the higher primates, the ego is developed to a stage of near-emergency. *My* territory, *my* space, *my* semantic excretions demark the most important system in the universe; no other system may encroach.

Since this contradicts the non-locality principle of quantum mechanics, most primate physicists perforce become mystics, claiming that the territory marked by the boundary is functionally identical with the territory outside the boundary.

Blake Williams hastily shoved the book back into the gap on the shelf, closing off the flood of metaphysical dread it had unleashed.

So far Blake Williams had accumulated only five explanations of what collapses that *verdammt* state vector and "causes" or leastways brings it about that a quantum leap occurs:

1). *Everything possible that can happen to the state vector does happen to it.* There are multiple universes, where everything that can happen, does happen. He had gotten this answer from physicists like Everett, Wheeler, Graham and DeWitt, from Clem Cotex and from numerous science-fiction writers.

2). *A decision in the consciousness of the observer collapses the state vector.* He had gotten this answer from many disciples of Niels Bohr who said that that was what the Copenhagen Interpretation meant. They were contradicted by other disciples of Bohr who denied that that was what the Copenhagen Interpretation meant.

3). *The Hidden Variable collapses it.* He had gotten that answer from Einstein, Walker, Bohm and several other physics biggies, and variations of it from Clem Cotex, who sometimes said the Mad Fishmonger did it, and Simon Moon, who said the Gentry did it.

4). *Pure chance does it.* He had gotten that answer from the majority of high school science teachers and readers of *Scientific American.*

5). *Eris, the Greek goddess of chaos and confusion, does it.* He had gotten that answer from a San Francisco computer expert named Gregory Hill, who wrote odd theological treatises under the pen-name Malaclypse the Younger.

Having met Hagbard Celine, Blake Williams knew that it was inevitable that there be precisely five explanations. Hagbard claimed that there were five explanations for *everything.* He called it the Law of Fives.

Hagbard had also secretively informed Williams that behind his usual mask of jet-set millionaire he was secretly the Grand Master of the Illuminati. Williams had no idea that Hagbard had Simon Moon and Josephine Malik convinced that he was the Chief Clown of the Discordian Society, the age-old anarchist conspiracy devoted to frustrating the Illuminati.

THE MAD FISHMONGER

There is no such thing as water. It is merely melted ice.

—FURBISH LOUSEWART V, *Unsafe Wherever You Go*

The Mad Fishmonger was the patron saint of the Warren Belch Society. He, or she, had originally appeared, or had been alleged to have appeared, in Cromer Gardens, Worcester, England, on May 28, 1881. He, or she, along with perhaps a dozen assistants, had rushed through Cromer Gardens at high noon, throwing crabs and periwinkles all over the streets. They also threw crabs and periwinkles into the fields beside the road. They climbed high walls to dump some of the fish into gardens and onto the roofs of houses.

It was thorough, painstaking work, and since the Mad Fishmonger and his, or her, associates accomplished it all at noon on a busy day *without being seen,* the citizens of Cromer Gardens claimed that the crabs and periwinkles had fallen out of the sky.

This notion was not acceptable to the scientists of the day, who held it as axiomatic that crabs and periwinkles do not fall out of the sky. A scientist from *Nature* magazine therefore offered the Mad Fishmonger an explanation, although he failed to explain how the Fishmonger and his co-conspirators had accomplished their feat without being noticed by any of the citizenry.

Charles Fort, founder of the Fortean Society, rejected the Mad Fishmonger indignantly and claimed that crabs and periwinkles *did* fall from the sky. After Clem Cotex was thrown out of the Fortean Society for his heresies, he reconsidered the whole puzzling case of the mysterious event in Cromer Gardens of May 28, 1881. Cotex decided to believe in the Mad Fishmonger. It was the fundamental hypothesis of his system of philosophy, and the guiding light of the Warren Belch Society, that the craziest-sounding theory is the most likely one. All things considered, the motives and methodology of the Mad Fishmonger were much more mysterious than shellfish falling from the sky; *ergo,* the Mad Fishmonger probably did exist.

There were many events which the science of that primitive period could not explain. Indeed, due to the failure of scientists to study neuroprogramming, such science as existed bore many remnants of the outdated dogmatisms of theology and priestcraft.* As a result, those events which science could not yet explain were not eagerly accepted as data which science should explain by generating more inclusive and sophisticated scientific theories, as happens on civilized planets. Instead, there was a whole profession of primates devoted to proving such events never *really* happened, but only "seemed to" happen.

The people who worked at this profession called themselves Skeptics. They were not skeptical at all.

---

* *Terran Archives 2803:* Theology was a system for explaining things by coining words which nobody could understand and pretending that the words meant something. Among the Western primates the chief word used for this purpose was "God." Among the Eastern primates it was "karma." Both words were, of course, crude primate gropings toward the system of quantum checks-and-balances which causes the greatest Whole System, and all the lesser Whole Systems, to cohere.

They were True Believers in the scientific paradigms of that barbaric and primitive age.

Among the things the science of that time could not explain, which Clem Cotex attributed to the Mad Fishmonger, were other Damned Things that fell out of the sky, such as iron balls with inscriptions on them or chunks of ice as big as elephants. There were also Damned Things on the ground, including jumping furniture, "haunts" and the Gentry. There were animals that shouldn't be and animals that couldn't be and trans-time and trans-space perceptions and religious "miracles."

The first clue to correct understanding of these things came when quantum causality was finally formulated correctly in Gilhooley's Demonstration of 1984, and nobody understood Gilhooley.

At the time of our story everybody was as confused as Clem Cotex. Most of them just expressed their confusion, or rather concealed it, in more conservative ways.

ANOTHER C.I.A. PLOT

The spirit of decision consists simply in not hesitating when an inner voice commands you to act.

—FURBISH LOUSEWART V, *Unsafe Wherever You Go*

Just before coming to Wildeblood's party, Blake Williams wrote one of the most heretical passages in his jealously guarded *Secret Diaries*. He wrote:

I am an anthropologist, *ergo* a professional liar. An anthropologist is a scientist trained to observe that every society is a little bit mad, including his own. He holds his job by never mentioning this . fact explicitly.

Perhaps 1983 as a whole had been too much for him.

In January, one of the biggest breakthroughs had occurred at Project Pan, and Williams and Dashwood had to reach new heights of eloquence to persuade the other scientists involved that any premature disclosure could be lethal. At that very time, they pointed out, the John Birch Society was staging massive sit-ins and protests against the introduction of anthropology texts to high schools in Orange County.

In February, the Government Accounting Office announced that all the gold in Fort Knox had disappeared sometime in the past decade.

In March, three new life-extension pills were placed on the market, during the controversy over FOREVER, the first life-extension pill, which was widely suspected of creating disastrous side-effects. All the data on FOREVER thus far had shown one consistency: scientists not employed by Blue Sky, Inc., the manufacturer of FOREVER, continually found evidence of these tragic side-effects, and all scientists employed by Blue Sky continually found no evidence of such problems. (That month Blake Williams wrote in his *Diaries,* quoting Lord Macaulay, "The law of gravity would be thrown into dispute were there a commercial interest involved.")

In April, average rent for a one-room apartment reached $1,000 per month and many families were renting broom closets at $600 to $700 per month or just sleeping in parks. Landlords were hanged in Berkeley, California, and Carbondale, Michigan.*

In May, the missing gold from Fort Knox was found buried at San Clemente. Nixon still denied *everything*.

The new *World Almanac* listed the first UFO cult to reach 20,000,000 members among the major world religions.

In June, the first human embryo transplant was accomplished and the U.S. troops in Tierra del Fuego mutinied.

In July, FEMFREE, a drug which allegedly removed mothering impulses, was banned by the F.D.A., and UFO cultists and Christians clashed in Belfast.

In August, astronomer Bertha Van Ation discovered two new planets in the solar system, and bootleg FEMFREE at ten times the free market price began to circulate through Women's Lib groups coast to coast.

In September, UFO cultists and Moslems clashed in Cairo.

In October, landlords were lynched in three more American cities, the first human brain transplant was accomplished, and UFO cultists clashed with Maoists in Peking.

In November, Mae Brussell on KPFA-Berkeley charged that Jesus had been killed by a C.I.A. plot.

---

* *Galactic Archives:* Rent was a form of tribute paid by non-"owning" users of land to non-using "owners." The "owners," known as *lords-of-the-land,* or *landlords* for short, were originally relatives of the alpha male or king (see Nomis of Noom, "From the Baboon Food-Gathering Band to Consciousness"), but among the higher barbarians, such as in Unistat at the time of this epic, anyone with enough "money" could buy land and become a "landlord."

A HIT ON THE HEAD

> Every society encourages some behaviors and puni-
> tively forbids others. Thus, although cultures were not
> scientifically designed, they act much like computers
> programmed for specific results. One can look at their
> cultural structure and predict: this one will have a
> high murder rate, this one will have many schizo-
> phrenics, this one will remain Stone Age unless in-
> terfered with, this one is going to the stars.
>
> —MARILYN CHAMBERS, *Neuro-Anthropology*

Benny "Eggs" Benedict never got home from Epicene
Wildeblood's party that night. On the corner of Lexington and Twenty-third, Benny was hit by a heavy lead
pipe which smashed his skull and killed him. The pipe
did not fall by accident; it was wielded deliberately by
a man named Francesco "Pablo" Gomez. Pablo did
not hate Benny or have any personal feelings toward
him at all and he did not grin sadistically. Pablo hit
Benny with the pipe because Benny was well dressed
and probably had money in his pockets. When Benny
was comatose but not yet dead, Pablo dragged him into
an alley and went through his pockets, finding to his
delight that his surmise had been correct and Benny
was actually carrying more than $50; he had $52,
to be exact. Benny died while Pablo was rifling the
wallet.

To Pablo, $52 was a lot of money. He went home
humming happily.

That's the way things were in Unistat at the height
of the Revolution of Lowered Expectations.

CLUES

Every string which has one end also has another end.

—FINAGLE'S FIRST FUNDAMENTAL FINDING

Clem Cotex had been nosing about the Lincoln Park Zoo for several days and was more puzzled than ever. The facts were undeniable: the zoo had, indeed, purchased over 200 gorillas in the past decade and only two of them were on exhibit; 198 were missing. Any sort of casual questioning of the primate house attendants brought instantly vague answers in a well-rehearsed manner. They were all in on the cover-up. The public was being protected against all knowledge of the inexplicable, the weird, the surrealistic. All part of the usual governmental pretense that human affairs were rationally administered by experts who knew what was really going on. They feared that if people ever discovered that those in power were as confused by this inexplicable universe as those out of power, then the whole charade might collapse.

There was no Black Hole in the zoo; Cotex was sure of that. All gravity conditions were normal. The gorillas were not falling through a Schwartzchild radius into the universe next door or anything really spooky like that. They were simply teleporting somewhere . . . maybe back to their homelands in Africa. Although, considering the unpredictability of teleportive currents as documented by Charles Fort—who had recorded cases of snakes landing in Memphis, Tennessee, and coconuts being deposited in Worcester, England—the gorillas might actually be reappearing *anywhere*.

103

Since anything might be a clue in such occult enigmas, Clem had carefully copied all the graffiti in the men's room at the primate house. It was the usual jumble of disparate and ambiguous signals: "Black P. Stone Run It," "For a good blow job call 237-1717 and ask for Father James Flanagan," "Help Prevent Von Neumann's Catastrophe!," "Arm the Unemployed," "Free our four-legged brothers and sisters. A zoo is a child's heaven and an animal's hell," "Save the Whales—harpoon a Honda," "Off the Landlords," " ♀⇌ ∆⊓♀△⊒✳. " "Stamp Out Sizeism," "Death to all fanatics!"

Probably, Cotex thought morosely, there is an important signal in there and I'm just not imaginative enough to see it.

THE ALTRUIST

God bless America.

—LAST WORDS OF G. I. GURDJIEFF

Everybody who had been at Wildeblood's party felt compelled to attend Benedict's funeral, even though none of them enjoyed it. Benny had been one of the funniest writers of his time, at least in the daily press, and it would have been appropriate to send him off with a showing of old Laurel and Hardy films or something equally in his own métier. Primate decorum forbade this. They packed him in with a dull and depressing "religious" ceremony.

"I am the Resurrection and the Life," intoned a primate with his collar on backwards. Nobody knew what the hell that meant, if anything, but they tried to feel better when they heard it.

At the time Benny was buried, a window-washer was at work on the seventeenth floor of the Morgan Guaranty Trust at 23 Wall Street. He was an expert lip-reader and knew more of the secrets of Wall Street than anybody outside the Illuminati. In fact, the second reason he had become a window-washer was to get work in the Wall Street district and pick up useful information.

The main reason he had taken the job would have been even more unnerving to Morgan Guaranty had they known about it. The window-washer was a member of Purity of Essence and had already managed to place 333 homemade nuclear weapons on ledges so high nobody but a pigeon was ever likely to see them.

All of the weapons were set to go off at a signal from the P.O.E. computer—another homemade contraption but awesomely efficient. P.O.E. was full of science grads who had dropped out of the career game in horror and revulsion at the uses to which science was being put in their universe.

At this point P.O.E. had 28 American cities mined. The window-washer hoped that, when push came to shove, P.O.E. wouldn't have to detonate more than one of those cities. He was an altruist, like everybody else in Purity of Essence.

PRIMATE ECONOMICS

With capital the line grows thick,
With capital there is no clear demarcation.

—KARL MARX, *Canto 23*

GALACTIC ARCHIVES:

Domesticated primates originally imprinted/hooked
their bio-survival circuit onto the extended primate
family (*viz:* the baboon band, the hominid tribe). As
domestication of the majority by the predator minority
advanced in complexity, the primates were increasingly
isolated and atomized; they referred to this process as
"alienation" or *"anomie."* They had many huge hives,
but no hive-bond. Their bio-survival circuitry was now
hooked to the peculiar tickets called *"money."*

Concretely, this meant that the average domesticated
primate needed to get these tickets in order to live.

Any attempt to remove their tickets, or cut off their
supply of tickets, caused them *acute bio-survival anxiety*. The tickets had become a substitute for the extended family, the tribe, the communal bond. Thus,
the usual symptoms when the tickets were withdrawn
were identical with those found in tribal persons suddenly isolated from the tribe: dizzy spells, paranoia,
nightmares, sweating palms, heart palpitations, delusions and hallucinations.

These symptoms were so common in Unistat that
there was a vast "Mental Health" movement to try to
alleviate them. This was because the Unistat alpha
males managed the ticket supply in such a way that
almost everybody always felt that they didn't have quite

enough tickets and would probably have less next week. The poor mammals lurched around in a state of acute bio-survival emergency, all neural signals sending vast quantities of adrenaline, adrenochrome and adrenalutin into their bloodstreams. These chemicals are the same that any animal produces in emergency situations; the same that tribal primates produce when ostracized from the tribe; the source of the neurosomatic symptoms such as nightmares and dizzy spells mentioned above.

The alpha males managed the ticket supply in this manner for the same reason they endowed churches and "Left Wing" organizations that preached that most primates are *no-good shits*. It is easier to control domesticated primates when they are anxious and depressed. Such chemical-emotional reflexes keep the poor hive-apes submissive and confused.

Unfortunately, the alpha males of Unistat, like most alpha males in other primitive societies, did not know when they had too much of a good thing going for them. They had increased the anxiety level of their society to the point where they actually had one violent crime every eight minutes. Still, they didn't realize they were approaching the explosive level, despite the fact that P.O.E. had been preceded by dozens of similarly desperate outlaw bands.

The alpha males kept financing the Revolution of Lowered Expectations and hoped that the domesticated majority would settle for the lives of medieval serfs. As the gasoline ran out, and the planet's resources dwindled, it became evident that this strategy was sound. The domesticates continued to submit.

What the alpha males had forgotten was that the science of weaponry had already evolved to the point where even a small minority of angry, rage-filled people could blow the whole planet to hell.

Even if they had understood this, it is doubtful that the alpha males would have tried to create a world in which it was impossible for anybody to get that angry. Such a goal would have seemed Utopian to them. They could not guess that it was actually a necessity on any advanced technological planet.

TAKE WHAT THOU HAST

Take what thou hast and give it to the poor.

—ATTRIBUTED TO SOME LONGHAIR COMMIE FREAK

The letter was sent out May 1, 1984, to the New York *Times-News-Post,* the Chicago *Sun,* the Los Angeles *Times-Free Press,* NBC News, CBS News, the White House, Mae Brussel, the Berkeley *Barb,* KPFA, ABC News, the London *Times,* Zodiac News Service, the *Christian Science Monitor,* the Archdiocese of New York, Chicago, San Francisco and St. Louis, the Church of Scientology, Mark Lane, Paul Krassner, Dick Gregory, Chase Manhattan Bank, the Bad Ass *Bugle,* the Nihilist Anarchist Horde, Norman Mailer and 237 miscellaneous other institutions and celebrities. P.O.E. wanted to be sure that their message would get out to the general public with the minimum of distortion by the Establishment.

The letter said:

May God forgive us. May history judge us charitably.

We have placed tactical nuclear bombs in over 1,700 locations throughout the United States. The targets are all enemies of the people: large banks, multinational corporations, government facilities. We will trigger one of these bombs at noon tomorrow, somewhere in the eastern United States, to demonstrate that we are not bluffing.

All of the other nuclear bombs will be triggered in succession until our demands are met. If any attempt is made to apprehend and arrest us—any attempt at all—all the remaining bombs will be detonated at once.

We demand:

That President Furbish Lousewart immediately confiscate all fortunes above one million dollars;

That this money, which we calculate makes a sum of approximately three trillion dollars, be distributed at once to the forty million families who are, according to the government's own standards, living below the poverty line, so that each poor family receives $75,000;

That all government money presently invested in weapons of war and preparations for war be immediately redirected to improving schools, homes and hospitals in poor neighborhoods, so as to make them fit for human beings;

That President Lousewart, in accepting our terms, shall further publicly repudiate all the lies he has uttered at the behest of the corporations and banks who secretly finance the People's Ecology Party; that he repudiate specifically all he has said about the necessity of lowered expectations; that he admit that human beings have the right to high expectations and to an ever-better and more humane use of technology for the benefit of all;

That George Washington be removed from the dollar bill and replaced by Walt Disney's Mickey Mouse to remind people forever of the idiocy of worshipping money.

A final word of warning: we have been working on this project for 16 years and have the full capacity to do all that we say. The Revolution of Lowered Expectations has been a monopolist's heaven and a poor people's hell. We intend to change that.

P.O.E.

COLLAPSE OF THE STATE VECTOR

> Records can be destroyed if they do not suit the prejudices of ruling cliques, lost if they become incomprehensible, distorted if a copyist wishes to impose a new meaning upon them, misunderstood if we lack the information to interpret them. The past is like a huge library, mostly fiction.
>
> —HENRY FORD, *Neuro-History*

The doorbell rang.

Josephine Malik said "Shit" quietly but fervently. She was correcting the galleys of the second printing of her *Clitoral Politics* and interruptions were not welcome.

Jo approached the door warily. The regular lock, the bolt lock and the police lock were all in place; the intruder would need an axe to get in, if he were one of the 2,000,000 violent criminals among the 20,000,000 citizens of New York in 1984.

"Who is it?" she shouted through the door.

"Ukraine."

"Who???" she screamed.

"Hugh Crane," came the voice, louder. "We met at a Wildeblood party last December. . . ."

"Go away. I don't know you and I'm busy."

"This is important. The novel we're in is coming to a horrible conclusion. . . ."

"You're nuts. Go away." Jo turned away from the

door and went to the closet for her Saturday Night Special, in case this maniac did have an axe.

"Listen to me, please, we've only got a few minutes," the voice shouted through the door. "Maybe you can almost remember the name Hagbard Celine. That's the name I had in the last quantum *eigen*state, the last novel, when we worked together. . . ."

Jo went to the phone. "Give me the police!" she shouted, forgetting that she wasn't yelling through a door anymore.

It was the last sentence she ever spoke.

At that moment, Manhattan Island became a nuclear furnace.

President Lousewart, guided by Intelligence Agencies that had collectively listened to enough "private" conversations to be stone-paranoid, had acted within minutes after the P.O.E. letter arrived in the White House. The Unistat government would not be blackmailed. Even before TV could broadcast the story of the threat, over 10,000,000 "radicals" and possible "radicals" had been placed under arrest coast to coast. One of them, more or less accidentally, had been Sylvia Goldfarb of P.O.E.

All 1,700 P.O.E. bombs detonated at once. Unistat as an entity ceased to exist. Nihilist Anarchist Hordes roamed what was left of the landscape.

Twenty-three hundred nuclear missiles, computer-guided to fire if Unistat were nuked, took off at the first blast and decimated Russia. The Beast had been programmed by Intelligence Agencies who were all convinced that any nuclear attack would come from there.

Twenty-three hundred Russian missiles took off the

111

moment the first Unistat missile entered Russian airspace. They all went to China. The Russian computer had also been programmed by very dogmatic, very inflexible primates; it "knew" that any nuclear attack would come from China.

Starhawk was coming out of a bar on Geary when Frisco went. He was incinerated before his brain could register that anything was happening.

Lionel Eacher, long since returned to Contract Law, outlived most of them. He had been on vacation in Upper Michigan and was well armed, since he had been hunting. He survived by hunting and eating other mammals, including formerly domesticated primates, for nearly twenty years.

Then another formerly domesticated primate, even quicker and slicker, hunted and ate Lionel.

F.D.R. Stuart went with New York City. So did Justin Case, Epicene Wildeblood, Jo Malik and most of the others.

Joe Malik was horrified. He didn't want the novel to end so abruptly and unpleasantly. He had a lot more work in mind for Wilson, a virtual epic, in fact. He tried frantically to regain control of the book.

Wilson had seen San Francisco go, from his window high in the Berkeley hills, while trying to work out a happy ending despite the grim circumstances.

He was blinded by the flash, of course, and stumbled about in a black world of mad chaos, like most Berkeleyans, until the radiation finished him off.

Markoff Chaney survived. He was on a Greyhound in Florida, between Miami and Hollywood, when the bombs went off. He took to the Everglades and eventually even found a mate—a Seminole woman who didn't think he was absurd at all.

Their tribe increased.

The tribal stage endured one hundred thousand years, as it had before.

Then, suddenly, when environmental conditions were right, genetic programs reasserted themselves. The hive instinct re-appeared in the primates. Cities appeared, sin and guilt were re-invented, technology advanced.

Nuclear energy was rediscovered, and misused again.

The tribal age endured twelve million years the next time.

Then, suddenly, when environmental conditions were right, genetic programs reasserted themselves. The hive instinct re-appeared in the primates. Cities appeared, sin and guilt were re-invented, technology advanced. . . .

The six-legged majority knew little and cared less about all this primate activity. They had solved all their social problems three billion years earlier, and saw no need to change. They followed their own DNA cycles, just as monotonously as the primates followed primate cycles.

GALACTIC ARCHIVES

And so ends the first movement of this mightiest of all Terran novels. Critics from Sirius to Betelguise, in a thousand years of commentaries, have not yet exhausted the richness of these few pages, in which the ancient Bard so cleverly and inventively introduces, in the dark mode, all those cosmic and glorious themes which are to be so beautifully realized in the subsequent developments. *Schrödinger's Cat* and Beethoven's *Ninth,* it is generally agreed, are the two Terran artifact-signals that most richly embody the experience—the agony, the anger, the ultimate joy—of domesticated primates evolving toward True Consciousness.

INTER-OFFICE MEMOS

J. C. to G. B.:

I've read through several barely related chapters now and I'm totally adrift. Even if Wilson somehow justifies all this deliberate eccentricity, his delusions of grandeur definitely need to be cut or toned down. Writing megalomaniac future scholarship about himself is a bit thick, I'd say. Why publish such drivel?

G. B. to J. C.:

Read on. It's all part of The Plot, as you'll soon realize.

BETWEEN WORLDS

Josephine Malik lies trembling on the bed, trying to be brave, trying to hide her fear. Where, now, is the mask of masculinity?

"The delusion that you are a man trapped in a woman's body can only be cured one way. I might be kicked out of the American Psychoanalytical Association if they knew about my methods. In fact, already had a spot of bother with them when one of my patients cured his Oedipus complex by actually fucking his mother, convincing himself that she really was an old lady and not the woman he remembered from infancy. Nevertheless, the whole world is going bananas, as you must have noticed, my poor girl, and we have to use heroic measures to save whatever sanity remains." [*The psychiatrist is now naked. He joins her on the bed.*] "Now, my little frightened dove, I will convince you that you really are a true-born, honest-to-God woman. . . ."

The psychiatrist was either Horus the War God or the mysterious Hugh Crane, master of magick, or else he was Hagbard Celine.

It's hard to be sure of anything when you're lost out here.

Faster than a speeding photon, Jo leaped to another *eigen*state.

THE UNIVERSE
NEXT DOOR

by Robert Anson Wilson

We doctors know
a hopeless case when—listen: there's a hell
of a good universe next door; let's go

—e e cummings, "pity this
busy monster, manunkind"

ROCKET BOOKS

Boston 1980

Take Two:

There Are No Fnords in the Advertisements

The influence of the senses have in men over-powered the thought to the degree that the walls of time and space have come to look solid, real and insurmountable. . . . Yet time and space are but inverse measures of the power of the mind. Man is capable of abolishing them both.

—Ralph Waldo Emerson

THE QUESTION OF REALITY

I still recall vividly the shock I experienced on first encountering this multiworld concept. The idea of $10^{100^\dagger}$ slightly imperfect copies of oneself all constantly splitting into further copies . . . is not easy to reconcile with common sense.

—BRYCE S. DEWITT, "QUANTUM MECHANICS AND REALITY," *Physics Today*, SEPT. 1970

TERRAN ARCHIVES 2803:

It was the nineteenth-century anarchist P. J. Proudhon who first warned that the number of laws, decrees, bureaucratic forms and miscellaneous paperwork being produced by governments might soon suffocate humanity in documents, a phenomenon he predicted future archeologists would refer to as "the papyraceous formation." He was nearly right. Before cybernetics and the information revolution, printed documents multiplied at an alarming rate in the nineteenth and twentieth centuries. And yet, in all this preserved pulp, we have been able to find only one reference to our sublime Bard, Robert Anson Wilson. This is certainly most astonishing.

Some claim that Robert Anson Wilson was abnormally shy and retiring, but this is an implausible theory considering the megalomania of *The Universe Next Door*. Others therefore urge that Wilson eventually got himself in trouble with the Neurological Police of that barbaric era and all his documentia were destroyed, *The Universe Next Door* and one other reference escaping by accident. This is somewhat more plausible, but has certainly not been established. All we can say for sure is that the Bard existed, wrote this one masterpiece, and left no further trace but a single news story.

For what light it might throw on the mystery, here is the one published reference ever found in which Robert Anson Wilson is mentioned. It is from a newspaper called *San Francisco Chronicle:*

NOBEL WINNER'S BAY AREA TOUR

A Crash Course in Occult

By Kevin Wallace

Edgy young Brian Josephson, 1973 British Nobel laureate in quantum physics, wasn't yet into blue jeans yesterday, but his shoes were off, and he padded around the Nob Hill apartment in maroon sox.

"Very, ah—well, different from Cambridge," the 36-year-old Welshman summarized his current two-week crash course in Bay Area physics, metaphysics, consciousness-raising, clairvoyance and inter-terrestrial intelligence probing.

He is here as guest of San Francisco's two-year-old Physics/Consciousness Research Group (PCRG), which finances physicists' mind expansion along lines universities ordinarily won't pay for.

"We got Brian into experiencing Cecil Williams at Glide Church Sunday, and turned him on to massage last night," declared his ebullient blue-jeaned host and guide, PCRG's physicist founder, Jack Sarfatti.

Josephson hastily changed the subject to his ESP inquiries at Stanford Research Institute, and talks at Lawrence Berkeley Lab on the question of reality—"they're very interested in the question of reality over there."

"Brian's very into Don Juan and Carlos Castenada," Sarfatti declared proudly, "though it all goes back to Maharishi."

Josephson said it was a Cambridge visit two years ago by Transcendental Meditation's Maharishi Mahesh Yogi that first piqued his puzzlement about reality in general and the occult learning of the Bay Area in particular.

"Initially," he said, "my

121

visit here was planned to study American artificial intelligence findings"—with a view to programming computers to deal with something like Maharishi's higher states of consciousness.

But the tour's horizons have been dramatically expanded by his host's broader concerns, including a speeding-up of the cumbersome speed-of-light factor in possible inter-terrestrial communications, adjusting the DNA molecule to extend the normal life span to 3000 years, tapping the latent energy supply in vacuums, and writing and producing a rock opera version of Goethe's "Faust."

"Quantum physics explains ordinary phenomena by real weird, surrealistic, psychedelic, occult things," Sarfatti said happily, and noted that his PCRG funnels donated funds not only for the Nobel laureate's visit, but to promote Lynn Hershman's environmental art, Tim Leary's space-migration research, Robert Anson Wilson's science fiction, and allied heavy questing—$40,000 worth in the past year.

"Werner Ehrhard of est gave us our first grant, and Mike Murphy of Esalen Institute advises us, and I'm in touch with Governor Brown, whom I call a real 'quantum politician,' " Sarfatti said. ("Quantum" refers in physics to the astonishing jumpiness of energy states.)

Josephson ventured timidly, "If the average person weren't too tied down to a rigid belief system, I feel it might, ah, change the nature of society."

"That's well said!" Sarfatti cried with gusto.

As far as we can determine, San Francisco was a city-state on the east coast of Unistat, although Professor Jubelum has proposed that it was actually an independent island or archipelago off the coast.

TO CROSS AGAIN

To cross again is not to cross.

—G. SPENCER BROWN,
Laws of Form

Mary Margaret Wildeblood had been born or reborn in November 1983, in John Hopkins Hospital. The very first sound she heard was a radio in the next ward playing:

> *God rest ye merry gentlemen*
> *Let nothing you dismay*

Localization was gradually determined: this universe, this galaxy, this solar system, this planet, this hospital. They were sawing off his penis.

Yes indisputably no doubt about it they were sawing off his penis. Seven dwarfs with evil grins were doing it. Then coming all the way out of the ether, this hospital, this bed, this morning in November 1983, Epicene Wildeblood knew at last who SHe really was. The radio sang cheerfully:

> *Remember Christ our Savior*
> *Was born upon this day*

SHe was still giddy from the ether, but that would pass; meanwhile the Voice of Dream was still talking, a fussy old professor lecturing: "One quantum jump away the ideal pretense is Real Presence. An S-T transformation. The English language limerick is restricted so that a cross carried up a hill is anisogamous but the essence

123

remains the Body and Blood of the first amoeba. Consider the following example which some consider Donne and others describe as overdone:

> *Quoth a merrie old judge named Magoo*
> *"Perversions? Yea, I've tried a few*
>   *But the best I e'er balled*
>   *Were Lee Harvey Oswald*
> *Seven dwarfs and a pink cockatoo!"*

"It doesn't scan," Wildeblood protested feebly.

A gay swish of starched cloth moved queerly and a nurse's bland blonde face appeared looking down at hir. "Anything the matter, dearie?" in a Brooklyn accent.

"What day is it?"

"Wednesday. Still Wednesday." The nurse spoke, as they always do after surgery, as if talking to an idiot.

The doctor recrossed on his pegleg (but that was slipping back into the dream again).

"Circumcision is a Jewish conspiracy. He bit it off, one great CHOMP! ! !—and off it came," Dr. Aháb was ranting. "I am the feet's lieutenant. Sprechen Sie Joysbrick?"

A dangling "e" fell past from another book.

They were opening the curtains to let in sunlight. The white wall was a hospital wall. A hand at his wrist told hir that now her pulse was being taken.

Epicene Wildeblood awakened again. "I'm Mary Margaret," he gasped happily, beached on the shore of reality, cast up from the ocean of dream.

"Yes," said the real doctor's voice [his name was Glopberger, not Ahab], "the operation was um 100 percent successful. You are most certainly Mary Margaret now." He beamed, an artist proud of his work, yet tentative, waiting for the Work's first live movement.

Mary Margaret Wildeblood looked about her at the New World. This is Johns Hopkins Hospital. This is 1983. Everything that went before was just a nightmare. I am alive. I am me. I am free.

"How soon do I get the Curse?" she cried. "When do I become a *real* woman?" Thinking: the Blood of the Lamb.

Glopberger's pink face, agape, was yet another Disney caricature, the waters of unconsciousness calling hir home. Home: back to the stars. And SHe went, she went, into the great ether drift, into the cosmic void again, from dina shaur to turban bay in a michaelsonmorley regurgitation to the Hawkfouledest Convention in Elveron. Yes a 44-year-old male rising like Venus on fours out of the waves but aglow gleaming as in Botticelli hir Self surprised at this astonishingly female body a really successful crossing and one hand crept as she slept toward the crypt rested there happy yes: it was true. A female body. She snored hoarsely.

And Dr. Glopberger, like Baron Frankenstein, looked on his work and saw that it was very good. So far.

MURPHY'S RELIGIOUS

Just as landowners preserve the game they are going to kill during the hunting season, so do lawyers preserve the criminal class.

—FURBISH LOUSEWART V, *Unsafe Wherever You Go*

They were sitting in a VW Rabbit on Market Street in San Francisco. The marquee across the street still said

DEEP THROAT after twelve years. "They never going to change that?" Starhawk asked. "Everybody and his brother been there to see that Linda Lovelace swallow peckers by now. Hell, everybody and his brother been there twice by now."

"She could swallow my pecker anytime," Mendoza said. Mendoza was a cop.

"I seen a funny one the other day," Starhawk said, starting to laugh. "In the men's crapper in the archeology building. 'Linda Lovelace for President,' it said. 'Let's have a *good-looking* cocksucker in the White House.' College kids."

"They're all a bunch of fags these days," Mendoza told him seriously. "Fags and dopers. And they call us pigs. Anyway, what were you doing in the archaeology building?"

"I like to study my people's history," Starhawk said. "There a law against that?"

"The fuck," Mendoza said, "I don't care what you do on your spare time. You make out with those college girls? Don't tell me, I know. You make out like a bandit. You're the greatest thing come down the pike since Burt Reynolds, you are."

Starhawk started to clean his nails with an attachment on his key ring.

"Tell me about the coke."

"Murph owns more guns than the army got, up in Presidio. He's a real nut on guns. I mean, it's your ass he catches you. He won't think twice about it. A police officer catching a burglar in his own house, it's your ass. You got to understand that."

"*Dig,*" Starhawk said. "It's always my ass. You think there's a crib worth knocking over they don't have guns these days? Christ, there's never been a better-armed country since we had the Revolution, is what it is. Even little old ladies. Even in Berkeley for Christ's sake. This is no business for anybody got shaky nerves, these days.

College professors, their houses are stacked with enough munitions for Black Panther headquarters. What I don't understand is how come everybody in the fucking country hasn't been at least wounded by now. Everybody's even more crazy-mad than they are shit-scared. It's like High Noon. You don't have to tell me, be careful. I wasn't careful, I'd be one dead Indian."

"Son of a bitch," Mendoza said suddenly, sitting up.

Starhawk was almost startled. "Huh?"

"That dog," Mendoza said. "You see that son of a bitch, shit right on the sidewalk? They do that all over the city, the ordinance doesn't mean a fucking thing. Dirty, filthy animals, I'd ban them from the fucking city entirely, I was mayor."

"Yeah," Starhawk said. "That's our chief problem here, dogs shitting on the street."

"It ain't funny," Mendoza said. "Filthy bastards spread all kinds of diseases. And you take your kid out for a walk and there's two of them humping and the kid says, 'Daddy, what are the doggies doing?' What are you gonna tell her, is what I wanna know. Dirty, filthy animals."

"Yeah, but about Murphy and this job."

"Okay, okay," Mendoza said. "I'm just telling you dirty filthy animals should be banned. With Murph you got to be in and out as slick and sneaky as a preacher's prick in a cow's ass. I mean, he likes guns, more than most cops. And he'd love an excuse to shoot you."

"Murphy?" Starhawk turned in his seat. "Murph and I, we never had any bad feelings."

"Well, okay, he loves the ground you walk on. Like all the hookers on Powell Street, and the housewives up in Marin, and the college girls now, too. But he hates what you are. He hates all minorities—Indians, niggers, it don't matter to him, he's democratic about it. The fuck, he doesn't like me much, and we been partners going on ten years this May. And he hates burglars

127

especially. An Indian burglar, that's almost as good to him as a nigger burglar. You got to realize that when you go in there."

"That's a hot one," Starhawk said, not laughing. "That really is a hot one. All the stuff he's fenced for me, and he hates burglars. That really is good. Next thing you'll tell me is the Vice Squad hates hookers."

"Murphy's religious," Mendoza said. "He'd love to make holes in you. That's what you got to understand."

"Support your local police," Starhawk said, "for a more efficient police state."

"Look, you on this caper or you just going to sit here and crack wise? I can get Marty Malloy, you know."

"You're religious, too," Starhawk said. "I went and made fun of the department and now you're going to get Malloy. Who'll fuck up the whole job and you'll both be up in Q for the next twenty years. But at least he won't crack wise about the department. He'll leave fingerprints all over the joint, and drop the snow in the bushes on his way out, and crash into an Oakland P.D. car going home, and then lead them right to your front door, but he's got proper respect for the police, Malloy. Yeah, you get Malloy."

"Look, no need to be touchy." Mendoza was ingratiating. "I want you. I don't want Malloy. Just lay off the department, is all."

"Okay, okay. No need for either of us to get antsy." Starhawk smiled like an actor. "How much coke you think?"

"Like I say, who knows? But it's got to be around 500 Gs. That's what Amato says and he's good at making estimates like that. Say Amato is wrong for once in his life, say it's only 300 Gs, still you don't get half of 300 Gs every night you go out and knock over a house."

"It's beautiful," Starhawk said. "It's so beautiful it stinks. A cop with a couple hundred thou in hot

128

cocaine, all I got to do is walk in and walk out, he'll never report it to anyone. That's just what bothers me. Murphy comes home and finds it gone, he's going to do something. Okay, he can't call the captain and say, 'Some thief just stole the cocaine I took from Freddy Fuckerfaster when I busted him, before I could sell it to Maldonado. Send over a squad car real quick.' That's what he don't do. So, okay, what does he do? You know him better than I do."

"He gets mad for a week, and anybody we bust better watch his ass or Murph will turn him over to wrecking crew. That's all. What the fuck can he do, you see? There's just nothing you can do when somebody snatches something you shouldn't have in the first place. Especially when you're a cop."

"There's me and Malloy," Starhawk said. "And five others Murph knows as well as me. And two I can think of that Murph doesn't know about yet. And maybe two that I don't even know, let's say. That's let's see, about ten or eleven guys who might have done it, afterwards. Ten or eleven really good cat burglars in the Bay Area that Murphy will come looking for, one way or another."

"So? You had a day in the last five years somebody on the force wasn't trying to put you away?" Mendoza grinned. "Or you worried that Maldonado will think the coke's already his and put the whole Cosa Nostra onto getting it back? Balls. There's ten guys around here could do it, like you say. And ten more might have come up from L.A. and another ten from Vegas or Chicago or Christ knows where. You go in as slick as you usually do, nobody'll ever have a lead. Murphy'll have a purple hard-on for a week or so, and I wouldn't want to be anybody he busts then, but that's all that'll happen, all. You in or you out?"

"Wait. When's Murph's next day off?"

"Tomorrow. Why?"

"Some people," Starhawk said, "they had this kind of merchandise, they'd hide it so you practically got to take the walls down one by one before you find it. You know? Case like that, you want to save yourself some time, you watch until they show you where it is."

"Hey, Murph's no dumbbell. You think you're the Invisible Man or something?"

"It's got to be tomorrow. Believe me, he'll never see me, but I'll see him. You was to ask me, going in today bare-ass, before I can case the house, would be the best way to get my balls in a sling. For all I know, he's got a friend staked out there for when he's at work. And I wait till the day after tomorrow, when he's at work again, he may have already sold it to Maldonado. Am I right or am I right?"

"Jeez." Mendoza turned to look straight at Starhawk. "You going in there, with Murph at home, I don't like that at all. What I don't want is somebody gets dead, him or you. That happens, my ass is grass and the whole department is the lawnmower."

"Anybody in the Department ever link me to a killing? Even suspect me? You know better than that, Mendy. I don't go in bare-ass, you know. Already, I got three plans."

"Then you're really in."

"Oh, I'm in." Starhawk stopped cleaning his nails and returned the key to the ignition. "I wouldn't miss it for the world. The only thing I like better than stealing from a cop is fucking a cop."

"Funny," Mendoza said. "Remind me to laugh on my day off. That attitude is going to get you in a lot of trouble some fine day, my friend."

PRIMATE PHYSICS

The tire is only flat on the bottom.

—Finagle's Second Fundamental Finding

GALACTIC ARCHIVES:

Terran primates had a great deal of difficulty in understanding how a thing could be in two places at the same time. This was because the evolution of the vertebrate nervous system had developed bio-survival intelligence first, as a prerequisite for any gene-pool that could endure the brutal conditions of planetary living.

Living planetside, as all primitives do, involves quick recognition of, and response to, potential predators. Thus, the bio-survival brain of vertebrates imprints first and most intensely of all those large, macroscopic constants that can be recognized as competitive organisms or dangerous places. This leads to the usual Euclidean-Aristotelian prejudices about concreteness, locality in space, either/or logic, etc.

When quantum mechanics began to demonstrate to the Terran primates that some things—the most important things in the universe: the sources of all energy and order—function non-locally in space-time, they were naturally confused. They resorted to the three fundamental ploys of the primate brain when baffled.

The first fundamental ploy, known as the Finagle Factor, adjusts the universe to fit the equations. This was the path of the primates of the Hidden Variable sect, under the leadership of a very clever and philosophical primate named Dr. David Bohm.

The second fundamental ploy, known as the Bugger

131

Factor, adjusts the equations to fit the universe. This was the path of the primates of the Teutonic-Agnostic sect under the leadership of a brilliant German primate named Werner Heisenberg.

The third fundamental ploy, known as the Diddle Factor, reconciles the equations with the universe without adjusting either too notably, by a process of smoothing. This was the path of the primates of the Copenhagen-Taoist sect under the non-leadership of a sly old Danish primate named Niels Bohr.

About then some primates began to wonder if the whole problem of the state vector couldn't be solved by just giving up the idea of separation in space and time. They were incited by a rascally English primate named G. Spencer Brown and a wily Unistat primate named John S. Bell.

The first dawnings of post-terrestrial brain functioning began to appear on Terra.

And those who understood what was going on realized that post-terrestrial thinking had been appearing in the primates for millenniums, in rare individuals known as mathematicians, musicians and mystics. Post-terrestrial thinking represents the transition from closed systems to open systems. Any species that achieves it, whether insectoid or primate or whatever, is ready to enter free space.

If they can pass the Entrance Exam.

THE FIRST FURBISH LOUSEWART

You must take the bull by the tail and look the facts
in the face.

—W. C. FIELDS

The first Furbish Lousewart was a retainer on the Greystoke estate in England in the thirteenth century. He
was a foundling, the bastard offspring of the local
curate and a nun who, oddly enough, later told Chaucer
a story he considered good enough to retell in verse.
The nun was also the model for the Prioress in the
earliest Tarot deck and her basic features remained
even after that card became the Female Pope and,
later, the High Priestess.

Lord Greystoke named the infant Furbish Lousewart
because he looked so dainty when they found him in
the manger. Furbish Lousewart was as dainty a name
as you could have in Merrie England in those days,
being the vernacular term for *herba pedicularis,* a most
lovely flower of the snapdragon species.

Furbish Lousewart grew to manhood, married,
fathered three legitimate children and died in the
Third Crusade. One of his illegitimate children, by
Lady Greystoke, was the only Greystoke to survive that
Crusade and carried on the Greystoke line, unknown to
his brothers and sisters who continued the plebeian line
of Lousewarts.

NOTHING

Everyone who is a lawyer must either be mentally
defective by nature or be bound to become so in time.

—FURBISH LOUSEWART V, *Unsafe Wherever You Go*

And Dr. Glopberger, like Frankenstein, looked on his
work and saw that it was very good. So far.

But the nurse, Ms. Ida Pingala, returning along the
long white hall permeated with Lysol to the snug white
cubicle of the nurses' lounge, seated herself smoothing
the starched white hem of her skirt over her pale white
knees and punched numbers quick and neat on the
phone console, white keys on white plastic the colorless
allcolor of antiseptic sterility.

"Ubu, here," came the Voice in her ear.

"Roy. It's Ida." Ms. Pingala was equally crisp.

Sounds of canine panting; Roy was always a cut-up.

Ms. Pingala laughed merrily. "Tonight?" she asked.

Sounds of louder, more passionate panting.

She giggled again. "Your place or mine?"

"Yours. You know how the Bureau is. . . ."

"Eightish?"

"Nineish, to be on the safe side. All hell is breaking
loose again."

"Nineish, then. You devil."

More panting.

"Oh you devil you wild man you animal."

"Nineish gotto go now love you bye."

Roy Ubu, in Washington,* hangs up and glances at
his wristwatch. Time for the meeting with Babbit.

---

* *Terran Archives 2803:* Washington was the capital city of
Unistat. It was governed ostensibly by a baseball team called

A listless Santa Claus dingdonging his bell with empty junkie eyes as light snow fell in sparse crystals, not sticking to the sidewalk, but a biting Washington wind stings Ubu's eyes as he leaves the FBI office, turning up his collar to slouch hands deep in pockets to his car. Shifting from first gear into second turning up Pennsylvania Avenue the snowflakes growing thicker and heavier as he drives, snaps on the car radio

and so the second black uprising in Miami has ended in flame and tragedy. In Washington, President Lousewart is meeting this morning with the Stentorian Ambassador to discuss balance of payments amid a mood of cautious optimism. Parents in Bad Ass, Texas, continue to keep their children out of school in the bitter dispute over biofeedback training. School Superintendent B. S. Curve, still hospitalized from the bomb blast which destroyed

Ubu parks carefully with neat precision flashing his I.D. at the Secret Service man to be passed quickly into the White House over thick carpets under brilliant chandeliers to the office of Mountbatten Babbit, scientific advisor to the President: a bald and ovoid head with impatiently piercing eyes that scanned for the exact measurement and the precisely calibrated number.

"This ah is a very delicate matter," Babbit began at once. "We give it an Urgent rating but at the same time we do not wish to alarm the public you understand the whole investigation must be carried on with kid gloves as they say The President Himself has instructed me to make it clear to you, to make it *abso-*

the Senators, but by the time of our story real control had fallen into the hands of the F.B.I. and the Beast.

lutely clear, that no leaks will be tolerated no leaks *whatsoever* or a very big axe will fall on the whole Bureau a *very* big axe have I made myself clear?"

"Yes sir absolutely sir."

"Good. Now, have you noticed a certain ah a certain decline in American science and technology in recent years a withering away of talent and originality so to speak?"

"Well sir law is my background you know sir I wouldn't know a test-tube from a bevatron sir. . . ."

"The decline has been accelerating and is becoming critical in some respects, *critical.*"

"Yes sir but so what sir a lot of science is classified as non-ec and not very popular with the Administration."

Babbit's eyes were scanning Ubu without warmth. "You think it is possible to draw a hard line a sharp boundary between ec science and non-ec science?"

"Well of course sir President Lousewart himself is always saying . . ."

"I'm not talking about Administration rhetoric Mr. Ubu I am talking about reality. Could you draw such a line and say this is ec research and this is non-ec?"

"Well sir I don't get involved in politics I investigate and find out the facts and that's my job sir administrative decisions are not our business at the Bureau."

"There is no difference between ec and non-ec science," Babbit said with icy deliberation. "I will never say that in public as long as I am part of the Administration you understand the President has a right to expect loyalty from Members of the Team of course but I tell you in private ec and non-ec are terms in theology in metaphysics in value judgment, *they have nothing to do with science.* It's all as absurd as saying some research is chocolate and some is vanilla and the chocolate is better than the vanilla."

136

"Yes sir I understand you sir you have my word I'll never repeat any of this sir."

"Good now officially the Administration only wishes to discourage non-ec science but in fact we are suffering a drastic a dangerous possibly a *lethal* decline in all science right across the board . . ."

"But sir isn't that what President Lousewart stands for? Tightening our belts, the simple rugged life of our pioneer ancestors, lowered expectations . . ."

"You damned fool we're not talking about political speeches we're talking about the realities of *survival.*"

"Uh yes sir yes."

"Survival damn it *survival.*"

But quantumly inseparable from Ubu nurse Ida Pingala peeks into the Wildeblood room to see if the patient is sleeping comfortably *(always got to be careful with these rich bitches especially the types we get here in Trans-sexuality Surgery rather be back in obs so helpless and adorable they are even if some of the mothers shouldn't be raising kittens much less humans)* and leans fixing the hem on her skirt as the figure in the bed gurgles a halfsnore mutter "master . . . escape . . ."

Another quantum jump:

"One hundred thirty-two?" Ubu repeated.

"Those are the figures that came out of the Beast," Babbit said evenly. "One hundred thirty-two of the top scientific minds who've left government since the ec programs were implemented are not working for private industry, teaching at universities or anywhere else to be found."

SEX, STATUS, SUCCESS

As it becomes obvious that terrestrial resources are
limited, the drive toward extra-terrestrial industry
becomes irresistible. We begin to realize that planetside
industry is a very primitive stage of energy-economy.

—ASTRONAUT CASSIUS CLAY, *The High Frontier*

It may have been coincidence or synchronicity or the
quantum inseparability principle (QUIP), but the very
same day that Epicene Wildeblood became Mary Margaret Wildeblood in Baltimore and Babbit briefed Roy
Ubu on the brain drain mystery in Washington, Blake
Williams was teaching a class at Columbia and Hugo
de Naranja was a student in it. Since Hugo was the first
human being who ever saw the Cat, he should have been
paying close attention to Williams, but in fact he was a
poet and felt it his duty to be bored by all the sciences.
Hugo would settle for a gentleman's C in "The Anthropology of Quantum Physics." Hugo was a *Santaria* initiate, the third ex-husband of Carol Christmas, and
(although he didn't know it) he worked for Hassan i
Sabbah X.

"It wasn't Einstein," Williams was droning along,
"and it wasn't even Heisenberg or dear old Schrödinger
who drove the last nail in the coffin of common sense. It
was John S. Bell, who published his memorable Theorem in 1964, nearly twenty years ago," and blah blah
blah. Hugo was more interested in the ass of the girl
in the row ahead of him. He wanted both his hands on
that ass. He wanted her thighs around his waist. He
wanted his cock way up inside her hot White Protestant
pussy. Screwing Latino girls rated 0 in his book (that

was only sex), screwing Jewish girls was 5 (that was Status), but screwing a White Protestant girl was 10 points and a gold star (that was SUCCESS).

Williams continues to transmit to blank bored faces:

"Bell's Theorem basically deals with non-locality. That is, it shows that no local explanation can account for the known facts of quantum mechanics. Um perhaps I should clarify that. A local explanation is one that assumes that things seemingly separate in space and time are really separate. Um? Yes. It assumes, that is to say, that space and time are independent of our primate nervous systems. Do I have your attention, class?

"But Bell is even more revolutionary. He offers us two choices if we try to keep locality, and if there are any students in this class who are seriously interested in the subject this would be a good time to take a few notes. Um. First choice: we can abandon quantum mechanics itself. That of course means inescapably that we abandon atomic physics and about three-quarters of everything we call science. Um. Now we really don't want to give up quantum mechanics so let's look at choice two. We give up objectivity. Well, that's not too great a sacrifice for those of us who have already given up sweets and male superiority and ha ha faith in the integrity of government or even cigarettes. We can give up objectivity. Ahhh yes but the trouble is . . . Yes Mr. Naranja?"

"Ees this goan be on the examination sir?"

"No you needn't worry about that Mr. Naranja we wouldn't dream of asking anything hard on the examination I believe the last examination with a hard question given at this university was in a survey of mathematics course in 1953 yes Mr. Lee?"

"Is possibre that quantum connection is not immediate and unmitigated? Then perhaps we take choice one and give up not quantum mechanics itself but merely modify the quantum connection in a sense that it is some way sir mediate or mitigated, does that seem possibre sir?"

"Ah Mr. Lee how did you ever land at this university there are times I suspect you of actually seeking an education but I'm afraid in this case your canny intellect has run aground. Recent experiments by Clauser and Aspect shut that door forever. The quantum connection is immediate, unmitigated, and I might say omnipresent as the Thomist God."

"So. You tell us, Professor Williams, how many times Crauser's experiment has been verified?"

> *Jingle bells, jingle bells,*
> *Jingle all the way*

Rebirth, Wildeblood was deciding, is messier than first birth, despite old Augustine and his *media feces et urine* trip . . . how much he had wanted to be Annette Haven in the clusterfuck scene in *China Girl:* one cock in Her mouth, one in Her snatch, one in each hand: ah, Wildeblood, 'twere paradise enow. But the reality of it, the adjustments to be made:

> *Sit down when you want to pee*
> *Sit down when you want to pee*
> *Sit down when you want to pee*

SHe was writing it out a hundred times, to avoid making *that* mistake again. Ego is much more a body-image than she had known. Psychologically, she was androgynous WoMan, the Baphomet idol; physically, she had to sit down to pee.

> *Oh what fun it is to ride*

But Roy Ubu, back at F.B.I. headquarters, was already briefing a five-man team on the brain drain mystery.

"You mean," Special Agent Tobias Knight asked, "we're supposed to find 132 missing scientists without letting anybody know that there are 132 missing scientists we're looking for? Is that it?"

"The President Himself," Ubu pronounced in Babbit's frigid tones, "gives this project Top Priority."

"In other words, it's impossible but you want us to do it, anyway," Knight translated.

"Now that's enough defeatism, Toby, let's get to work and believe in ourselves and by Christ a busted flush can win when the guys behind it have the balls for it. . . . Now, here's the names in alphabetical order. One: Dr. George Washington Carver Bridge, sounds like a spade, graduate Miskatonic University; it says last worked for the government on Project Cyclops in the late '70s. Two: Dr. Charles Chance, nickname Fat, graduate Miskatonic, also last worked for the government on Cyclops. Three . . ."

"It's very simple," Blake Williams was telling Professor Sylvia Goldfarb from the music department. "Just memorize the sentence, 'Mother very easily made a jam sandwich using no peanuts, mayonnaise or glue.' "

THE SECOND FURBISH LOUSEWART

A man with one watch knows what time it is.
A man with two watches is never sure.

—Segal's Law

Percy Lousewart was born in the Ohio River Valley in
1866 and by then Lousewart was no longer considered
a euphonious name. His Christian name didn't help,
even though his mother had picked it due to her fervent,
almost erotic, admiration for Shelley. She might as well
have named the poor lad Cissy. Every time he introduced himself as Percy Lousewart, some bully or other
felt compelled to make a witty remark, and a fight
usually followed. Eventually poor Percy decided to
change his name and went to see an educated man, a
lawyer, about having the job done legally; he also
wanted some advice on choosing a better, more popular
title. The lawyer, alas, was more than erudite; he was a
bibliomaniac, an alcoholic scholar, and the kind of
crank who delights in writing letters to the *Britannica*
correcting their errors. He told Percy all about the
Furbish Lousewart plant and even showed him a picture
of one. He was eloquent on the subject, and his passion
was contagious. Percy Lousewart had his name
changed only to Furbish Lousewart and took his lumps
as they came. His first son was named Furbish Lousewart II and a tradition was begun.

MALLOY DON'T SING

The variables vary too much and the constants aren't
as constant as they seem.

—FINAGLE'S FIFTH FUNDAMENTAL FINDING

"The fuck," Malloy said. "Where you get an idea like
that? I don't sing, I never sing. Who's been handing
you that shit?"

It was a small furnished room on Taylor Street in
the San Francisco tenderloin. A sign outside the window advertised an establishment on the ground floor,
Les Nuits de Paris Massage.

Starhawk said, "Marty, I know three guys up in
Folsom because of you. They're not sure. Each one of
them, he says it might of been you, it might of been two
other guys. I'm sure. I make it a point of honor to be
sure about things like that. You pick up $20 here from
Mendoza, $15 there from Murphy, and you tell them
what you think they want to hear, mostly crap. To keep
them interested, you give them a live one now and then,
somebody you don't like. You and twenty other guys in
this town. Don't crap me, Marty. I'm here to make
money for you, not to give you a hard time about it."

Malloy said, "You're crazy. You should go see a
psychiatrist. You must of been back on the reservation
eating peyote again. I don't know what the fuck you're
talking about."

"Okay," Starhawk said. "You're smart, Marty. You're
so damned smart you don't admit anything, even when
the other guy knows more about it than you do. My
ass. You're so damned smart you're stupid, is what
you are."

Malloy started to get up.

"Sit down," Starhawk said. "I keep telling you, I'm not here to give you a hard time. Listen to me, Marty, just a minute. I've got a century that's not doing anything, and it's yours." He opened his wallet and laid a $100 bill on the table. "Now, do we talk about its four brothers, and what you do to get them, or do you go on shitting me until I go out the door and find another guy that talks to cops?"

The massage sign below the window flickered on-off, on-off.

"Suppose I do it," Malloy said. "I mean, I'm not admitting anything, but suppose just this once I go talk to The Murph. What I got to know is, whose ass is in the sling, who goes up? You understand, I don't want somebody comes looking for me from the Syndicate."

"Nobody goes up, that's the beauty of it," Starhawk said. "You're just going to tell Murph about a guy got in today from L.A. He's here to do a job for Maldonado, see, and he got drunk and started shooting off his mouth about how funny it was, the guy he came to do the job on is a cop."

"Jesus," Malloy said. The massage sign flickered off and on again. "Don't tell me, let me guess. Starhawk, the man of bronze, two balls of cast iron and no more brains than a hamster. You got it in your head it's cop-hunting season and you're going to shoot one of them. And they trust good old Marty Malloy so much they'll spend all their time looking for an imaginary hit man from L.A., just because good old Marty tells them so. I take it all back. You don't need a psychiatrist, you need a new brain."

"Don't get your bowels in an uproar," Starhawk said. "It's not that kind of job. It's just a heist."

"What's this cop got, somebody comes all the way from L.A. to heist it? The crown jewels?"

144

Starhawk raised his fingers to his nose and made a sniffing motion.

"Jesus, Mary and Joseph," Malloy said. "This cop, what he's got is a bag of snow, so he won't be talking to anybody else in the department when it turns up missing. I got to hand it to you, kid. Nobody could have set this up for you but another cop. The fuck, it would have to be his partner. Who's pissed because he didn't get his half, right?"

"Don't think about that, you might get so excited you'll talk about it in your sleep. The thing is, you just got to tell Murph about this Syndicate gun from L.A. and how funny he thinks it is, that this crooked cop is trying to sell some hot snow to Maldonado's boys and they just went and brought up this gorilla to take it from him, no down payment, no monthly installments, for free."

Malloy was grinning broadly. "Murph'll shit," he said. "He'll absolutely shit a brick."

"Yeah," Starhawk said. "I kind of think he will. You like it?"

"Kiddo," Malloy said, "if I wasn't so broke this week, I'd do it free. Just to watch him trying not to look like the cop I'm telling him about. The fat prick."

"I sort of figured you'd like it," Starhawk said. "Me, the only thing I regret is I can't be there to see his face myself."

"Yeah," Malloy said. "The fat prick."

IS VLAD A SYMBOL?

A class made up solely of intellectuals will always have a guilty conscience.

—FURBISH LOUSEWART V, *Unsafe Wherever You Go*

"Defection?" Ubu suggested at the second conference on the Brain Drain. "Russia or China . . ."

"The C.I.A. was the first agency into this," Babbit said, "and they say it's impossible. They know what color drawers every commissar wears these days with the latest surveillance techniques. One hundred thirty-two top American scientists are not working over there unknown to the C.I.A. Take that as axiomatic." Babbit was firm.

"Well there are only twelve people in H.O.M.E. . . ."

"They haven't left the planet," Babbit said briefly. "People of that caliber do not travel about without somebody noticing—Intelligence, newspapers, TV, other scientists, *somebody*. It is as if they have crawled into a hole and dragged the ground in after them." His chair creaked screeee as he leaned forward for emphasis.

"Hell, they're not loose *inside* the country sir," Ubu said firmly. "Americans can't just disappear these days. Why to cash a check any kind of check you've got to write *both* your Social Security number and your GWB number and have them both scanned by the Beast. Sir there's never been a people better watched and protected than the American people of November 1983. And we expect to do even better sir when the new circuits are put in the Beast next month."

146

But the snow falls thicker making a blanket of foam against the window of Babbit's office and piles against the door of The Upstart Crow bookstore off Dupont Circle across town, where Marvin Gardens is autographing copies of *Vlad Victorious*.

"I never got a real live autograph from a real live author Mr. Gardens tell me why did you write two books about a man like Vlad?"

"To make money," Marvin said in his Peter Lorre cokehead voice. He had prepared for the ordeal of the seventeenth autograph party in twenty-three days by snorting more than his usual morning quantity of the snow and was in no mood to conceal his divinity from the blind uncoked Earthlings. "I have always been possessed by a *mad, passionate,* almost *erotic* desire for a very large bank account. In fact, I love the *feel* of money the crisp *crinkle* of bills the metal *solidity* of coin the visual impact of a large check with *seven figures,*" and he was scrawling not just "To Mary" as she had asked but "To Mary in memory of that glorious night beneath the stars in Miami when we tasted true ecstasy in each other's arms, your devoted" and Marvin with a big M and Gardens with an even bigger G "Yes?"

"Is it true John Wayne will play Vlad again in the sequel?"

"That's just in the talking stage now and frankly I don't care if they cast Raquel Welch the important thing is *cash on the barrelhead* my agent is asking a million for the screen rights and we won't settle for a penny less . . . Yes?"

"Is Vlad really a symbol?"

O come let us adore Him
O come let us adore Him

The twelve people in H.O.M.E.—High Orbital Mini-Earth—were construction engineers, six male and six female. They had originally been sent there to build, with materials shipped from Lunar Mining, H.O.M.E. II, a space village for ten thousand occupants. This program had been canceled as "non-ec" by President Lousewart and the twelve colonists restricted to "ec" research, mostly astronomical, which President Lousewart turned over to his astrologers for a mystical interpretation.

H.O.M.E. was located in the area called Libration Point 5, where the gravitational fields of Luna and Terra were equally balanced. This null-gravity area had been mathematically discovered by the astronomer Lagrange and was therefore sometimes called the Lagrange Area. The name for the space town, H.O.M.E., had been coined by psychologist Timothy Leary in 1977.

A friend of Leary's named Robert Anson Wilson, who wrote overly complicated novels, had suggested a team song for the colonists, "HOME on Lagrange." To popularize this idea, he had written letters about it to many space research groups and included it in a novel called *The Trick Top Hat*. Still, by 1984, the song hadn't caught on with the twelve colonists. They were not at home on Lagrange because they feared that the whole project would soon be classified as "non-ec" and they would be dragged back to the womb-planet.

TOP GOVERNMENT SECRET

Don't tell anyone, he said. It's a secret.

—CARL JUNG, *Odysseus*

Mountbatten Babbit had a secret which he guarded more jealously than a bitch watches over her puppies.

The secret was that he, Dr. M. F. Babbit, former Vice-President of Weishaupt Chemicals, Grey Eminence of the People's Ecology Party, was as mad as a hatter.

ULYSSES AT HOME

My dog understands perfectly everything I say to him.
I am the one who does not understand.

—FURBISH LOUSEWART V, *Unsafe Wherever You Go*

Mary Margaret Wildeblood's parties were the place to go that winter because of the penile adornment above the mantelpiece. Some even began to suspect that Wildeblood had undergone the trans-sex operation only to engage in the most flagrant excess of exhibitionism in world history.

This was an uncharitable oversimplification. Wildeblood's mind was vast, not simple, and had more kinks than a Pollack painting; SHe was not deep, but wide and complex. SHe actually intended to become a nun. When SHe quoted from the gospel of hir youth, "Humility is endless," SHe really meant it. Submission was salvation; and who is more submissive than a nun? Above all, SHe longed to embrace the Lamb, all woolly and fleecy and pure, but very definitely horned and Ram-signed with Pentecostal fire. SHe had the hots for Divine intercourse. Where Natalie Drest was merely cock-mad, Mary Margaret Wildeblood was possessed by the god Priapus.

The idea of mounting and, so to speak, enshrining Ulysses occurred to Mary Margaret at her very first reception after returning from Johns Hopkins.

Benny "Eggs" Benedict started it by suggesting, "Norman Mailer might try to get revenge for some of your reviews by raping you."

"Let the male chauvinist pig try it," Mary Margaret said demurely. "I've been studying kung fu."

"Oh, are you planning to join Women's Lib?" Justin Case inquired.

"I have given it some thought," Mary Margaret replied, practicing her new simpery-Marilyn-Monroe smile and positively reveling in the feel of the nylons on his, no dammit her, thighs.

"JUST A GODDAM MINUTE," a booming masculine voice cut in. This was Josephine Malik, chairperson of God's Lightning—an outfit long suspected of terrorist firebombings against porny movie houses, adult bookstores and other sexist enterprises. Jo was an ideological descendant of those who thought copulation was bad for the crops. "I don't know about lib-lab wishy-washy groups like NOW," she went on, "but God's Lightning certainly isn't accepting any members who weren't *born* female."

"Oh, now," a fluty feminine voice intervened— "Figs" Newton, spokesperson for the Necrophile Liberation Front, sporting a lapel button that said: OUT OF THE MAUSOLEUMS, INTO THE STREETS. "That's hardly fair," he pronounced—like most Terrestrials, he regarded himself as an expert on morality.

"People are what they make themselves," he said, good Existentialist that he was. "To hold the accidents of birth against them is practically *racism,* isn't it?"

This led to some lively debate, and it was finally decided that to hold the accident of genitalia-at-birth against somebody was definitely not *racism,* but might be *sexism,* or possibly *genderism.* Josephine Malik, meanwhile, smoldered.

"Well," she said finally, "God's Lightning is not influenced by all this *baroque* civil rights and civil liberties horseshit out of the eighteenth century. According to semantics, people don't *have* rights; they just make demands and call them their rights. It's purely a pragmatic problem. If we let this—*person*—in, what's to prevent other men from hacking off their prongs, infiltrating our ranks and subverting our whole organization?"

This was a poser, admittedly; and while the assembled company grappled with it, Josephine delivered her crusher: "Besides, there's a lot of doubt about how complete these operations are. How do we know Ms. Wildeblood is in all respects a true woman and not just a truncated man?"

Mary Margaret Wildeblood, who had a mind somewhat bizarre even for the twentieth century, had been waiting for such an opportunity. "I can certainly prove I'm not a man," she smiled sweetly, and drew Ulysses out of her purse. Although two men fainted on the spot, the women merely blinked, at least at first. Then some of them began to titter.

Thus began the great Wildeblood *scandale* of that winter. She had maliciously saved the relic of her previous masculinity with the thought that it might provoke some sort of spontaneous Group Encounter sessions, and now she knew she had the potential for some truly memorable Freak-outs. The relic was placed in the hands of a skilled taxidermist and soon emerged, in a natural-looking erect state, handsomely mounted on a redwood plaque. This hung over the mantelpiece of her posh Sutton Place apartment, and there she began to hold parties to which were invited (along with the usual New York V.I.P.s) precisely those persons most likely to be neurologically galvanized by the sight of a penis without a man, which is considerably more memorable than mathematician Dodgson's grin without a cat, although perhaps not as memorable as physicist Schrödinger's cat, who was dead and alive at the same time.

Blake Williams became a regular at these *soirées,* and often retired sneakily to the kitchen to make notes, which later resulted in a scholarly article, "Priapism Recrudescent: Hellenic Religion in a Secular Context." The "ithyphallic eidolon," as he insisted on calling Ms. Wildeblood's obscene joke, seemed to produce markedly different effects on various personality types. One football player, for instance, had to be removed in a straitjacket. Strangely enough, certain shy, timid, and stoop-shouldered men took it all in their stride, quite as if Wildeblood's brutally explicit rejection of masculinity reinforced their own loose grip upon that (after all) somewhat mystical estate. The Gay set developed a superstition, almost a *mystique,* and the tradition of "kissing it for good luck" was even joked about, obscurely, in certain newspaper columns. ["A new religion, of which Linda Lovelace might almost be the prophet, is now sweeping the Way-Out People, all the way from Fifty-seventh Street to St. Mark's Place."]

WHY?

Why me, O Lord?

—ANCIENT PRIMATE QUESTION

"I said FUCK THE BLOODY CAPITALISTS," the California writer was howling amid the group at the mantelpiece, below the ithyphallic eidolon.

"Mother very easily made a jam sandwich using no peanuts, mayonnaise or glue," Blake Williams was reciting patiently to Natalie Drest.

"TV, publishing, movies, everywhere—the extraterrestrials have *taken over*," Marvin Gardens was warning in his passionate Peter Lorre intonation.

Benny Benedict suddenly had enough of the Wildeblood high-I.Q. set. He wandered out on the balcony, to look at the stars and wonder, half-drunkenly, why he was so depressed.

After three years, the question still came to him when he had too much booze aboard: *Why me?*

Which was selfish and maudlin. The real question should be: *Why my mother?*

Or, more to the point: *Why anybody?*

The world must be mad, that we go on living like this, and tolerate it. The primordial jungles were probably less dangerous than the streets of any city in Unistat. Was this the resultant of the long struggle upward from the caves—a world more frightening, more full of hatred and violence, more bloody than the days of the saber-tooth?

Every time I look at the TV news at seven, he thought miserably, I end up feeling this way before midnight. It's almost as if they're afraid somebody

153

might have a flicker of hope or a good opinion of humanity (at least in potential) or a brief moment of delusory security. Every night, to prevent such unrealistic moods, they have to remind us that the violence and brutality is still continuing.

With a shock, Benny discovered that he was weeping again, silently, guiltily, privately. He had thought he was past that.

So much for booze as a tranquilizer.

He fought against it. It was self-indulgence, disguised self-pity actually. He dabbed his eyes and tried to think of something else. *Om mani padme hum, Om mani padme hum . . .*

"Nice night." An Unidentified Man had walked out onto the balcony.

"You don't feel the smog up here," Benny said, embarrassed, wondering if he had gotten rid of the last tear before this stranger had seen him.

The Unidentified Man looked up at the stars, smiling slightly. He was good-looking enough to be an actor, Benny thought, and at second glance he did look remotely familiar, as if his face had been in the newspapers sometime. "The stars," he said, "don't they get to you?"

Benny looked up. "I used to think I'd live to see people go there," he confessed, suddenly sure he had met this man somewhere before, a long time ago. "Not likely with Lousewart leading us back to the Stone Age."

"You're non-ec," the man said, in mock-accusation.

"Guilty," Benny replied, realizing that this man was remarkably easy to talk to. "I think that if we used more of our brains, we'd be able to create a world where people would have a right to High Expectations."

"Hopelessly reactionary," the man said, grinning. "You probably still read science fiction."

"Guilty again," Benny said.

154

"Suppose I were an extraterrestrial," the man said quietly. "Suppose I were several million years ahead of this planet. What one question would you ask me?"

"Why is there so much violence and hatred among us?" Benny asked at once.

"It's always that way on primitive planets," the man said. "The early stages of evolution are never pretty."

"Do planets grow up?" Benny asked.

"Some of them," the man said simply.

"How?"

"Through suffering enough, they learn wisdom."

Benny turned and looked at his odd companion. He *is* an actor, he thought. "Through suffering," he repeated. "There's no other way?"

"Not in the primitive stages," the man said. "Primitives are too self-centered to ask the important questions, until suffering forces them to ask."

Benny felt the grief pass through him again, and leave. He grinned. "You play this game very well."

"Anybody can do it," the man said. "It's a gimmick, to get outside your usual mind-set. You can do it, too. Just try for a minute—you be the advanced intelligence, and I'll be the primitive Terran. Okay?"

"Sure," Benny said, enjoying this.

"Why me?" The stranger's tone was intense. "Why have I been singled out for so much injustice and pain?"

"There is no known answer to that," Benny said at once. "Some say it's just chance—hazard—statistics. Some say there is a Plan, and that you were chosen to learn an important lesson. Nobody knows, really. The important thing is to ask the next question."

"And what is the next question?"

Benny felt as if this was easy. "The next question is: What do I do about it? How ever many minutes or hours or years or decades I have left, what do I do to make sense out of it all?"

"Hey, that's good," the stranger said. "You play Higher Intelligence very well."

"It's just a gimmick," Benny said, feeling as if a great weight had been taken off him.

They laughed.

"Where did you ever learn that?" Benny asked.

"From a book on Cabala," the man said. "It's a way of contacting the Holy Guardian Angel. But people don't relate to that metaphor these days, so I changed it to an extraterrestrial from an advanced civilization."

"Who are you? I keep feeling I've seen your face. . . ."

The man laughed. "I'm a stage magician," he said. "Cagliostro the Great."

"Are you sure you're not a real magician?" Benny asked.

SCHRÖDINGER THE MAN

> Your theory is crazy, but it's not crazy enough to be true.
>
> —NIELS BOHR, QUOTED BY BEYNAM,
> *Future Science*

Erwin Schrödinger did a lot more than just make up mathematical riddles about fictitious cats. His equations describing sub-atomic wave mechanics, which earned him a Nobel Prize, were among the most important contributions to particle theory in our century. Later, he turned his attention to biophysics and in a small book called *What is Life?* he offered the first mathematical definition of the difference between living and dead systems, throwing off as a side reflection the idea that life is negative entropy. This insight was to trigger quite a few new ideas in many of his readers, including Norbert Wiener of M.I.T. and Claud Shannon of Bell Labs, who got so deep into negative entropy, due to Schrödinger, that they created mathematical information theory and laid the foundations of the science of cybernetics, resulting ultimately in the Beast.

Schrödinger didn't even believe in his own Cat riddle; he had propounded it only to show that there must be something wrong with quantum theory if it leads to conclusions like that. Schrödinger didn't like quantum theory because it pictures an anarchist universe and he was a determinist, like his good friend, Albert Einstein. Thus, even though he had helped to create quantum theory and used it every day, Schrödinger kept hoping to find something seriously wrong with it.

The Cat problem presupposes a Cat, a device of lethal nature, such as a gun or a poison-gas pellet, and a quantum process which will, eventually, trigger the weapon and kill the Cat. Very simple. An experimenter, if he wanted to find out when the device had fired and killed the Cat, would look into the laboratory where all this was transpiring and note what actually happened. But—Schrödinger points out with some glee —modern physics, if it's all it's cracked up to be, should allow us to find out what is happening without our actually going into the laboratory to look. All we have to do is write down the equations of the quantum process and calculate when the phase-change leading to detonation will occur. The trouble is that the equations yield, at minimum, two solutions. At any given time— say one half-hour—the equations give us two quantum *eigen*values, one of which means that the Cat is now definitely dead, *kaput, spurlos versenkt,* finished, and the other which tells us that the Cat is still alive as you and me.

I never died, said he;
I never died, said he.

Most physicists preferred to ignore Schrödinger's damned Cat; quantum mechanics *worked,* after all, and why make a big thing about something a little funny in the mathematics?

Einstein loved Schrödinger's Cat because it mathematically demonstrated his own conviction that subatomic events couldn't be as anarchistic as wave mechanics seemed to imply. Einstein was a Hidden Variable man. He claimed there *must* be a Hidden Variable—an Invisible Hand, as Adam Smith might have said—controlling the seemingly indeterminate quantum anarchy. Einstein was sure that the Hidden Variable was something quite deterministic and mechanical, which would be discovered eventually. "God does not play dice with the world," he liked to say.

Decade followed decade and the Hidden Variable remained elusive.

In the 1970s, Dr. Evan Harris Walker solved the Cat paradox (to his own satisfaction) and defined the Hidden Variable (to his own satisfaction). The Hidden Variable, he said, was consciousness. There was muttering in some quarters that Walker was smuggling pantheism into physics disguised as quantum psychology, but many younger physicists—especially the acid-heads—accepted the Walker solution.

Professor John Archibald Wheeler of Princeton found another way of dealing with the Cat; he took it literally. Every quantum indeterminacy, he proposed, creates *two* universes; thus, the equations are literally true and in one universe the Cat lives and in another universe the Cat dies. We can only experience one universe at a time, of course, but if the math says the other universe is there, then by God it *is* there. Futhermore, since .5 probabilities occur continually—every time you toss a coin, for instance—there are many, many such universes, perhaps an infinite number of them. With two graduate students named Everett and Graham, Wheeler even worked up a model of where the other universes were. They were on all sides of us, in super-space.

Some were heard to suggest that old Wheeler had been reading too much science fiction.

Actually, Schrödinger had given the beginning of the real solution to the Cat paradox in his great essay on biophysics, defining life as negative entropy. Nobody understood that, however, until Sarfatti's Demonstration in 1986. At the time of our story, physicists were adrift without a paddle and trying to conceal the fact from the general public.

SILENT SNOW, SECRET SNOW

If the scientific and medical resources of the United States alone were mobilized, aging would be conquered within a decade.

—DR. ALEX COMFORT, 1973

When Freddy Fuckerfaster found that he had been booked for possession-with-intent-to-sell of two pounds of marijuana, he immediately realized that two options, equally unsatisfactory, were open to him.

One: He could keep his mouth shut, take the fall for the weed (which meant a year and a day under current California law) and just try his damnedest to forget that he had been robbed of half a million in cocaine. This was unsatisfactory to him because he was, like most primates, jealous of his property and resented being robbed—especially when the thief was a policeman.

Two: He could sing to the D.A. This was equally unsatisfactory, since then he would take the fall for the coke (five to twenty; and even with the D.A. requesting clemency because he had cooperated, he'd probably get at least a deuce), and though he would enjoy considerable gratification in seeing Murphy take a fall, too, he still wouldn't have his property back.

Freddy also knew, glumly, that Murphy was counting on the extremely high probability that, all things considered, Freddy would elect undesirable alternative One as less painful than undesirable alternative Two. He didn't know that was very close, structurally, to a famous unsolvable problem in mathematical Game Theory, known as the Prisoner's Dilemma, which had baffled the best mathematicians of this century, but he did realize that it was, however you looked at it, a royal pain in the ass.

Not being a mathematician, and not knowing the hopelessness of his situation, Freddy proceeded by intuition. He sent a message out of the San Francisco jail, by way of a trustee, to Banana Nose Maldonado.

The box of cocaine had originally been smuggled into Unistat by the robot who traveled under the name "Frank Sullivan." It was sold, as per "Sullivan's" usual *modus operandi,* to Hassan i Sabbah X, a.k.a. Frank Delano Roosevelt Stuart. Hassan, however, did not in turn sell it to his usual retailer, a Times Square dealer known as Panama Red. Instead, Red got only a small sample which he sold to Marvin Gardens, for a substantial increase in price. The greater part of the coke was sold to a representative of a terrorist* group called Morituri, who resold it, at a still higher price, to finance their latest munitions purchase. The buyer who received the hot snow from Morituri was Marlene Murphy, a young lady of altruistic and psychotic passions who was, it so happened, a member of P.O.E. It had only been cut twenty-five percent in all these transactions but the P.O.E. collective cut it fifty percent more before selling it again to Freddy Fuckerfaster at a really meaty profit. P.O.E., of course, used the cash to add further plutonium to their already large stock of that rare metal.

---

* *Terran Archives 2803:* Terrorists were bands of desperate persons much like governments in that their chief occupations were murder and extortion. In his excellent study, "From Baboon Food-Gathering Bands to Consciousness," Nomis of Noom demonstrates at least three differences between terrorists and governments: (1) the alpha male in a terrorist band was usually an intellectual, whereas in government he was usually a lawyer; (2) terrorists did not print their own currency, but governments did; (3) terrorists usually murdered small groups (from two or three to a few dozen), whereas governments murdered millions. Otherwise, the two types of organization were indistinguishable from any other hominid predator-band from the australopithecines circa 4,000,000 B.C.E. to the dawn of True Consciousness begun by the evolutionary mutation recorded in this Romance.

TO CROSS AGAIN

If I offer a child the choice between a pear and a piece of meat, he'll immediately take the pear. That's his instinct speaking.

—FURBISH LOUSEWART V, *Unsafe Wherever You Go*

Mountbatten Babbit, being methodical in all things including his madness, could pinpoint exactly the date on which he had started sliding over the porous membrane separating the sane from the insane. It had been long, long ago—back in 1941, actually, in July, the 23rd of the month, a Thursday.

Or perhaps it had actually started the night before, on the 22nd. It was hard to say, actually, even though Babbit was a man who detested imprecision of any sort. Say it was the 22nd, then, even though the overt symptom did not manifest until the 23rd. We do want to be as accurate as possible when we're lost out here.

So say the 22nd: Mountbatten was a freshman at Antioch College then and the Carter Brothers Carnival was playing in nearby Xenia. Mounty and some friends went over to have a look-see. Since Mounty personally didn't wait around for the post-midnight private exhibition of the lustful mulatto lady and the randy pony, advertised by shills in the crowd, the high point of the show for him had been the Mentalist, Cagliostro the Great.

A girl assistant, in as brief a costume as the carnival could get away with back in nearly antediluvian 1941 and barbaric Ohio, circulated through the audience, while Cagliostro, youngish and handsome for this racket, sat blindfolded on the stage.

162

"Now what am I holding?" she would ask, when somebody handed her a watch.

"I get the image of a timepiece . . . yes, a wristwatch . . ." the magician intoned.

"What do I have in my hand this time?" The answer was a locket.

"Can you tell me what this object is?"

A wallet photo.

Driving back to Yellow Springs, the students fell into a debate. One guy from the psychology department gave a long spiel on Rhine and parapsychology and scientific data for ESP, which convinced almost everyone. Babbit was the exception. He was not only a chemistry major but a leading firebrand for the Atheist Club on campus and he knew damned well that ESP was pseudo-scientific balderdash and hocus-pocus.

He spent the next day, the 23rd, in the library, researching stage magic and, in a biography of Houdini, he found the answer. A simple substitution code. *Now what* = watch. *What do I have* = locket. *Can you tell* = photo. And so forth. Fraud, pure and simple, like everything that goes under the name of religion or magic.

Sirius shone very bright that night in the southern sky and Mounty Babbit was back at the carnival, loaded for bear. When the girl approached his part of the audience, he handed her a prized and illegal possession: a dragon-headed Japanese condom.

"Tell me what I have been given by this person."

That wasn't in the Houdini code, but neither was a condom, with or without a dragon-head.

"It's against the law in this state," Cagliostro intoned somberly, causing heads to turn. "And I would advise the young gentleman from Antioch to restrain his sense of humor in the future."

And don't marry Suzie from Red Lion

The second voice was-and-yet-wasn't Cagliostro's.

Mounty took quite a riding from the other students on their way back to Yellow Springs that night. "How did he know you were young?" "How did he know you were from Antioch—where was that in the code?" "Christ, a condom—you coulda got us all arrested." But nobody said anything about Suzie from Red Lion, Pennsylvania. Mounty finally forced the issue. "What was that business about the lion?" he asked with maximum indirection.

It was as he had feared; nobody else had heard anything about a lion, or about Suzie.

It was simple logic, then. ESP is fraud. Hearing voices in your head is insanity. Mountbatten Babbit, he told himself, you are in need of psychiatric help.

But a psychiatric record would be a handicap in the career he already had mapped out for himself.

Self-control, then, was the answer. Nobody really goes bananas, after all, except weaklings.

A man like Mountbatten Babbit simply would not go mad.

But Mountbatten Babbit never did marry Suzie from Red Lion; there was a rather nasty war concluded with the exclamation point of a rather nasty bomb and then there was a marriage to a more suitably upward-mobile partner and eventually there was a title of Chief Engineer at Weishaupt Chemicals in Chicago. It was 1967 and he was no longer a brash young atheist-scientist but a middle-aged scientist-businessman who knew enough to keep his mouth shut about controversial issues and steadily feed a growing six-figure savings account. He had it made. If Cagliostro didn't keep getting in the newspapers for one shocking incident or another, Babbit might even have been able to forget the whole episode in which he had thought he might be going mad.

Then he crossed the boundary again.

A juvenile delinquent named Franklin Delano Roosevelt Stuart, from the black ghetto on the South Side, stole Mounty's car from in front of the Babbit residence in Rogers Park at precisely a moment when Mounty was looking out the window. In his trained and methodical way Mounty memorized fifteen details about the boy as he ran out the front door only to catch the briefest glimpse of the car zooming away (at least six feet, blue sweater with turtleneck, Afro hairstyle, very black skin, nose more Caucasian than Negroid, drives well, face more narrow than norm, high forehead, no beard, slim build to judge from shoulders, ring on left hand with green stone, clenched fist button on sweater, earring in right ear, get more, damn there he goes around the corner . . .).

At the trial Mounty pronounced his positive identification in the same tones he used specifying materiel orders at Weishaupt Chemicals. The jury brought in a guilty verdict in five minutes.

That was the second time Mounty went mad.

For as the boy was led away Mounty glanced at him one more time and saw a blue halo form around his head just like in Catholic art.

Mounty blinked and tried a few other heads. No haloes. He looked back at F.D.R. Stuart. The halo was still there.

I will ignore it, and tell nobody about it, and concentrate on my work, and in time it will be forgotten like that crazy business at the carnival before the war; all it takes is self-control and a strong Will.

Two weeks later he was promoted to Vice-President of Weishaupt and began to see haloes around random individuals in the street.

LED, LED, LED

> If every case of aging can be corrected, we might all
> be Methuselahs, living 1,000 years or more.
>
> —Dr. Robert Prehoda, 1969

A Chinese named Wing Chee was Cagliostro's closest
friend in those early carnival days. Wing was the
world's great master of karate, kung fu, akido and
Comprehensive Advanced Machismo, but a gentle soul
when not pushed too hard. In Bad Ass, Texas, he got
pushed too hard by local cops, who objected to his
use of the white toilet facilities at a gas station. They
told him "A chink is just a yellowed-out nigger,"
roughed him up and accidentally knocked his right
eye out in their enthusiasm. At that point, Wing lost
his temper and was subsequently apprehended and
quickly tried and convicted for the murder of four
police officers.

Judge Draconic V. Wasp pronounced sentence in
this wise: "Young feller, you've been tried and convicted and every man in this courtroom knows your
guilt is as black as hell. I have no regret in passing
sentence in such a case. Soon, you little bastard, it will
be spring and the robin will sing again, the flowers will
bud, little children will laugh on their way to school—
and you will hear and know nothing of that, for you
will be dead, dead, dead. You chink bastard. Sheriff,
take the yellow son-of-a-bitch out and hang him."

Wing Chee received this with no show of emotion,
but then he arose and addressed the court in a steady
and terrible voice. "As I rook upon the whiskey-fogged

faces of judge and july in the tlavesty of a civirized coult," he said, "I know furr werr that I was foorish to ever expect justice from such degenelates. You, Judge Wasp, speak of the sweet singing of lobins in the spling and the brooming of the prants, but what can you know of the gleat Tao that moves arr of us, you four-mouthed, cunt-ricking, donkey-fucking led-neck? You desclibe the gentre voices of chirden, you glafting, thiev-ing, monkey-faced, frat-nosed idiot offspring of a feebre-minded goat by pulple-plicked baboon! What do you know of the innocence of rittle chirden? What do you know of anything but colluption and highway lob-bery, you syph-spocked, clap-lidden, amoeba-blained white lacist? You say that Wing Chee sharr be hanged by the neck until he is dead, dead, dead, but Wing Chee says"—he paused dramatically, swept the court-room with a withering glance and concluded—"you can kiss my ass until it is led, led, *led!*"

It is said that nineteen peace officers were torn limb from limb in the course of the hanging of Wing Chee.

FRANK: But he was hanged anyway.

ERNEST: But they knew they had hanged a *man*.

FRANK: Like hell. They thought they'd just hanged a crazy gook.

AN ABREACTED CATHEXIS

It will soon be possible to double or triple human life-span.

—DR. JOHN BJORKSTEIN, 1976

ARCHIVES OF GENERAL PSYCHIATRY, JUNE 2003:

Wilson was fascinated by Houdini and clearly modeled Cagliostro in some ways upon the famous escape artist. Needless to say, the trained clinician recognizes what fantasies of escape from bondage mean in the language of the unconscious. It is no surprise that Wilson was also obsessed with rocketry and the technicalities of reaching what is called escape velocity in order to attain zero-gravity. All schizoid types have these fantasies of floating off into space, of astral projection, of weightlessness, etc. This merely indicates an abreacted cathexis of the Oedipal desire to return to the womb and float within the protective amniotic fluid.

THE VALUE OF THE CONTENT

When a people begin to cut down their trees without making any provision for reforestation, you may be sure it is a sign of the beginning of their cultural degeneration.

—FURBISH LOUSEWART V, *Unsafe Wherever You Go*

In the weeks following the car theft in 1968, Mounty Babbit's luck at poker became so pronounced that he had to start losing by deliberation on occasion, to avoid the suspicion of cheating. Haloes were everywhere on earth; UFOs everywhere above.

I am a genuine mad scientist, Mounty Babbit thought. Well, nobody is ever going to know about it.

Then, a month later, it all passed. He didn't know what cards the other poker players had, and he wasn't seeing haloes. He moved his family to Evanston, settled into his new job as Vice-President at Weishaupt Chemicals, worked actively for the Nixon-Agnew campaign and finally quit smoking.

The pickets outside the walls of Weishaupt Chemicals (which was now the nation's second largest producer of napalm) were the only harassment in an otherwise perfectly satisfactory life.

The Invasion (as he came to call it) began in early 1969. He was driving home from work, came off Lake Shore Drive onto Sheridan, crossed the Howard Street border into Evanston and noted a large billboard with an eye atop a pyramid. A teaser campaign, he thought. The reverse side of the dollar bill. After a month or so of making people wonder, the advertisers would add their slogan. Probably another Friendly Loan Company.

The next morning he awoke in total horror. He recalled the symptoms from some of the psychology books he had read back when he had feared for his sanity. The Activation Syndrome: thirst, rapid heartbeat, dizzy wobbles—the body preparing for emergency. What emergency? He couldn't remember anything from the previous evening.

Beside him, Mary Lou snuggled closer. "My, you were passionate last night," she murmured affectionately.

I drove home. I must have had dinner. And I made love—better than usual, it sounds like. And I can't remember any of it.

Micro-amnesia.

Babbit kept a very close watch on himself in the following days. Not close enough, evidently. At the end of the month, he found among the canceled checks returned by his bank one in the sum of $100 to the Chicago Peace Action Committee. This was the sentimental old ladies who often appeared with the raggedy students picketing Weishaupt Chemicals. "EAT WHAT YOU KILL." "NO MORE WAR." "DRACULA LIVES ON BLOOD, TOO." "BLESSED ARE THE PEACE-MAKERS." All those silly sentimental signs.

He had not written this check. And yet the signature was his.

Alone in his study with the bank book and checks, Mountbatten Babbit wept. He knew horror.

Some alien entity had taken over his mind and written that check.

My God, he thought, I am *possessed.*

POLITICS OF THE IMPOSSIBLE

> Politics is the art of the possible. Art is the politics of the impossible.
>
> —Simon Moon

The robot whose passport said "Frank Sullivan" landed at Kennedy International on December 26, 1983, and brought $500,000 worth of hashish through customs without any trouble, since the customs officials had orders from the C.I.A. never to interfere with him.

"Sullivan" affixed his gas mask and hailed a cab which took him to the Hotel Claridge on Forty-fourth Street.

In rapid succession, following a genetic script, he took a quick shower, shaved, changed into his best suit, went out for a slow stroll on Forty-second Street and picked up a boy lounging outside the Fascination pinball arcade.

They returned to "Sullivan's" room and the boy there received a slurpingly hedonic blow-job, for which he was paid $25.

The lad was then covered with rapturous kisses and compelled (out of politeness) to listen to an interminable monologue on the world's injustices to Ireland, the villainy of England and the perfidy of the Masonic Jews. More kisses followed, the boy told a lugubrious story of poverty and legal problems, "Sullivan" coughed up $5 more and the transaction was ended. "Sullivan" lounged on the bed for a while after the boy left, discovered that another $15 had disappeared from his wallet, cursed mildly, showered again and set out on his night's business.

Another taxi delivered him to the Signifyin' Monkey, a nightclub on Lenox Avenue in Harlem. He checked his Luger before getting out of the cab and darting across the sidewalk; he knew what was likely to happen to melanin-deficient persons on that street at that hour.

The maître d' recognized "Sullivan" and made an almost imperceptible movement with his head. "Sullivan" ascended the stairs in the back, knocked quickly three times, then five times, then three times more and was admitted to the private office of Hassan i Sabbah X.

"Ah," said Hassan, "the goodies from Afghanistan have arrived."

A sordid commercial transaction followed, distasteful to both parties—Hassan and "Sullivan" each regarded himself as fundamentally a philosopher unwillingly forced to grub and hustle in the jungle of commerce. Nonetheless, each bargained professionally and they were both quite happy by the time they came to the ritual of sharing one sample of the merchandise to seal their friendship anew.

"You know," Hassan said when they were both floating, "I don't really believe you're I.R.A."

"That's funny," said "Sullivan" with a hash giggle, "I don't believe you're really C.I.A., either."

They both chortled happily, having their keys.

"Complicated world," said Hassan.

"Getting more complicated every day," pseudo-Sullivan agreed benignly.

"Could you place a Klee with a European collector?"

"A Paul Klee?" Sullivan had heard "clay" originally and wondered if he were being asked to peddle pottery.

"An honest-to-Jesus Klee original. From his mescaline period, I would say."

"Hold on to it a day or two," Sullivan said grandly. "I'll have to make a few phone calls first." He was thinking that Hassan i Sabbah X wore the most bril-

172

liantly maroon ties he had ever seen. For that matter, the rug danced with hues worthy of a sultan's harem. Definitely superior-grade hash, he decided.

A door opened in the back of the office and another man stuck his head into the room. He was a black man, white-haired, gold spectacles, rather conservative blue suit and vest: "Sullivan" automatically memorized his features and sent them through his computer to records-and-identification.

"Oh, pardon me," the man said, backing out.

But Sullivan—who was not I.R.A. at all, as Hassan surmised, but was C.I.A., at least part-time—had already come up with a "make." The man was George Washington Carver Bridge, one of the top scientists on Project Cyclops in the '70s. Now what was a man of that caliber doing skulking about the den of so large and carnivorous a mammal as Hassan i Sabbah X?

"Who was that?" he asked idly.

"One of the boys," Hassan replied carelessly. "Just one of the boys."

But Sullivan went back to his hotel mulling over the perversities and paradoxes of the hashish state, and the ever-maddening question, "What is Reality?" for his memory kept insisting that just before the door closed he had noted that the esteemed Dr. Bridge was carrying in his hand the amputated penis of a white man.

WE MIGHT WAKE UP

We mustn't sleep a wink all night, or we might wake up—changed.

—*Invasion of the Body Snatchers*

After the day in 1968 when he found that he had written a check to the Chicago Peace Action Committee while in an altered state of consciousness, Mountbatten Babbit decided, once and for all, that he would see a psychiatrist.

But not right away. He would fight for self-control first.

He realized that his mental condition was highly illegal. ESP in 1941. Haloes and ESP together, after that black kid stole his car. Now he was having blackouts in which he performed abominable acts that might threaten his security clearance and even his bank account. That was absolutely terrifying. Anything that endangered the bank account must be a symptom of the most aggravated psychosis. Yes: he would definitely absolutely irrevocably commit himself to psychiatric counseling.

But not right away. He would fight for self-control first.

One night the Babbits had the Moons from across the street as guests for dinner. Molly Moon, as usual, got Mary Lou into a discussion of the occult. All the usual hocus-pocus and rubbish. She was especially keen on some Neon Bal Loon, a Tibetan monk who had allegedly transferred his consciousness into the mind of an Englishman and was now writing books through the Englishman's mediumship.

"It's just the beginning," Molly enthused. "Our materialism has become a threat to the whole world. Sure, more and more of the great Masters will be taking over Occidental bodies, to bring us their wisdom directly."

Mounty Babbit concentrated on discussing the financing of an anti-drug pamphlet with Joe Moon, detective-lieutenant on the Evanston police. Even that was disconcerting. "It probably won't do any good," Joe said once, rather bitterly. "The kids don't believe anything *we* tell them."

The next step into psychosis was unexpected and oddly pleasurable. It occurred in the lunchroom at Weishaupt, a few days later. Babbit was pouring sugar into his coffee when he suddenly *looked at* the sugar dispenser. The simplicity of the design, the one small flap that opened to let the sugar pour, abruptly delighted him. It was as if he had never seen it before.

After that, he was noticing more and more things in that heightened vision. One day in the Loop, he saw a mother whirl suddenly and slap a whining child. His heart leaped with shock—and then he remembered that this was an everyday occurrence in America. It was as if he had seen it from the perspective of some culture where whining and hitting were not normal communication between parents and children.

He wanted less and less meat in his diet; meat now appeared heavy and hard to digest.

The strangest and most disturbing thing of all was the way Weishaupt Chemicals itself began to change. But everything was the same; he was just seeing with different eyes. The contrast between the executive offices and the workshops was an overwhelming experience. Architecture, coloring, decoration, upkeep— every kind of communication except words themselves said with total clarity, "The Masters" and "The Serfs."

The typical primate pack-hierarchy, unnoticed and taken for granted before.

Strange visions came to him whenever his mind relaxed from financial or scientific problems. He would be in a burning jungle, running from helicopters that caused the burning. Or he would be in a temple with the eye-on-the-pyramid design practicing strange breathing exercises. Once he even had a name: *Ped Xing:* and he watched as one of his teachers burned himself to death in protest against the war. He was Ped Xing seeing through the eyes of Mountbatten Babbit.

His monogamy, which he usually succeeded in maintaining fifty-one weeks of the year, was falling apart on him. He worried that Mary Lou would be growing suspicious. Women turned him on constantly, incessantly, tormentingly, as in early adolescence. Not all women: just white women. Ped Xing couldn't get enough of them. He couldn't even get enough of any one of them. Even after an orgasm, I would want to start again, rubbing and caressing their moist pussies until they came a second time. This excited me so much that I would often go down and suck them into a third orgasm. Then Ped Xing would ask them to suck him and drift off into aeons of tension and pleasure, glimpsing the temple of the eye-on-the-pyramid, occasionally even coming a second time himself, which hadn't happened since he was in his early twenties.

The homosexual phase almost drove me to suicide. But my ESP (I accepted it now, knowing it was all hallucination of course, but following it blindly, being dragged along by it) was both infallible and specific. Ped Xing picked only men of Babbit's own status and importance; and he was never wrong. Evidently, there were more closet cases in the world than even Kinsey had estimated. I always took the male role, coming in their mouths, and would reciprocate by no more than masturbating them. Once, when the partner was not

176

merely an executive but a Pentagon official, I started laughing at his moment of ejaculation, losing all control, laughing louder and louder, revealing the psychosis and not caring.

That night I looked at the tree in his yard and knew it was an intelligent being. Not with human intellect, not with the mind of a dog or a rat or a fish even, but with its own life and indwelling consciousness. There was even a scientist in New York measuring the emotional reactions of plants with polygraph equipment. And there it stood, a blue spruce, stranger in structure and more alien in intelligence that any creature in science fiction.

How can we live among so many wonders and not be overwhelmed by the sheer mystery of existence? Mounty Babbit, former atheist, asked himself. Our knowledge is so small, and our conceit is so great. . . .

Then he realized in horror that that was Ped Xing, the Buddhist, thinking.

PARTNERS

Man will never be contented until he conquers death.

—DR. BERNARD STREHLER, 1977

When Murphy got into the car, Mendoza asked, "Bad news?"

Murphy pulled out into the traffic, carefully.

"It must be bad," Mendoza said, looking at Murphy's face.

They drove. Murphy stared straight ahead.

"Man's your partner," Mendoza said. "He shouldn't hide things from you."

"Malloy," Murphy said, "I got to go see Marty

Malloy. Only he's got a new bug up his ass; he only talks to one cop at a time."

"Shit on one at a time. You let him pull that, the next thing happens is he thinks he runs the police force. Marty, a cheap hood like Marty, you never give him an edge. On anything. You know that, Tom. Let them get out of line and all of a sudden you got another Jack Ruby. Guy like that gets an edge, he can't keep his mouth shut, going around telling everybody about his friends the cops. Dropping in to see you at home, you know? When he takes his fall, half the force falls with him."

"Your principal problem," Murphy said, "is that you're a dumb spic with a loud mouth. Me, I don't take shit from any of them, least of all from a Marty Malloy. But this is different."

"It sure is," Mendoza said. "I didn't know you so well, I'd think you got a guilty conscience about something. Some hood off the street, you can call him a spic anytime, but not me. Just who the fuck you think you are?"

"All right, that just slipped out. You don't have to eat my ass about it."

"All right, *shit*. First you're keeping secrets, then I'm a spic, now *I'm* the one who's being unreasonable. This is being partners? After ten years?"

Murphy turned onto Van Ness. "Nobody's keeping secrets," he said. "It's just one of those, what they call intangibles. Malloy doesn't have as much balls as a cockroach anymore. I mean I *know* Malloy. Pushing fifty, getting shaky, scared shitless of me for years now. He doesn't fancy-pants, not with me, he doesn't. He says he won't talk to anybody but me, that's the way I play it this time around. I keep telling you, I know Malloy."

They turned down Geary. "Okay," Mendoza said. "You know Malloy. He's got the whole solution to the

Kennedy assassination, or something. But, I don't know what it is, something's come over you this last week, Tom. Clam up all you want. A man can't be partners ten years without knowing."

"Joe," Murphy said, "it's just I didn't want to talk about it. Some things a man just keeps a tight mouth about. It's my sister."

"Your sister?"

"The doctor thinks she's got cancer. You know a man like me, the wife dead, family means a lot. I been lighting candles for her at church."

"Tom," Mendoza said. "Jesus, Tom. I'm sorry. Your sister. Christ, what can I say?"

"It's okay, Joe. Partners, it's like being married in a way. I should have known you'd realize something was up. A man like me, something in the family, he don't like to talk about it."

"Christ. Yeah. Which sister is that, the one in L.A. or the one up in Mendocino?"

"Oh . . . the one in Mendocino. Irene."

"Look, she needs more money and you can't raise it . . ."

"Thanks, Joe. It's not money, her husband is loaded, but thanks. I'm glad I talked about it."

"That's what a partner is for."

Murphy parked near the corner of Taylor. "You go down to Gulliver's, have a cup of coffee," he said. "I'll join you after I get whatever it is Malloy is selling."

"Partners," Mendoza said.

"Partners," Murphy replied warmly. They shook hands.

INSIDE OUT

America is a white man's heaven and a black man's hell.

—HASSAN I SABBAH X

Hassan i Sabbah X gave up on hashish. He went to the safe and got out the LSD. Remembering . . .

Using the transitional concept that the lock is a hole in the door through which one can exert an effort for a topological transformation, one could turn the room into another topological form other than a closed box. The room in effect was turned inside out through the hole.

(The tramp fell slowly to the ground and stayed there, unmoving. The child stared in horror.)

Remembering a lad of twelve having *Ivanhoe* rammed down his gullet by the Chicago Public School system and walking out the door at 3:05 P.M. to mingle with the junkies, whores, pimps, thieves and assorted varieties of revolutionaries (Black Panthers, Black P. Stone Rangers, acid-electrified Weatherpeople) who provided the real education in the Hyde Park neighborhood of the late 1960s. Remembering the assassinations of Malcolm and of Martin Luther King. Remembering the endless epic of Stackerlee and the famous couplet:

I got a tombstone disposition and a graveyard mind.
I'm a black motherfucker and I don't mind dyin'.

Call this the first metaprogram. It led Hassan (then

called F.D.R. Stuart) far outside the ghetto into an entirely new and different world. It was easy. By acting out the imperatives of the Stackerlee "black mother-fucker" script, the boy earned a term in the Audy Home, an institution for the further training of apprentice outlaws who slash tires on police cars, heave bricks through school windows, peddle merchandise from stores without first purchasing them and answer policemen's questions with, "Fuck you, ya honky mother-fuck'n cocksucker." F.D.R. Stuart received the standard Audy Home training, which consists of sophisticated expert coaching in: (a) sodomy; (b) sado-masochism; and (c) assorted crimes more lucrative than selling shoplifted merchandise.

He was, after graduation, ready for post-graduate work at Springfield, once he passed the admissions test, which consists of being captured by the police while in the possession of something hot. He was in possession of a Ford Mustang registered to a Mountbatten Babbit of Evanston. Post-graduate work at Springfield included a refresher course in sodomy and S-M, together with advanced study in grand larceny; but by this time F.D.R. Stuart had begun to doubt that the Stackerlee metaprogram contained the whole answer to life's problems. A former Black Muslim, now a Sufi, was his cellmate, and taught him various things about the less-publicized qualities of the human nervous system.

F.D.R. Stuart spent many hours staring at one wall of his cell, gradually creating a hole through which he could pass into another world. There was a different kind of time over there, and eventually he discovered that angels and fairies and elves and witches and Bodhisattvas and conjurs and all sorts of super-human folk could be contacted and persuaded to become allies.

The Sufi cellmate, a heavy cat in more ways than F.D.R. Stuart ever understood, pretended to be unimpressed with this achievement and laid down some stern

181

raps about the perils of "Opening the Gate" without first "clarifying the soul." The upshot of it was that young Stuart spent an hour a day memorizing a page in the dictionary until he had a vocabulary that would grace a Harvard graduate. Alas, the Sufi was paroled around then and Stuart continued his explorations unguided.

In 1983, in Harlem, New York, Hassan i Sabbah X was the Horsethief of a group known as the Cult of the Black Mother. This was ostensibly devoted to the worship of Kali, goddess of destruction (and rebirth); the police suspected, but couldn't prove, that it was also a kingpin in international hashish smuggling. The F.B.I., meanwhile, had their own suspicions; they believed it was a Black Revolutionary Army disguised as a church. An Army Intelligence agent of appropriate Negritude and duplicity managed to gain admission to one of the lower ranks but learned only that: (a) Horsethief was a term for head-honcho or boss-man borrowed from the gypsies; (b) the rituals were fairly close to those of orthodox Hindu Kali-worship, except for certain Masonic elements; and (c) every time a black F.B.I. agent managed to infiltrate the Cult of the Black Mother, he died very soon of a heart attack.

The last fact was well known, and often discussed, at the Bureau. The word "witchcraft" popped up at least once in each of these conversations, and was quickly laughed down, but each agent went away harboring his own very private opinions. Some of them even began attending the church of their choice even more often than was expected by the rather Puritan standards of the Bureau.

The C.I.A., which actually employed Hassan i Sabbah X as a spy on ghetto affairs, was well aware that he planned to double-cross them at the first opportunity; but that didn't worry them. They had their own plans for him, which were expressed in their usual jolly euphemism, "termination with maximum prejudice," a remark illustrated by a finger drawn across the throat to make the meaning clear to neophytes. But that was only for the future, when he began to show signs of shifting allegiance.

Now (it is the night of December 23, 1983, again) while a miniature sled with eight tiny reindeer was allegedly dodging past commercial airliners, communications satellites, flying saucers and other techno-craft in the skyways, two human beings of reprehensible character drove up to the Sutton Place digs of Mary Margaret (Epicene) Wildeblood in a truck hired from U-Haul only a few hours earlier. These were Edward J. Smith and Samuel R. Hall, and they had been purged from the Black Panther Party a few months earlier because of their fondness for the null-circuit neurological program induced by injecting diacetylmorphine ($C_{21}H_{23}NO_5$) directly into their veins. This compound was known as *heroin* to white people and *caballo* to Ed and Sam's Puerto Rican neighbors. Ed and Sam called it *horse* and mainlined it as often as they possibly could—"riding the horse over the rainbow" was their expression for the null-program, and it meant as much to them as Samadhi to a Hindu or the Eucharist to a Catholic. In fact, it allowed them to forget for a while that, to ninety percent of their fellow citizens, they were unmistakably identifiable as *niggers,* a species generally regarded as twice as ugly and ten times as dangerous as wild gorillas. It didn't matter, to Sam and Ed, that the people who believed this also believed in the existence of a gaseous vertebrate of astronomical heft named God, in the Virgin Birth of U.S. Senators, in the accuracy of TV news, and in pre-marital chastity for women.

Sam and Ed also believed in the existence of the gaseous vertebrate, the immaculate generation of senators, the pictures on the tube and pre-marital chastity

183

for at least *some* women (their own sisters, wives and daughters). They also believed that they *were* twice as ugly and ten times as dangerous as wild gorillas, but that they had a right to be that way. They called it Black Pride.

Once inside the Wildeblood apartment, Ed and Sam were as efficient as a pair of vacuum cleaners. To say they took everything that wasn't nailed down is to underestimate their rapacity. If something that looked valuable *was* nailed down, they employed pliers and other tools. When they finally drove away, the U-Haul truck was as stuffed with goodies as the miniature sled allegedly circling the skies at that moment. When Mary Margaret Wildeblood returned from her month in Vermont, she was heard to compare her condition to that of the Chinese farmer in *The Good Earth* after the locusts had passed.

Ed and Sam drove directly to the Sugar Hill apartment of Hassan i Sabbah X, which is not listed on the mailboxes and can only be reached through another apartment with the name LESTER MADDOX on it. Ed, who knew this scene better than Sam, knocked.

"White," said a muffled voice from inside.

"Man," Ed replied.

"Native," came the voice again.

"Born," Ed completed the formula.

The door opened, and they were ushered into the home of a very respectable Afro-Methodist clergyman who had never been publicly connected in any way with Hassan i Sabbah X.

"What was that jive?" Sam demanded.

"Password," Ed explained briefly.

"Borrowed from the Ku Klux Klan," the clergyman added with some glee. "He got himself one weird sense of humor, Brother Hassan." He ushered them into the kitchen, slid the refrigerator around easily on specially

184

built ball-rollers and they passed through to an apartment that did not exist in anybody's records anywhere.

The air was heavy with the smell of Indian hemp; an enormous statue of Kali, the Black Mother, dominated the room. A group of black men sat in a circle and Sam recognized two small cigarettes circulating in opposite directions, which he called clockwise and counterclockwise, not knowing the technical magical terms deosil and widdershins.

"You will now ascend to the sixth plane, without my guidance," said Hassan i Sabbah X to the circle. "I am returning to the earth-plane briefly. Aummmm . . ."

"Aummmm . . ." came the blissful reply from the students.

Hassan led Sam and Ed to another room.

"What's all that sixth-plane shit?" Sam whispered to Ed.

"Astral projection," was the brief reply.

Hassan seated himself at his desk and smiled genially. "Been out celebrating the Lord's birthday?" he asked pleasantly. "Expropriating the expropriators?"

"We got a fuckin' *truck*load downstairs," Ed replied.

"Mmmm-*mm!*" Hassan said. "A merry Yuletide indeed. Class merchandise from Honkyville, or were you ripping off our brothers and sisters again?"

"Class," Sam said emphatically.

"And a truckload." Hassan smiled dreamily. "Why, brothers, if I'm as generous as my reputation, you likely to end up owning more horse than the Kentucky Derby!" He pressed a button and another black man entered the room. This was Robert Pearson by birth, Robert Pearson, Ph.D., according to the anthropology department at U.C.-Berkeley, El Hajj Stackerlee Mohammed during a militant period in the '60s, Clark Kent (with his Supermen) during his commercial rock music years and now Robert Pearson again. "Accompany these cats to our warehouse and *e*-valuate the cash value of their merchandise," Hassan instructed.

Another trip brought Ed and Sam, with Pearson, to a building on Canal Street bearing the legend BHAVANI IMPORTS. Here the truck was unloaded, catalogued and priced.

"A genuine Klee or I'm a brass monkey," Pearson said once. "Your uh client has bread as well as taste."

"Now, what's this shit?" he said later, scrutinizing a saccharine rendition of two naked boys preparing to dive into a swiming hole, framed by a gingerbread copper-plated oval. "Oh, well, we can sell it as camp."

His sharpest reaction came when he confronted the redwood plaque bearing the ithyphallic eidolon.

"Jesus H. Christ on a unicycle," he breathed.

Sam and Ed exchanged glances. "We can't figure that one out, either," Sam ventured. "Beats the hell out of our ass."

"Looks like some bozo's joint," Ed suggested helpfully.

Pearson put out an exploratory hand. *"Feels* like some bozo's joint," he amended. "Sure as shit ain't plastic." He shook his head wearily. "What I want to know is *what kind of bozo would do this to his joint?"*

Sam and Ed shrugged. "He was a white bozo," Sam contributed finally.

"I can see that," Pearson said. "A *crazy* white bozo." He rolled his eyes heavenward. "Lawd, Lawd," he said in down-home accents, "the things that white folks do, it's just too much for this simple cullud boy."

"Skin!" cried Sam.

"Skin," Pearson agreed. They slapped palms. And there the mystery rested until Hassan i Sabbah X arrived personally to inspect the new imports a few days later.

"Namu Amida Butsu," he said, peering closely. "Shee-it."

"Where do you think we can sell it?" Pearson asked dubiously.

"That I do not know," Hassan i Sabbah X pronounced slowly. "But when we do find a buyer, the price will make your head swim. This is a one-of-a-kind item."

Things were coming to a head. The key was no key.

Hassan had other things on his mind that weekend; he was well aware that "Frank Sullivan" (probably, in his estimation, a double agent for both Washington and Peking) had recognized "Washy" Bridge and *that* opened a very wiggly can of worms, indeed. Ever since Washy had told him about Project Pan, in fact, Hassan had felt increasingly like the Sorcerer's Apprentice in the legend. A line from an H. P. Lovecraft story came back to his consciousness over and over again: *"Do not, I beseech you, call up any that you cannot put down."* Like many another occultist before him, Hassan i Sabbah X now wished he had taken that warning a bit more seriously a bit sooner. . . .

Even before he left Bhavani Imports he was startled by an incident that seemed a definite *Santaria* synchromesh. "Hey, listen, man," an art appraiser cried, catching his sleeve, "I've just heard the greatest limerick. Listen, just listen: 'A habit obscene and unsavory—' " He broke down, laughing, caught himself and repeated urgently, "Listen." He tried again:

"A habit obscene and unsavory
Holds the Bishop of Boston in slavery.
'Midst hootings and howls—"

He broke down again, then went on:

" 'Midst hootings and howls
He deflowers young owls
Which he keeps in an underground aviary!"

Hassan looked at him with paranoid suspicion. "Very funny," he said, unsmiling, and hastened out to his limousine.

"Back uptown?" the chauffeur asked.

"Broad Street," Hassan said, giving an address. He was in mild first-circuit anxiety all the way to his destination.

He remembered his first conversation with Washy Bridge. "How many?" he had asked, not in shock or in outrage but in simple unbelief, inability to believe. *They are our creation: we are their creation.*

"Fifty-seven of us." The scientist was perspiring with anxiety, now that the secret was finally out, the reason he had fled Project Pan.

"Fifty-seven," Hassan said hollowly. *Heinz 57 Varieties,* he remembered absently from the advertisements. "And all of them with Ph.D.'s and M.D.'s and more diplomas than a dog has fleas . . ."

"You've got to realize it works," Washy said then. "You just can't understand if you don't keep that in mind. It works."

"And 200 to 300 years in jail for each of you, if it ever gets out," Hassan added harshly. "You just better keep that in mind, too."

"That's why I'm here," the scientist said.

Hassan had paced the room briefly. "Wheels within wheels," he said once. "Wheels within wheels *within* wheels." Once he grinned. "At least I know why the Cincinnati cocaine market is thriving," he said with a lewd chuckle. "Cincinnati," he repeated, shaking his head. "What do they call it again?"

"Knights of Christianity United in Faith."

A habit obscene and unsavory, Hassan remembered suddenly, jostled back into present time. He had arrived at his destination.

The man to whom he spoke then was a stockbroker

188

according to public knowledge but pursued certain other careers in a private and clandestine manner.

" 'Frank Sullivan,' " Hassan said. "I want to know *everything* about him. Everything."

The part-time stockbroker turned ashy-white. He got up, glared suspiciously at a window-washer outside his office and walked over to check that the window was closed all the way.

"Impossible," he said then, in a near-whisper. "If I told you the one most amusing and interesting fact about him, I'd be dead tomorrow."

"That hot?" Hassan asked.

The man leaned back in his chair and gazed absently toward the ceiling. He recited some names, beginning with Jack Ruby of Dallas and ending with a senator whose private plane had crashed just the week before, on Christmas Eve. "Those are just a few," he ended, "who happened to find out too much about Frank Sullivan."

Hassan spoke only once during the drive back to Harlem.

"Secrecy!" he said with a profound grimace.

The chauffeur looked back nervously. He had never heard so much obscene emphasis in a single word.

AN n-DIMENSIONAL KLEIN BOTTLE

At the end of the last century the progress of science and technology led liberalism astray in proclaiming the mastery of man over nature and announcing that he would soon have dominion over space.

—FURBISH LOUSEWART V, *Unsafe Wherever You Go*

Mountbatten Babbit refused to believe he was also Ped Xing, but Ped Xing adamantly insisted that *he* was also Mountbatten Babbit.

"This body isn't big enough for the two of us," Babbit said in a menacing tone, fingering his gunbelt. "I want you out of my neurons by sundown, stranger, or I'm hittin' leather."

"Go fluck yourself," said Ped Xing.

Babbit, suddenly unable to contain his furies, pulled the key from his holster. The room was turned inside out through the keyhole and Babbit passed through an n-dimensional Klein bottle, entering Hell. The Devils all rode helicopters and dropped his own napalm on him. "Yankee, go home, Yankee, go home," they chanted.

Burning with perspiration, Babbit awoke.

It was only a dream, only a dream, he repeated, gasping air desperately. Only a dream only a dream . . .

But the next day Ped Xing fucked a secretary during lunch hour. Babbit couldn't stop him, and couldn't help but share in his exultation as the thought pounded in their cells: I'm fucking a white American girl, in an office where the war against my people is being created.

GWB-666

Perhaps we are now in the process of building a culture that will know immortality on earth and in heaven.

—Pauwels and Bergier, *The Eternal Man*

He knows when you are sleeping
He knows when you're awake

Within three days the storm had become a blizzard in most of the Northeast and Roy Ubu was feeling snowed under in every sense of the phrase, driving with extreme caution, thinking that the new Head of Programming for the Beast, whatzisname, Moon, really seemed to take some kind of fiendish pleasure in producing reams and reams of records to prove that the records were all defective. . . .

The snow whipped Ubu again as he parked and skittered into GWB to find Moon once again cheerfully perusing printouts that demonstrated, for the thirty-third time, that every single one of the missing scientists had simply stopped leaving ink or magnetic tape traces some time between summer '81 and spring '82. Which was impossible in the age of bureaucracy: it was like an animal not leaving footprints on a wet beach.

"But the Beast is *supposed* to know," Ubu had protested once.

"GWB-666 knows *everything* that has been recorded," Moon said patiently. "It does not know what has never been recorded. You can't see behind your head; GWB-666 can't scan what was never recorded anywhere."

"But dammit nobody can do anything in this country dammit without making a record."

"Nobody but these 132 very elusive men and women," Moon replied placidly. "If you'll notice, I marked the bios where it deals with experience in programming. Seventy-eight out of the 132 have such experience. They obviously learned a great deal about Erase and Cancel codes. . . ."

Roy Ubu made a despairing gesture. "How many bits can this thing access?" he asked wearily.

"Over one hundred twenty billion bytes," Simon said. "Nearly a trillion bits. There's never been an information system like this in all history," he added with some pride.

"But it has amnesia where these scientists are concerned," Ubu said bitterly.

TO HAVE KEYS

Government is an agency not of law and order, but of law and disorder.

—WILSON AND SHEA, *Illuminatus!*

The robot whose passport said "Frank Sullivan" was in Washington that weekend and reported to a high official in Naval Intelligence, who suspected him of being a double agent infiltrating them for Air Force Intelligence.

After the usual sordid business was disposed of, "Sullivan" asked casually if N.I. had any interest in Hassan i Sabbah X.

"Good Lord and Aunt Agnes, no!" said the official emphatically. "Congress will have our ass if we get into anything domestic." Then he asked, elaborately disinterested, "What did you happen to pick up?"

"Well, if there's no real interest . . ." Pseudo-Sullivan gazed off into space absently.

There was a short silence.

"If it's something big . . ." the official said finally.

"Sullivan" held out his hand. Another commercial transaction took place.

"It's about a government scientist named George Washington Bridge . . ." pseudo-Sullivan began. . . .

AD TENEBRAS

800-YEAR LIFE-SPAN PREDICTED

—HEADLINE, SAN FRANCISCO *Chronicle,* 1979

"Miska-*what?*" Roy Ubu demanded.

"Miskatonic," Special Agent Tobias Knight repeated. "Here's their catalog." He held up a booklet blazoned with a Gothic sketch of book, candle, inverse pentagram and the motto:

MISKATONIC UNIVERSITY
founded 1692
EX IGNORANTIA AD SAPIENTAM
EX LUCE AD TENEBRAS

"Where the hell is that?" Ubu asked.

"New England, somewhere in Massachusetts . . . ah, here it is, Arkham, Massachusetts."

"And how many of the 132 were students there?" Ubu was hot on the scent.

"Sixty-seven of them," Knight said triumphantly. "All in the classes of '66 through '69. . . ."

"By God, it's a *live* one," Ubu cried. "Two or three might be happenstance, even ten might be coincidence, but Jumpin' Jesus sixtyfuckin*seven* means something. Let's look into this Miskatonic U. and find out what was going on back there in '66 to '69, besides dope."

> *'cause Santa Claus is coming
> to tooooooown!*

GORILLA THEATRE

Mounty Babbit took a walk in Lincoln Park one day in 1969, trying to relax and calm his mind. Every tree spoke to him; the lions looked at him as a brother; the nervous armadillo pacing its cage stopped to stare at him and he received clearly the message, "How did we get trapped in these ridiculous bodies?"

"We need bodies," Ped Xing replied, "just as we need minds, to function in this 3-dimensional continuum. Surely you remember that we are actually n-dimensional?"

"Oh, yes," the armadillo signaled, "how could I have forgotten?"

Socrates had his *daemon,* Mounty thought in despair; Jesus had the Father in Heaven; Elwood P. Dowd had his giant white rabbit, Harvey; but why do I have to have a crazy Vietnamese Buddhist?

"You make the napalm," Ped Xing told him.

Thoroughly agitated, Babbit wandered into the primate house, not noticing the sign which said "CLOSED TODAY." There he saw two grim-faced men, in green uniforms, and a gorilla, in a blue uniform, going through a most remarkable pantomime. One of the men would raise a sign saying "WE DEMAND JUSTICE" and the gorilla would then spray him with a can of shaving cream; the other man would then feed the gorilla.

Operant conditioning. But what the hell . . .

Even Ped Xing was confused by that one.

WHERE THE FUCK

The night watchman at Bhavani Imports, a Puerto Rican poet and *Santaria* initiate named Hugo de Naranja, was reading a novel called *Illuminatus!* when the mysterious incident occurred. Hugo was so absorbed in the book, which he considered the greatest novel since *Don Quixote,* that he didn't notice the strange sound at first. Gradually, the sound's persistence invaded his consciousness, dragged him out of the most esthetically exquisite blow-job in all modern fiction, jerked him into an alert awareness that out there in the darkness there was something odd going on.

Rats, he thought.

No, the quick trot of rat paws was different.

A thief with soft slippers, or in his stockings . . .

Not that, either.

Hugo put down his book and picked up flashlight in left hand groping right-handedly and then finding pistol in holster. Something was going on in the vast darkness of the warehouse and he had to go and look for it and do something about it. He wished he hadn't read so many Women's Lib diatribes against *machismo* and Papa Hemingway. He wished he could still believe in the *macho* values. He wished he had more *cojones* or another job.

Then he walked out of his cubbyhole office, flashing

the light ahead of him, and quoted to himself from his favorite philosopher, "The ordinary man has problems. The warrior only has challenges." Then he saw the intruder.

A *cat*. It was only a cat, held for one moment in his lightbeam, then skittering away into deeper darkness as the light raced after it. Then it was caught again, higher up, standing for Christ's sake on the ghastly amputated penis plaque, its golden eyes glittering half-whitely in the flashed lightray. A cat standing on a penis, something right out of Surrealism or Dada.

"Scat!" Hugo shouted, really amused now. "Rrrow! Scat! Beat it!"

Then the cat leaped and Hugo's flash leaped after it jumping to the floor, where it would, should, must, *didn't* land. The light moved back quickly, swept several arcs, while Hugo was beginning to think: *Christ, it didn't make any sound when it landed, not even a muffled cat-thud.* And his beam swept back and forth again in searching arcs, as the words formed "it disappeared in mid-air," were rejected *(it couldn't)* and the beam rested for a minute on the challengingly erect Penis Without a Man (what *hijo de puta* would do a thing like that?) and the question burst from his lips, aloud, the nightwatchman's vice of talking to himself, which he had always resisted before:

"Where did it the fuck jump to? Where the fuck?"

THE DISPOSSESSED

Mounty Babbit never did learn to live with Ped Xing. In fact, he eventually had a full-scale psychotic breakdown. Of course, because of his wealth, the doctors always referred to it as a catathymic crisis.

The breakdown occurred at a dinner party, worse luck.

The Moons were guests again, and this time they had their nephew, Simon—a bearded young mathematician whose father had been the black sheep of the Moon family, a Wobbly agitator. Simon himself had been arrested during the Democratic Convention riots the previous year but got off on probation.

Everything went pleasantly enough until Molly Moon got on her obsession about Oriental Masters invading Western bodies to pass on their transcendental mysticism.

Joe Moon must have noticed the look on Mounty's face because he said, "Molly, remember our host is a scientist."

"And a Taurus," Molly said quickly. "I know how hard it is for him to accept spiritual truths."

"He doesn't bore you with the latest chemical shoptalk," Joe said gently. "I'm sure you don't have to bore him with all this astrology or whatever it is."

"It's not astrology. It's astral projection."

"It sounds half-astral to me," Joe said, laughing as loud as he could, trying to get them all laughing and turn the topic into a joke.

Young Simon, however, had ideas of his own. "Aunt Molly might be right," he said thoughtfully. "The Einstein-Rosen-Podolsky paradox does lead to some freaky possibilities. But why assume only the high adepts are coming? Every primitive group in the world has some kind of magical tradition. And they've tried everything else to get out from under white domination."

"Now don't start with your radicalism—" Joe warned.

"I'm not talking politics," Simon said innocently. "Everywhere in the world there are people who'd like to change places with us. Live in our rich homes. Eat our extravagant diet. Drive our cars. We know a lot about the space-time-matter continuum, but we're more ignorant than Asia or Africa about space-time-mind continuum. How about the American Indians, for that matter? Wouldn't their magicians love to take over some white bodies for a while? Is that why so many young people are wearing Indian headbands, taking Indian drugs like peyote, moving out of the cities into the woods . . . ? Ever have your car stolen by a black kid from Chicago's ghetto? Wouldn't they like to steal your body, too?"

PRIMATE EVOLUTION

> The hedonic neurosomatic circuit and the relativistic metaprogramming circuit must have some evolutionary function. I assume they are preparing us for post-terrestrial migration.
>
> —SIR HENRY ADAMS, "THE VAGINA AND THE BEVETRON"

GALACTIC ARCHIVES:

Every domesticated Terran primate was a walking archeological museum. The primate nervous system contained the whole of evolution.

The bio-survival circuit, imprinted in the oral-suckling stage, was chemically bonded into the autonomic nervous system and brainstem. It existed in null-class neurological time; that is, it acted without any conscious decision-making process, so no *time* was experienced when it operated. "I just found myself doing it," said the baffled primate as he was being decorated for bravery or court-martialed for cowardice.

The emotional circuit, imprinted in the anal-territorial toddling stage, was chemically bonded into the thalamus. It existed in medium-fast neurological time; that is, primates often reacted mechanically to emotional stimuli but sometimes agonized over emotional decisions, becoming acutely aware of *time* as they hesitated.

The semantic circuit, imprinted by hominid speech-forms and artifacts, was chemically bonded into the left hemisphere of the cortex. It existed in medium neurological time; primates were always conscious of themselves thinking as they juggled their verbal categories around.

The socio-sexual circuit, imprinted by the first mating or orgasm experiences, was chemically bonded into the left neo-cortex. It existed in medium-slow neurological time and caused the primates to plan for the future, to think of old age and death and to have hopes for their children.

The neurosomatic circuit, imprinted by extraplanetary travel (zero-gravity) or neurotransmitter chemicals, was chemically bonded into the right neo-cortex. It existed in very-slow neurological time and gave the primates who had developed it a hedonic, laid-back attitude—a brain High.

The metaprogramming circuit, imprinted by disciplined training in neuro-science, was chemically bonded into the frontal lobes. It existed beyond time, giving the primates who had it a multiple-choice view of reality and allowing them to understand quantum physics and the laws of magick.

BACK TO THE FLAMES

Today when we speak of immortality and of going to another world, we no longer mean these in a theological or metaphysical sense. People are now seeking immortality. People are now traveling to other worlds. Transcendence is no longer a metaphysical concept. It has become reality.

—F. M. ESFANDIARY,
Upwingers: A Futurist Manifesto

"That's nonsense," Molly Moon said angrily in 1969. "All those backward people you're talking about couldn't learn the higher spiritual arts. . . ."

"Mounty, you're a scientist," Joe Moon said imploringly. "Tell Simon what's wrong with his theory."

"Anybody can spin theories," Babbit said carefully. "Science is a mâtter of proof. You can make up a million and one theories, Simon, but if you go to work for a corporation you'll have to produce theories that engineers can use. The one theory out of a million that can be proven. Everything else is just idle speculation."

"Exactly." Joe Moon beamed, delighted. "Let the coons earn the right to live in Evanston, I say."

"Well, this theory *could* be checked out," Simon went on guilelessly; but Babbit knew he was baiting everybody. "If such an uh invasion were occurring, it would be aimed at people with important positions. Business executives. Government officials. The people who control the media. Check them out and see if they're all growing a little bit weird lately. . . ."

The helicopter descended and the earth turned to flame. My daughter ran toward me, burning, screaming. Why was it an American flag on the helicopter instead of a swastika? Was it Calley or Eichmann who was looking at me with imploring eyes begging my understanding and forgiveness?

Day after day the napalm fell from the skies. Day after day children died screaming at 1,000° Centigrade. Month after month, year after year, the fire continued to consume the world, Ped Xing's world. He sat in the lotus, his *shakti* mounted on his penis, their eyes locked, until the neurological synergy occurred: they were One. And then the Others were there, too, all the minds of space-time who turned on the neuro-atomic circuit, the beetle intellects of Betelgeuse, Nicholas and Perenella Flamel, Bruno and Elizabeth, Cagliostro, and, as the time-warp opened, galaxy after galaxy joined in, the Starmaker appeared dimly and the first jump was possible.

He was a flower on a rose bush in England and a poet was staring at him as he stared back at the poet: "The roses have the look of flowers that are looked at" emerged from that moment.

SHe was a microbe flailing tentatively in a soupy ocean.

He was a Terran archivist looking back at the decline and fall of the American Empire.

SHe was Mountbatten Babbit in Evanston, Illinois— a good one, grab quick, this was one of the murderers, hold on—

Mountbatten Babbit, Ph.D., became aware that everybody at the table was staring at him. Then he realized that he was sobbing. "Oh, God," he said, a mind at the end of its tether. "Oh, God, God, God . . ."

It was explained as a breakdown due to overwork. There was no psychiatrist; ambition forbade the risk, so a clinical psychologist of Behaviorist orientation was found, on the faculty of Northwestern University, and the visits were listed as consultation in social psychology for business management.

Mounty and the psychologist defined Ped Xing as a hallucination caused by the negative conditioning of the pacifist pickets surrounding Weishaupt Chemicals. A method of de-conditioning was worked out, using hypnosis and aversion therapy against all manifestations of the Ped Xing persona. The aversive stimulus was apomorphine, a non-addicting morphine derivative that provokes vomiting and sensations of death. At first, Ped Xing would speak directly at these moments, begging and pleading, "Don't send me back to the flames. . . ." Later, he became defiant. "We'll be back, millions of us, from all over the Third World. Living in your fat white bodies. Running your corporations and bureaucracies. All through the seventies and eighties. We'll be back." As the theory of aversion therapy predicts, Ped Xing was finally extinguished.

Safely established beyond freedom and dignity, Mounty Babbit became the ideal conditioned subject. In 1982, he resigned his position as President of Weishaupt Chemicals to become Special Scientific Advisor to the White House.

ANOTHER EIGENSTATE

That which is forbidden is not allowed.

—JOHN LILLY, *The Center of the Cyclone*

O how money makes me hum O how money makes me hum O how money makes me hum

Benny Benedict was working on his mantra, and didn't realize that he had wandered quite a bit from the Sanskrit original.

O how money makes me hum O how money makes

202

me hum O how money makes me hum the purpose of suffering is to make us ask the important questions what a guy a stage magician he said O how money makes me hum O how money makes me hum

He had reached the corner of Lexington and Twenty-third Street.

Pablo Gomez stepped out of a doorway and hit Benny from behind, hard, with a lead pipe.

Oh mommie take me home Oh mommie take me home . . . Benny exploded into the white light.

Fortunately the last remaining citizen of Manhattan with a sense of civic duty, one James Mortimer, came around the corner at just that moment. James Mortimer carried a police whistle at all times, since he knew he was living in a still-violent society. He blew several blasts, loud and shrill. Pablo Gomez fled without getting any money, and an ambulance arrived in time to rush Benny to the hospital and save his life.

THE ROOMS WERE TURNED INSIDE OUT

The division of labor between the linear left lobe of the brain (Pavlov's Dog) and the quantum right lobe (Schrödinger's Cat) is pre-scientifically anticipated in Nietzsche's dichotomy of the Apollonian-rational and Dionysian-ecstatic.

—LEARY AND WILSON, *The Game of Life*

The "nervous breakdown" (as it was called) of Hassan i Sabbah X did not attract much attention; the Cult of the Black Mother had never been as well publicized as the Nation of Islam or the Black Panthers. The New York *News-Times-Post* actually referred to

Hassan as a "well-known nightclub owner in Harlem," in their very brief story, and their reporter hadn't even investigated far enough to learn that Hassan was also the head of a cult with more members than the Missouri Synod Lutherans. But, then, the Cult of the Black Mother had never been publicity-minded; even the *Amsterdam News,* unaware of its membership, described it as "a small church."

Hassan had been delivered to Bellevue in a state of raving mania, under physical restraint by two of his former aides. The psychiatrists quickly pronounced him "paranoid schizophrenic" and prescribed the heaviest tranquilizer then available, which in fact kept him fairly drowsy even when he wasn't comatose. Nonetheless, when able to summon the energy to rise out of his lethargy and talk again, he would monotonously repeat to any other inmate or orderly who came near, "Look, I don't belong here. Something terrible has happened. I'm really the President of this fucking country . . ." and so on, with endless elaborations and details.

"A deeply defended psychosis," the psychiatrists decided, and began a course of electro-shock treatments.

Whenever the flipped-out black came out of his daze, however, he would begin the same schizzy ranting all over: "Hey, listen, I'm the President of this fucking country. . . ."

The electro-shock was stepped up. Hassan retreated into a permanent daze and ceased to annoy anybody. By this time his brain had been fried to the consistency of a White Tower scrambled egg and his impressions of the external world were mostly olfactory and aural, like those of a sub-normal toy poodle; he no longer argued about anything, since he no longer understood such abstract concepts as ego-persistence or identity. The psychiatrists were satisfied: "If you can't cure a nut," their tacit motto was, "at least you can keep him from running around the ward annoying people."

Two F.B.I. agents later discussed the matter privately.

"You think C.I.A. did it?" asked the first, Tobias Knight.

"You figure he'd been working for them?" the other, Roy Ubu, asked in return. "I always had that notion myself. But why would they fuck his head like that, when God only knows what he might spill to somebody who'd get released from the nuthouse and repeat it to a reporter? Nah, C.I.A. doesn't work that way. They'd just—" he drew a finger across his throat.

"I don't believe in coincidences," Knight said stubbornly. "Somebody got to him."

"Some*thing*," Ubu corrected with a sinister intonation. "You know as well as I do what he was. A witch."

"Voodooist," Knight corrected.

"Whatever. Everybody we ever sent in died of a heart attack, right?" Ubu looked over his shoulder. "Officially, the Bureau doesn't believe in witches. But I'll tell you what happened to Mr. Hassan i Sabbah X in *my* opinion. He called up something that he couldn't put down."

THE LOCK IS A HOLE

Everything not compulsory is forbidden.

—T. H. WHITE, *The Book of Merlin*

Dr. Francis Dashwood—neat, clean, rich and not yet forty—drove into the grounds of the Orgasm Research Foundation on Van Ness in San Francisco at precisely 8:57 in the morning. He checked his wristwatch again after he parked his sleek M.G. in the executive parking lot. It was 8:58. Excellent. A quick trot and he was at his desk before the office clock reached nine. Once again he had demonstrated the punctuality (anal-retentive personality, silly pre-scientific Freudians called it) which had contributed so much to raising him to his present high position in the medical research bureaucracy of the United States.

Frank Dashwood, M.D., L.L.D., Ph.D., at the age of only thirty-eight, headed the most heavily funded and hotly debated institution in the world: Orgasm Research, a multi-million-dollar project dedicated to filling in the psychological intangibles left out of the pioneering research of Masters and Johnson two decades earlier. Since these psychological intangibles were —as Dr. Dashwood sometimes wittily remarked—"both psychological and intangible," there was no end to the research. Meanwhile, the funding money came rolling in.

Frank was, according to a survey by a management analyst, one of the seventeen men in the United States who was totally happy with his job.

Other researchers sometimes expressed envy of this fact. "What red-blooded man," one of them had once asked with some warmth, "wouldn't be happy supervising other people's orgasms and pulling down a *swift sixty grand* a year for it?"

This was somewhat unfair to a dedicated scientist. Dr. Dashwood was truly fascinated by orgasms—as Edison was by electricity—and had an inexhaustible curiosity about every possible factor involved in every possible twitch, itch, moan, gibber, gasp, sob, shudder or howl connected with that dramatic biological tremor. Even more, however, he was mesmerized by lines, curves, averages, graphs and every aspect of mathematics that could be clearly visualized. The world, for him, was not made up of "things," crude Disneyland animations projected by our lower nervous circuits, but of energy meshes. With no knowledge of Zen Buddhism, he intuitively shared Sixth Patriarch Hui Neng's vision that "from the beginning there has never been a *thing*." Dr. Dashwood lived in a universe of transactions that could be written as equations and traced on graph paper.

Above his desk was a motto suggested ironically by a skeptical friend. Dr. Dashwood saw nothing funny about it and adopted it as his own banner:

> SCIENCE, PURE SCIENCE, AND DAMNED BE HE
> WHO FIRST CRIES "HOLD, TOO MUCH!"

As he often said in his highly paid lectures to medical societies, psychiatric conventions, Y.M.C.A.'s and P.T.A.'s, "It's just not true that 'if you've seen one orgasm, you've seen them all.' Why, Heraclitus—a great Greek philosopher who wrote over 109 fragments —once said that you can't step into the same river twice, because the water is changing and so are you. Well, you can't put the same penis into the same vagina twice, either."

Dr. Dashwood had supervised 23,017 orgasms to date, and his curiosity was still strong.

As he settled himself at his desk, he observed that Ms. Karrige, his secretary, had already poured his coffee for him. Fine: the girl (femperson, he corrected) was really getting broken to the harness. He whipped out his thermometer and measured the black liquid in the cup: 98.4 degrees. Excellent: she was learning to meet his exacting demands.

Dr. Dashwood could not abide inexactitude or slovenliness in any human activity. "A thing worth doing," he would explain to his subordinates, "is worth doing *right*." He said this often, and malicious members of the staff said it even more often, when he was out of earshot, with a tone and a facial expression that were caricatures of his own.

With a smile on his lips and a glint in his eye, Frank Dashwood buzzed Ms. Karrige. "What's first for today?" he asked cheerfully.

The Jabberwock was growing: the key was no key. . . .

FUNNY VALENTINE

Megalithic monuments were certainly not places of worship but places of refuge for people fleeing the advance of mud.

—FURBISH LOUSEWART V, *Unsafe Wherever You Go*

While Dr. Dashwood was pressing his buzzer in San Francisco, Starhawk was carefully screwing two mountain-climber's hooks into a hill across the bay in Oakland. The first rope was wrapped around his waist outside the trousers, ran through a pulley and came back to his hand. The second rope circled his chest, ran through the second pulley and was secured to a tree. He began lowering himself down through the redwoods.

At first there was no visibility at ground level, but he descended the roof of Murphy's house and a bit of yard came into view. None of the neighboring houses was visible at all.

Approaching Murphy's roof, Starhawk slowed and then stopped his descent. In mid-air, he turned, every muscle straining, and continued his descent head first, legs tightly together, the style of a professional high-diver. A small film of perspiration formed around his lips. He was totally silent.

Twice, redwood branches almost tangled his ropes. He remained totally silent while disengaging.

Finally, he gripped the roof edge with his left hand, let out more slack with his right and lowered himself until he was looking in the corner of a window upside down. It was the bedroom. Murphy wasn't there. The bed was unmade.

Starhawk raised himself, swung and descended again to inspect another window. The living room. Murphy was sitting in a red plush chair, his face expressionless. He was listening to music on the stereo. A shotgun leaned against the wall behind him.

Very slowly, Starhawk raised himself again and swung to the next window. In five minutes, totally silent, he was sure that there was nobody in any of the other rooms.

He slowly raised himself again and found a perch in a redwood that commanded a view of the front yard and doorway. He waited.

The music from the stereo drifted up to him. Peggy Lee was singing "My Funny Valentine."

PRIVILEGED PERSONS WHO POSSESSED THE KEYS

Gotta crash out . . . gotta crash out . . .

— HUMPHREY BOGART, AS ROY EARL, HAVING A NIGHTMARE IN *High Sierra* (SCRIPT BY JOHN HUSTON)

TERRAN ARCHIVES 2803:

Robert Anson Wilson was, of course, well aware of the context in which Allen Ginsberg had written, "We are all living in science fiction," in 1970; but it was not until April 1976 that Wilson began to believe that he himself was, indeed, living in science fiction. This came upon him during a week spent at the U.N. Habitat Forum in Vancouver (part of what was then called "Canada"). Wilson was acting as public relations and publicity writer for the L-5 Society, a group who believed that space industrialization was the answer to the energy problems that Habitat Forum was considering.

"I'm living in a science-fiction novel I read over twenty years ago," Wilson wrote in a letter. "It was called *The Man Who Sold the Moon* and was by Robert Anson Heinlein. The hero in the novel was a guy named Harriman who saw that the time for space migration had come. In our world, that's Gerard O'Neill, who designed the L-5 space-town. In the novel, there were a bunch of media people hired by Harriman to sell the idea. In this world, I'm one of them, one of O'Neill's press agents. We're all living out Heinlein's script."

In the following weeks, after returning to his Berkeley home, Wilson developed this idea with his characteristic monomania.

He was doing publicity for the local cryonics group, scientists who were concerned with life extension through cryogenic suspension. Was this not another S-F theme, a novel that had been written a thousand times?

Wilson was also a lecturer with the Physics Consciousness Research Group, in San Francisco, a group of physicists seeking to understand the so-called "occult" events of parapsychology through new quantum theories. This was a plot he had read in several science-fiction classics.

Even Wilson's off-again, on-again notion that he might be in touch with Higher Intelligence at Sirius via telepathy was another science-fiction script.

"I'm living in S-F," he concluded, "while all my old occult friends are still living in fantasy-fiction, and most of the population—especially East Coast intellectuals—are stuck in a very gloomy naturalistic novel out of the 1930s."

THE SQUIRREL

Anyone who paints the sky green should be sterilized at once.

—FURBISH LOUSEWART V, *Unsafe Wherever You Go*

After waiting forty-five minutes, Starhawk descended again. Murphy was no longer in the living room. The shotgun was missing also.

"The fuck?" Starhawk muttered.

He swung carefully over to the bedroom window. The shotgun rested against the wall beside the closet.

Murphy came out of the closet and picked up the shotgun again. Careful man, that Murphy; never go anywhere without your shotgun, when you're holding maybe half a million in hot snow.

Murphy looked quite happy now. He looked like the happiest man Starhawk had ever seen.

Starhawk returned to his perch in the redwood tree. Murphy had obviously taken a snort of the coke and was probably feeling like Luke Skywalker heading for the Death Star. Starhawk waited silently. It was good to know where the cocaine was.

A few minutes later a squirrel came along an overhead branch and almost walked over Starhawk's rope.

211

He stopped, frozen: unable to believe that a human being was way up here in the tree.

Starhawk and the squirrel stared at each other, both immobile. Then the squirrel ran.

Starhawk smiled. He went on waiting, quietly.

FIRST MAMMAL-ROBOT DYAD

> Human beings (including scientists) are larval robots programmed by: (1) genetic wiring, (2) neural imprints, (3) social conditioning.
>
> —LEARY AND WILSON, *The Game of Life*

Dr. Dashwood buzzed Ms. Karrige. "What's first for today?" he asked cheerfully, eager to plunge directly back into the thick of things, as was typical of him on Monday mornings.

"The uh colored gentleman from New York," came the tinny voice on the intercom.

"Send him right in!" Frank said eagerly.

Robert Pearson was dressed in his "dealing with the straight establishment" clothes, which meant that he looked like the black equivalent of a Mafia don moving in on a legit corporation. You had to look twice to realize that he was too resplendent to appear really conservative.

"You really have the um merchandise?" Dr. Dashwood asked.

"I wouldn't waste your time otherwise," Pearson said carefully.

"And it's not flaccid? I can get them in flaccid state from Johns Hopkins' sex-change department, by the gross. This must be totally erect, and I can't imagine how you managed that. . . ."

Pearson removed a package from his briefcase. "See for yourself," he said.

Dr. Dashwood spent several minutes examining the ghoulish trophy. Pearson sat back and lit up a black Sherman cigarette. He was wondering just how surprised Dashwood would be if he mentioned his own long-ago Ph.D. or his career as lead guitarist with Clark Kent and his Supermen. He was just another black gangster as far as Dashwood knew or cared.

"It's real," Dr. Dashwood said finally. "A beautiful specimen," he added with total scientific detachment. Then he looked directly at Pearson with unblinking curiosity. "You either have a friend with a truly desperate need for money, or an enemy who now knows what it means to rouse your anger," he commented mildly.

The haggling over money began at that point. Pearson left on the noon flight to New York, bearing $10,000 which later found its way to Afghanistan and came back in the form of bricks of pure hashish.

Dr. Dashwood, meanwhile, was in m.o.q.—the multiple-orgasm-quotient laboratory—making certain technical adjustments on the A.C.E. equipment. ACE—for *a*rtificial *c*oital *e*quipment—had been devised by the Masters-Johnson team and allowed a plastic imitation penis, containing micro-photographic devices, to stimulate the inside of a vagina while obtaining clear photographic evidence of the actual physiological changes occurring therein. Orgasm Research had used the same model in their investigation of m.o.q.—the endeavor to find out precisely how many orgasms a multiply orgasmic woman could actually have without untoward side-effects. It was Dashwood's conviction that, the physiological data being already determined, a real penis was more practical now; but a year-long search

213

for the once-famous Cuban Superman had failed to locate that stalwart stud. ("Those bloody puritanical commies have probably *rehabilitated* him into *more socially useful work,*" Dashwood concluded mournfully.)

Now at last with the relic of Wildeblood's quantum jump across the gender gap attached to ACE, Dashwood had the ideal scientific instrument to measure m.o.q.

A subject had been obtained via ads placed in underground newspapers throughout the state of California. ("What do Easterners know about fancy fucking?" Dashwood asked, ruling out everybody on the other side of the Rockies. All that part of the country, he firmly believed, was a puritan's heaven and a hedonist's hell.) The ad said bluntly:

SEXPOT WANTED

We are not making porny movies. We are not kinks or creeps. This is a serious scientific project. If you think you qualify, and would like to earn $1,000, write Box 56, San Francisco, in strict confidence.

Weeding out unlikely prospects had been time-consuming and somewhat wearying, although a few had set some interesting records with the old plastic ACE apparatus. The subject selected to have the trial run on the new reincarnated ACE was a Ms. Rhoda Chief, vocalist with a rock group called the Civic Monster. Known to critics as the best heavy rock singer since Janis Joplin, Rhoda was originally renowned back in the '60s for her own curious mutation of old-fashioned Dixieland "scat-singing"; what few realized was that her riffs were not mere Jabberwocky but actually fragments of the Enochian Keys used by Dr. John Dee, Mr. Aleister Crowley and other magicians. People who

214

came out of Civic Monster concerts seeing auras, hearing strange voices, catching odd fugitive glimpses into fairyland and Oz, or seeing the djinns gathered about the throne of Allah, attributed this to the heavy marijuana fumes always circulating in the air at rock concerts. What Rhoda herself saw during those moments was a secret between herself and her occasional lover in that decade, the controversial stage magician Cagliostro the Great.

Rhoda had gained another reputation in the 1970s: "That chick gives head better than anybody in show biz," it was often said in High society. But this rumor had not reached the aseptic scientific world in which Dr. Dashwood moved.

Twirling his dapper bow tie debonairly, Francis Dashwood, physician and scientist, strode down the hall to Laboratory Three.

Rhoda Chief, already nude but with a single sheet demurely spread over her full and obviously still-glorious body, smiled brightly as she saw the doctor.

"Where's ACE?" she asked cheerfully.

"We've been making some improvements," Dashwood said with professional unction. "You might find today's research a distinct improvement over the test runs last week."

The sheet slipped a bit, revealing several inches of round, tense breast. "You mean a bigger-size gizmo on it? I already been through the Errol Flynn, the Primo Carnera and the King Kong." These were technical slang for various models of robot dildo.

What a fantastic piece of hot lustful woman she was, Frank thought irrelevantly. Despite his scientific attitude, he felt himself secretly longing for the moments ahead when the sheet would finally be swept aside to reveal that incredible body which had appeared in his dreams twice over the weekend. With an effort, he resumed his professional manner.

"No," he said quietly. "No larger sizes. The King Kong is the biggest we have in stock. Today is something entirely new. We are using the real thing—but still attached to the ACE machine, so you can control it as always, calibrating speed and depth of thrust and so forth to your own special requirements. Ah, here it comes now."

A technician wheeled in the new improved ACE apparatus.

Rhoda sat up, staring in frank astonishment—and the sheet slipped another inch, revealing that gorgeous right nipple, like a chocolate gumdrop, Frank thought. Not for the first time, he cursed the professional ethics which would ruin his career if he ever touched one of his experimental subjects.

The technician, who always insisted on being called "Jonesy" or "R.N"—his real name was Richard Nixon Jones, but he kept that a careful secret, and never sent Mother's Day cards—wheeled the ACE over to the bed and affixed it at the proper angle. It looked like a science-fiction version of the Great God Baphomet. The pink phallus seemed extra-erotic amid the sculpted white plastic of the machine, dangling a few inches above the Venusian bush slightly visible through the thin white sheet. "All set," Jonesy said stiffly, and retreated to the door, He had never quite gotten over his initial embarrassment at working for Orgasm Research.

Rhoda Chief reached out a tentative hand and felt Ulysses hovering above her midsection. There was a pause. Dashwood watched her hand moving along the pink shaft. In imagination, he vividly felt the same hand groping within his trousers. I am a professional, he reminded himself sternly.

"Well," he said, "anytime you're ready."

"It's for science," Rhoda said hoarsely.

"That's right. For science."

"Take the sheet off me," she whispered.

"I can't do that," Frank said, straining to avoid a break in his voice, his eyes on the crotch beneath the sheets.

"Oh, yes," she said. "I forgot."

There was another pause.

"For science," he said gently.

"For science," she agreed. Slowly, she pushed down the sheet, revealing those globes that had twice tormented his sleep. She must be at least a forty-two, he thought, and who ever saw such enormous nipples before? Then, with more determination, she pushed the rest of the sheet off the bed in one quick motion. She was as sweet a sight as dawn itself.

Dr. Dashwood thought fleetingly of how Fourier series combine to produce, on occasion, perfect sine waves, valley and crest, valley and crest, in a harmony that was like the signature of intelligence and grace. A contemporary pop novelist might say, "She had a figure that would make the Pope kick a hole in a stained-glass window." Rhoda Chief, one of the trillions of multi-cellular bio-esthetic models worked out by the DNA during its three-and-a-half-billion-years' design-work on this planet, was only five-feet-two inches tall, but in that space were the breasts of Babylonian goddesses, the trim waist of a Petty Girl, the pubic bush that Titian strove so hard to paint, the legs of Venus Kallipygios. Dr. Dashwood, who sought always to uncover *significant form* (and did not know that Clive Bell had once defined art in those two words), responded both cortically and phallically. Were it not for his scientific discipline, he would have knelt in worship, to present her the Pentecostal Gift of Tongues.

"Um you can use it on the clitoris first, gently, to lubricate yourself," he said, feeling like a ninny.

"I'm lubricated already," Rhoda said in a strangled voice and moved the handle which spun the wheel which thrust Ulysses into the house where love lived.

Her eyes, Frank noted, were still open for a second, but completely out of focus. Then she closed them and began pulling the handle rhythmically.

Frank began jotting rapidly. "Nipples fully erect at twenty-three seconds. Sex-flush on breasts and neck at thirty seconds. Subject says 'Jesus' quite clearly at thirty-six seconds . . ."

Ulysses, as the scientist was writing, was creating a neurological uproar in Ms. Rhoda Chief, the mammalian study-unit in the first robot-mammal sexual dyad. As the rejected stone in Wildeblood's cathedral became the cornerstone in Rhoda's consciousness, she felt as if she were floating and allowed her left hand to run down her body, over her breasts, down over her belly into the garden of Nuit. Rhythmically, in time with the hot, fast thrusting motion of the shaft of Priapus, she rubbed her bush, while the other hand slowly increased the thrusting motion. In her mind's eye, she was simultaneously enjoying a second penis, in her mouth. Not all witches are cocksuckers, but all cocksuckers are witches (whether they know it or not); Rhoda knew it. Her reputation for "eating Peter like no chick since Cleopatra" was not unconnected with the versatility of her singing and other personality traits. Then ACE was talking, in the gentle, slightly Gay tones of HAL, the whacked-out computer in *2001:* "To the center of the galaxy," he was saying. "This is the center of space-time, and it is also the center of your womb, darling Rhoda." His soft purr went on, as he thrust deeper into her. "It is way, way out and it is also way, way in. You can only enter this mystery on vibes of sheer ecstasy, because all matter at a lower vibratory rate gets destroyed in the Black Hole. So, in order to navigate this dangerous crossing, I must fuck you even more deeply, my darling."

"Oh, do it, ACE, do it to me good," she murmured. "I want to see the center of the galaxy."

"There, there," he purred, "you'll see the center of the galaxy when your pretty little cunt gets hot enough."

"Take me," she moaned, "take me to the center of space-time." And deep, deep into the cosmic vaginal barrel and deep, deep into the spiral of her moist galaxy, ACE piloted her. Slow permutations, like the growth of crystals, her sensations were hardly contaminated any longer by thought or vision; deep, deep they went, down into a cavern of strange floral energies, each petal shape tingling with the languid joy-dance in the petals of her own warm pussy (happiness is a warm pussy, she remembered), the shaft of the actual ACE machine digging deeper and deeper into the starry dynamo. "Oh, ACE, oh, ACE, you fuck so divinely," she gasped.

"It's the only way to travel," he crooned electronically.

"Oh, keep fucking me. Keep fucking me. Please, please . . . fuck the universe, fuck every atom, turn the cosmic key in the galactic Black Hole, fuck and fuck and fuck, my God, my Baphomet, fuck forever, fuck the flowers and the starlight and thunder and rain. Fuck Heaven and Hell, too."

Dr. Dashwood's face had a curious, ashy-white color. He wanted to leap upon the bed, throw the ACE machine to the floor and take her. His erection was pulsating and his vision was red with pain and need. "Fuck the A.M.A.," he muttered thickly, lurching forward.

Just then the phone rang.

SURPRISE PARTY

That which is allowed exists.

—JOHN LILLY, *The Center of the Cyclone*

A car stopped about a hundred yards down the road from Murphy's house. Starhawk quickly began untying his ropes, listening intently. In a few moments he heard them: two or three men coming through the woods. They were very silent for white men.

Starhawk, free of the ropes, began to move across the trees. The men stopped. Starhawk waited. They still didn't stir. Starhawk moved again, without a sound. The men were still unmoving. He closed in on them, remaining always about thirty feet above the ground, until he found them.

Three men. Sitting quietly. Two of them smoking. Waiting.

Starhawk moved back toward the house, always testing each branch carefully before trusting it.

Two mourning doves began to sing a sad little duet.

Starhawk waited, ten feet above the roof, hidden in the redwood. The three men in the woods waited.

Inside the house, the phone rang. The men in the woods, who couldn't possibly have heard it, began moving again.

Starhawk smiled for the second time that day, and glanced at his watch. It was exactly half past ten. Murphy, on the phone, was probably insisting on a meet in downtown Oakland, some congested street corner he had already picked, where a double-cross would be too risky for all parties. Careful man, that Murph. He'd come out the door, with the coke under his arm,

220

thinking how careful he was, and the surprise party would be waiting in the bushes with their guns.

Starhawk moved quickly to a new perch. Carefully, he pulled up his trouser leg, tore the adhesive tape and took a pistol from his calf. He was not smiling now.

CHEESE

The caterpillar cannot understand the butterfly.

—LEARY AND WILSON, *Neuropolitics*

Robert Pearson said "Shee-it" in a tone of profound skepticism.

He was watching the TV hearings on the nomination of Rockwell Morgan Squeeze for Vice-President. Squeeze was an oil millionaire famous for such monumental parsimonies as installing pay phones in his mansion so guests couldn't run up his phone bill and bringing his lunch to the office in a paper bag for forty years. He was being quizzed about his generous contributions to seven out of ten of the senators on the committee investigating him.

"Now, I resent that," Rockwell was saying. "That's a very nasty word, Senator. 'Bribe,' indeed!"

"Well, just what *would* you call it?" asked the senator—one of the three who hadn't received Rockwell's largesse.

"I regard it this way," Mr. Squeeze said unctuously. "If I had a lot of cheese, and I looked around and saw a lot of mice without any cheese of their own, well, it would be the normal, generous thing. . . ."

"Now, wait a minute, I smell a rat," the senator interrupted.

"Shee-it," Pearson said again. The door buzzer was humming.

When Pearson opened the door he was greeted by a whiff of violets, even before he saw the man pointing the water pistol at him.

And when he awoke (a day later, and with Rockwell Squeeze approved by the committee with a vote that stood—coincidentally, no doubt—at 7 to 3), he was in a basement surrounded by men with canvas bags over their heads. And his genitals were wired up to some electrical apparatus.

"Shee-it," he said again, and closed his eyes, concentrating furiously on the formulas Hassan i Sabbah X had told him.

The men from Naval Intelligence began pouring electricity into Pearson's penis and trying to extract information from his mouth (two procedures that usually worked well together). It was quite irritating when they were unable to learn anything about George Washington Bridge's link with the Cult of the Black Mother, and perplexing when Pearson began to insist that he was Rockwell M. Squeeze, Vice-President of the United States. It was revolting when they finally realized that he wasn't play-acting and really believed he *was* Rockwell M. Squeeze. By then his whang was charred to a gruesome extent and his obvious insanity was hopeless. They smothered him with a pillow and left.

They were all very nice men when their duty did not call upon them to perform such regrettable tasks.

A CARNIVAL OF LOONIES

I am not what I am.

—IAGO, in BACON's *Othello*

The F.B.I. finally found G.W.C. Bridge living in a flop-house in Miami's ghetto. Having learned something from Naval Intelligence's bungling in the cases of Hassan i Sabbah X and Robert Pearson, they moved in with great delicacy; a black agent was employed to form a friendship with him, over a period of a month.

"Weird cat," the agent reported after a week. "Seems to be hiding something *all* the time. . . ."

"Can't make him at all," he reported the second week. "If I didn't know better, I'd say he was a white reporter in blackface, trying to find out what it's like to be black. . . ."

In fact, Bridge seemed more than a little bit psychotic in a methodical sort of way. He read no less than six newspapers a day and clipped numerous stories from them. The agent eventually had a chance to investigate these files while Bridge was visiting a patient in a nearby madhouse, and they were rather oblique. They all concerned Very Important Persons in government and industry, but that was about all they had in common. Bridge seemed to have a minute curiosity about the men who rule America; that was all that was evident. The agent could make nothing at all of the crazy notes scribbled on the margins of these news stories: "Possible," "Probable," "Still himself," "Definitely occupied". . .

The mystery grew worse when the agent realized that Bridge spent a lot of time visiting madhouses and psychiatric wards. "Sure knows a lot of crazy people," he reported the third week. "A hell of a lot of crazy people," he amended at the end of the month.

Another team of agents began revisiting the nuthouses, and it was soon realized that the patients Bridge visited had a few things in common, *viz.*, none was white, but not all were black (some were Oriental, Indian or Chicano); all, without exception, were diagnosed as paranoid schizophrenic with delusions of grandeur; all were listed as *chronic* rather than *acute* psychotics; all claimed to be somebody else rather than who they actually were—one said he was Secretary of Commerce, one that he was Chairman of the Board of Morgan Guaranty Trust, one that he was Chief Engineer at Cape Kennedy, etc.

The agents remembered their experience with Robert Pearson, former aide to Hassan i Sabbah X, and jumped to a conclusion. "That crazy church drove them all nuts and made them think they were white people." Alas, a little checking refuted this easy assumption. Most of the loonies Bridge had visited had no previous connection with the Cult of the Black Mother at all. . . .

Things were coming to a head.

A SPECIAL NUT

Rage, rage against the dying of the light.

—DYLAN THOMAS

There was also a guy who claimed to be Woodrow Wilson in a nuthouse in Napa, northern California, and oddly enough he was white and looked old enough to be Woodrow Wilson. In fact, his name really was

Wilson and he was an unsuccessful writer. He had two personalities. One claimed to be the famous Woodrow and was quite pompous and a bit of a bore. The other claimed to be a sane man *imitating* a lunatic.

"You see," he would explain to visiting clinical psychologists [who had read about him in *Clinical Psychology* and were interested in further acquaintanceship with such an odd specimen], "it is actually much safer in here. There are more violent lunatics loose on the outside than there are here on the inside.

"It's a jungle out there," he would say bitterly, with typical psychotic overreaction. "One rape every eight minutes. One assault every fourteen minutes. One murder every twenty minutes. Those bastards are armed and dangerous, out there.

"In here, it's different, more peaceful. The violent cases are much less common, and the orderlies know them all and keep an eye on them. You people from that much bigger madhouse called Unistat can't begin to realize the peace I have found here, the tranquility. I can go to sleep at night without worrying that some junkie is going to break in to steal the stereo and bash my skull in if I wake up and frighten him. I can walk down any hall at three in the morning without being mugged. Can you say that about any street in your cities out there? None of the violent cases in here have guns or atom bombs or napalm. Gentlemen, to you this is just an insane asylum. I say that it is, by comparison with the outside, a sane asylum."

This odd nut had many colorful and original symptoms. Whenever little girls were mentioned, he would immediately say, angrily, "Be gentle with them. They are very fragile jewels." He would weep in anguish at the sight of a BankAmericard stamping machine. In his Woodrow Wilson persona, he often claimed also to be the Secretary General of the United Nations and would issue manifestos ordering all peoples of the world to lay down their weapons and begin practicing the Corporal Works of Mercy.

He believed he had written a great book once and that Dell, after holding it five years, never published it.

THREE MINUTES, FORTY SECONDS

That which exists is allowed.

—JOHN LILLY, *The Center of the Cyclone*

When Murphy came out the front door, Ed Goldfarb, in the bushes, shot him twice with Mendoza's police special.

Murphy, thrown back against the door, was reaching into his shoulder holster, his mouth open, still alive.

The two shots hung in the empty mountain air, echoing.

Tomas Esposito fired at Murphy and missed as Murphy's hand slowly and steadily came up, firing at Goldfarb.

Goldfarb fell back, hit.

The echoes still rolled across the hills.

"Mama, Mama," Goldfarb said, rolling around, holding his stomach. He was weeping.

The third man, Juan Ybarra, ran from the bushes to Murphy.

Murphy was trying to raise the gun again. He was looking at Ybarra and trying to point the gun. His eyes were totally mad and would not focus anymore.

Esposito was trying to shoot at Murphy again, with Ybarra in the way. He had an erection and his hands shook.

Goldfarb continued to weep.

The shots were still echoing.

Birds were rising from the trees, flapping their wings noisily, twittering with anxiety. A crow cawed angrily.

Murphy's gun-hand dropped. His mad eyes went empty.

"Mama!" Goldfarb screamed. "I'm sorry!"

Esposito and Ybarra ran lithely down the hill.

"Mama," Goldfarb wept. "Not me. Please. I'm sorry."

The birds swept down the hill, flapping.

A black Mustang came up the hill. Esposito and Ybarra leaped out, ran around to the back, and opened the trunk compartment.

"Not me, please," Goldfarb was protesting.

Esposito and Ybarra lifted Detective Mendoza, gagged with adhesive tape, out of the trunk and carried him onto the lawn. He was dazed but his eyes were aware and frightened.

Esposito ran over to Murphy and took his gun. Standing there, he fired twice into Mendoza's head. He put the gun back in Murphy's hand.

Ybarra tore the adhesive tape off Mendoza's mouth. It came away bloodstained.

Goldfarb stopped crying and was still.

Ybarra retched, almost puked, caught himself. He stood white-faced, breathing hard.

Esposito picked up Murphy's package, a brown paper bag. He opened it, found a box within, raised the lid. He inserted a finger and tasted.

"The Jew," he said.

Ybarra looked at him, shaking.

"Get on the stick," Esposito said. "We can't leave the Jew; he doesn't fit."

Ybarra stood looking at him. "Come out of it," Esposito said. "Help me with the Jew."

They carried Goldfarb into the back of the car.

They drove off.

Starhawk landed lightly on the lawn, running as he alighted. He ran into the house and to the bedroom. He found what he expected in the closet, another box, and tasted it. He ran softly, on the balls of his feet, back outside. He leaped, caught the roof and pulled himself upward. He disappeared into the trees.

The two dead men sprawled on the lawn.

Birds began to return.

Elapsed time since Murphy had come out the door was three minutes and forty seconds.

THE SEA! THE SEA!

Rolypolyboys tell lasses.

—SIMON MOON,
"HAWKFULLEST CONVENTIONS EVER"

The loudroaring sea was calling. The moon was full, the Gentry were active, the howl of the wind was as mournful as a 1950s poem. Markoff Chaney, unable to sleep, sat up in his Y.M.C.A. bed and hatched mischief.

Through leaflets nailed on walls around Orange County, he had managed to create a Committee to Nuke the Whales, something that appealed to a lot of rich-wingers purely and simply on the grounds that it would make the eco-nuts and liberals scream. The Committee was an outstanding success; after only a year it had forty-two members. This was enough, together with such an outrageous cause, to get maximum media attention—Chaney was aware that anything, however small, can get the eye of the media if it's *repulsive* enough—and the eco-nuts and liberals *were* screaming.

Good; but now for something equally abominable on the other side.

Chaney contemplated the Radical Lesbians wistfully. He felt like Voltaire contemplating God; if the Radical Lesbians hadn't existed, he would have had to invent them. But what could he offer along those lines to balance the Committee to Nuke the Whales? The Child Molesters' Liberation Front? That couldn't begin to compete with "Figs" Newton's Necrophile Liberation Front. The Council of Armed Cocaine Abusers? Nobody would believe it. . . .

The midget suddenly remembered the Council of Armed Rabbis he had used in his letter to Dr. Frank Dashwood of Orgasm Research. He had meant to follow up on that. Gaining access to heavily guarded nuclear plants to tamper with the coolant systems had kept him so busy lately that he had almost forgotten the damnable Dashwood and his shitheel statistics.

The midget abominated above all things the three concepts of the "average" (a damned mathematical fiction), the "above average" (a mental construct of no objective validity aside from purely mathematical formalism) and, above all, the idiotic and carelessly used idea of the "below average" (a semantically meaningless null-class and a fucking sizeist insult, as well). And Dr. Frank Pig Dog Swine Dashwood, damn his eyes, was trying to drag these statistical fictions, these formal mathematical abstractions, to bear even up so intimate a thing as a blow-job. Seventeen Spelvins of Tenderness, indeed! This was the mind of the enemy at its most pestilential.

Chaney was awake most of the night planning a campaign to bring quantum wobble into Dashwood's charts and graphs.

When he finally slept, his tiny body curled into the orgonomic spiral and he looked as innocent as a schoolboy.

He awoke in the morning full of piss and vinegar.

The sea! The sea! Waving their long green hair, the sea-hags were calling him. Finding a dark-lit bar, he ducked into the phone booth, attached his Blue Box equipment and soon had a Washington operator convinced he was a White House official on important business.

"This is a call from the White House," the operator told the secretary at Orgasm Research. "The President is waiting on another line. He wishes to talk to Dr. Dashwood at once."

"I—I'll put you through at once," said Ms. Karrige, quite awed and flustered. The midget listened in glee as the phone rang.

"F—F—Frank Dashwood," came the doctor's voice, rather breathlessly.

"This is Ezra Pound of the Fair Play for Bad Ass Committee," the midget said, shifting his story now that he had the victim on the line. "Your name has been given to us as a leader of the scientific community, and, quite frankly, we are looking for all the distinguished support we can get for our next full-page ad in the Sunday *News-Times-Post*. I assume you're aware of the plight of Bad Ass," he said significantly, bluffing, of course (but with some assurance, since every place in the world had some plight or other by 1984).

"Oh, yes, of course," Dr. Dashwood said evasively. "Why don't you send me your literature and I'll give it a careful reading."

"Doctor," the midget said sternly, "if you were living in Bad Ass, wouldn't you want action now?"

"Well, undoubtedly, but if you'll just send me your literature . . ."

("Oh, Ace, darling, *darling*," a female voice near the phone said distinctly.)

There was a startled pause; the midget deliberately let it drag out until the doctor spoke again.

"Er, mark the envelope to my personal attention. You can be sure that the Bad Ass crisis has been very much on my mind. Terrible, simply terrible. But ah now I must be back to my business—"

("Fuck my cunt, Ace! Oh, fuck my cunt!")

"Doctor," the midget said sternly, "are you *fornicating* while you're talking to me? Is that your answer, sir, to the desperate people of Bad Ass?"

("Now, now!!!" the voice screeched. "Oh Jesus Jesus Jesus NOW!!!!!!!!")

Beautiful, the midget thought; I couldn't have called at a better time. "Doctor Dashwood," he said stiffly, "I don't think you are really the sort who will add *stature* to the Fair Play for Bad Ass Committee." He hung up jarringly.

Beautiful. Absolutely beautiful.

He set off for the post office and Stage Two of his campaign, smiling all the way—except once when he encountered one of the giant women, walking her enormous Saint Bernard, and he prudently crossed the street.

DIFFERENT INTERPRETATIONS

Walker finds that every process in the universe, down to the tiniest particle, must be conscious. Indeed, if non-locality is to be accepted, things cannot be otherwise. Every point in every reality must be conscious, though each one projects (or "perceives") a different reality. . . .

—BEYNAM, *Future Science*

TERRAN ARCHIVES 2803:

Scholars have long debated about the quotations attributed to Furbish Lousewart V in *The Universe Next Door,* some holding that Wilson invented them himself and others trying to trace them to some prominent anti-technology fanatic whom Wilson was caricaturing. This mystery, at least, has finally been solved. The Lousewart quotations are all taken from an obscure landscape painter who had flourished in Bavaria in Wilson's youth. Why Wilson picked this sentimental and banal artist, Adolf Hitler, as the model for Furbish Lousewart remains unclear. One school of occult and overly-imaginative students of the ancient Bard holds that, in fact, Robert Anson Wilson had access to knowledge about numerous parallel universes, in one of which the forgotten painter went into politics, like Lousewart, with equally disastrous results. No sober scholar, of course, accepts this preposterous hypothesis.

It is noteworthy, however, that the Physics/Consciousness Research Group, with which Wilson was associated, according to the sole surviving reference to him (in the San Francisco *Chronicle*), did contain several physicists who accepted *both* Walker's theory of consciousness as the hidden variable in the collapse of the state vector *and* Wheeler's multiple-universe solution to the same problem. If Wilson was not merely engaging in his favorite sport of playing jokes on the naïve reader, *The Universe Next Door* does strongly suggest that he believed each quantum jump in consciousness produced a separate and real new universe. If that theory were in any sense true, then the other universes in this saga are just as "real" as the universe in which we actually live—and there may even be other commentators in those universes writing different interpretations of this most enigmatic novel.

THE DREADED NEUROLOGICAL ARMY

Being keys themselves, their keylessness does not matter.

       —RICHARD ELLMAN, *Ulysses on the Liffey*

On March 2, 1984, Simon Moon found a peculiarity while scanning the Beast's memory banks for the Chicago police.

There seemed to be two possible totals for the number of police officers in Chicago.

Simon was intrigued. He began searching all the Chicago police records. What he found was so interesting that he mentioned it to Clem Cotex, whom he happened to be meeting for lunch that day.

Cotex was not concerned with things as mundane as police records, so it took a while before he heard what Simon was saying.

"Hold it," Clem said when it finally registered. "Did you say *198?*"

"Yes, exactly," Simon said. "There are pay vouchers for 198 officers less than there are uniforms for. In other words, there are 198 cops in Chicago who aren't being paid. Weird, huh?"

"One hundred ninety-eight," Cotex repeated, eyes wide. "The exact number . . . Were they all over the department, these extras, or were they clustered?"

"That's even stranger," Simon said. "They're all in the Red Squad. . . ."

That same day, Markoff Chaney was hiding in a coffee urn at Orgasm Research, hatching further mischief.

The clock struck midnight; the cleaning women left; and out crept Chaney with an evil grin.

Alas, he was not the only intruder that night, for as he padded lightly down the hall he suddenly heard a hoarse voice in one of the laboratories.

"Better than human, are you, you @*)@'&¢ing #$%&'#er? Better than human, my %$#&! Take this, you $%#)*$#-eating #$%%$*er!"

The voice was near inarticulate with rage, but it was clearly that of a jealous male, as any ethologist would easily recognize. Markoff slowly opened the door and peeked around the corner.

There in the dim light, fully dressed and in his wrong mind, stood the idol of millions, the world's leading rock guitarist, Knorton ("Grassy") Knoll, feverishly working with a monkey wrench upon an object the likes of which Markoff Chaney had never seen—a Giacometti robot with a gigantic human phallus.

"I'll take you apart, you $%$#," the demented rock musician was muttering. "I'll tear your $%$@¢ out by its roots, I will." And he continued his assault, gargling and panting like one obsessed—which he was. "Man against machine," he gasped. "First they out-think us, now they out-fuck us. It's time for all-out war, by $%*@$. . . ."

Markoff watched, silent as a cat, until the hebephrenic cuckold was finished with his foul work, and the machine stood, a heap of scrap metal, with the phallus removed. Then, after the musician slouched off into the night, the midget crept into the room and carefully wrote on the wall in stark purple crayon:

THE PIGEONS IN B. F. SKINNER'S
LABORATORIES ARE POLITICAL PRISONERS.

EZRA POUND, FOR
THE DREADED NEUROLOGICAL ARMY (DNA)

Spur-of-the-moment inspiration was his specialty.

"In the typical Beethoven *scherzo*," Justin Case explains with precise emphasis, "the elements are so mingled that, even though some may be the musical equivalent of cries of pain or grief, the total construction is both grotesque and gay."

Like most rock musicians, "Grassy" Knoll was a Second Circuit neuro-genetic type, quite incapable of the Machiavellian mentations of Third Circuit schemers like Markoff Chaney. When "Grassy" carried Ulysses away from Orgasm Research, he planned only on throwing it in the first garbage can he passed. On the spur of the moment, he threw it in an alley instead.

There it was found by a cat named Acapulco Gold—an ugly yellow Tom belonging to San Francisco's best-known gossip columnist. The cat, with typical perversity, dragged it home.

The columnist was at work on a book of reminiscences (*The Roving I,* he planned to call it) when his wife staggered in from the kitchen, white-faced but with a devilish grin. "Honey," she said coaxingly, "come see what the cat dragged in. . . ."

Now, it so happened that the columnist was (like most writers in capitalist society) abominably underpaid, and, like Hassan i Sabbah X, he knew a one-of-a-kind item when he saw it. "This," he pronounced, "will bring a pretty penny, when I find the right buyer."

He found the right buyer at police court only two nights later, when a tip informed him that the notorious Eva Gebloomencraft had been arrested again, this time for putting laughing gas in the air-conditioning system at a benefit concert for the Epileptic Liberation Front.

The infamous Eva did not get called right away; the columnist had to sit through a dreary hearing on a black man who had caused a riot in a bar, throwing sixty fits and screaming that only a few minutes ago he had been a white atomic scientist at Los Alamos. When this obvious lunatic was finally removed from the court in a straitjacket (still shouting atomic secrets which he had evidently learned somewhere in the early stages of his delusion), Eva's case was called.

Ms. Gebloomencraft, the only daughter of the most defiant and unrepentant Nuremburg war criminal, had been the holy terror of the international jet set ever since she reached puberty in the 1960s. Imagine the mind of Markoff Chaney in the body of Raquel Welch; good, you've got dear Eva. It was she who had spiked the punch with aphrodisiac PCPA at the Spanish embassy in London, precipitating an orgy and several subsequent suicides among members of Opus Dei. She and she alone who smuggled Norman Mailer in drag to a top-secret strategy meeting of the Radical Lesbians. She again who hired the best free-lance electronics experts to obtain tape recordings of J. Edgar Hoover's boudoir adventures, and then sent them to Rev. Martin Luther King. (That gallant *naïf*, alas, destroyed them.)

Eva saw the possibilities of the Wildeblood relic as soon as the columnist broached the matter.

"Hot shit," she said, eyes dancing.

THE LAW OF CONTAGION

> When a pattern is set up in time by the activation of
> an archetype, however, the crucial factor does not
> seem to be an external agency of any kind but rather
> an *ordering principle* that is inherent in the fact that
> a pattern is being formed.
>
> —IRA PROGOFF, *Jung, Synchronicity and
> Human Destiny*

"This instantaneous communication between particles,"
Dr. Williams went on earnestly, "is *strictly forbidden* by
Special Relativity. Therefore, either quantum mechanics
is wrong or Special Relativity is wrong."

"Well, which one is it?" Natalie Drest was stoned,
spaced and wasted.

"That's the problem, my dear. Neither of them seems
to be wrong. Both of them work out perfectly in prac-
tice. The whole nuclear arsenal is based on *both* of
them. So is the TV set in the corner there, for that
matter."

"Well, then, the watchacallit, the goddamitexperiment
must be wrong—" Natalie really wanted more music
and less philosophy.

"*Gedankenexperiment,*" Williams corrected. "It can't
be wrong. The mathematics of it is ironclad. Every
particle in my body and yours, my dear, is communicat-
ing faster than the speed of light with every particle
of everybody else who was at Mary Wildeblood's party
tonight. Or with everybody who ever touched Marvin
Gardens' cocaine. *Faster than the speed of light,* mind."

"Cripes. That's spooky when you say it that way."

"Spooky, indeed. It is identical with what we anthropologists call the Law of Contagion, which is the um

savage superstition ha-ha that if you can get hold of the hair or fingernails of somebody you can control him at a distance."

"You mean that any particle of Marvin's cocaine that ever was in contact with any other particle of anything . . ."

BAD FOR BUSINESS

Banana Nose Maldonado ate silently. He ate three kinds of cheese and pepperoni and black olives and sliced red peppers and anchovy, for antipasto. Then he ate beef fillets in parmigiana and a side of lasagna, drinking occasionally from the Chianti glass. He did not speak until after he had finished the last sip of the wine and pushed back his plate.

"Proceed," he said.

"The food was excellent, don. As always," said Starhawk, pushing back his own plate.

Banana Nose nodded formally, smiling. "Proceed."

"You got a box of sugar today," Starhawk said. "With some cocaine on top. You went to a hell of a lot of trouble to get it. Three guys got dead."

"Imagine that," said Maldonado. "You know a great deal about my private business."

"Two of the guys were supposed to get dead," Starhawk said. "But one of them was a thick Irishman and he didn't die easy. The funny thing is, what with the excitement and all, he got shot once with the wrong gun. He was only supposed to be shot with his partner's gun. It was supposed to look like they shot each other, fighting over the coke."

"Son-of-a-bitch," Maldonado said, softly as a prayer.

238

"They tell me you're a thief. They didn't tell me you're the Invisible Man. What were you doing, riding around in one of my boys' back pockets?"

"You was to ask me," Starhawk said, "I'd guess that your boys goofed up twice. After they got excited and shot Murph with the wrong gun, they forgot something."

"Yes? Tell me."

"They forgot to leave some of the coke behind. After all, that was supposed to be what Murphy and Mendoza were fighting over. You probably told them to leave a sizable amount."

"Not a sizable amount. It doesn't take much to cause two pigs to fight and kill each other."

"The reason the cops had to be offed," Starhawk said, "is that they didn't treat you with proper respect. Trying to sell you your own merchandise, at street prices. They should have been satisfied with a commission, the way I see it. You can't afford for guys to get out of line like that, it's bad for business. And I kind of figure you also didn't like it that they were trying to cut each other out. So you decided to off both of them and just take your stuff back. The fuck, you probably got a grudge against cops going back seventy years or more."

Maldonado nodded sadly. "My mistake was I didn't imagine what a crazy son-of-a-bitch this Murphy was. He was coming to the meet with a box of shit and thought he could just laugh at me afterwards."

"Hell," Starhawk said. "You're old, right, and you own a lot of respectable businesses. He didn't think you had the stones to kill a cop anymore, is all. And he didn't know Mendoza was planning to hijack him and had already contacted your boys for a price on the coke. So he couldn't guess you'd set it up that two crooked cops shot each other."

"We are all very careful," Maldonado said, "and we

239

all make mistakes. So: you come into this as the man Mendoza hired to hijack Murphy. Let me ask you: Why do you come to me and talk of the standard commission for returning the snow? You could be on a plane right now, and sell it at street prices somewhere, and nobody the wiser. What does Maldonado have for you?"

"I bought an airplane ticket, first thing this afternoon. Then I started thinking. With Murph and Mendoza dead, I need new friends, and there just aren't that many cops I am that close to. Don, I want you to be my friend."

"The coke is worth at least three hundred fifty grand on the street. Standard commission is thirty-five grand. You are sure you will not later regret losing so much to make a new friend?"

"Don," Starhawk said, "nobody ever regrets making a new friend."

"It is agreeable to me," Maldonado said. "Will you have some more Chianti?"

"Only a little," Starhawk said. "It is bad for the reflexes."

TOKE WITHOUT HASTE

The letter was sent out May 1, 1984, to the White House and all the major media. It said:

> May God forgive us. May history judge us charitably.
> We have placed tactical nuclear bombs in over 500 locations throughout Unistat. The targets are all enemies of the people: large banks, multina-

240

tional corporations, government tax offices. We will trigger one of these bombs at noon tomorrow, somewhere in western Unistat, to demonstrate that we are not bluffing.

All the other nuclear bombs will be triggered in succession until our demands are met. If any attempt is made to apprehend and arrest us—any attempt at all—all the remaining bombs will be detonated at once.

We demand:

That President Lousewart immediately confiscate all fortunes above one million dollars. . . .

And so on. P.O.E. had come into materialization again—caused by the same historical and neurogenetic forces.

"I think it's a hoax," said President Lousewart, who was really, of course, Franklin Delano Roosevelt Stuart, a.k.a. Hassan i Sabbah X.

"Can we be *sure?*" asked Mounty Babbit, who was now nought else but a walking automaton, controlled by the quantum information system that had been a Vietnamese Buddhist.

"We can never be sure," said Vice-President Squeeze, who used to be Robert Pearson. "This is an absolute piss-cutter."

There was a depressed silence.

"How did our karma ever land us here?" asked Hassan i Sabbah X.

Even Ped Xing wasn't sure of the answer to that.

"Well," Hassan said. "Let's distribute the fucking money. This just accelerates what we had in mind all along. . . ."

"We can't do it," Pearson said. "You'd be assassinated before the day is over."

Hassan contemplated.

"We can *fucking try*," he said.

"There are many mindstates and universes," Ped Xing added serenely. "If we don't succeed here, we will continue elsewhere."

THOSE MEMOS AGAIN

J. C. to G. B.:

The trilogy is getting better—but I don't see how it begins to justify the deliberate eccentricities at the beginning. Meanwhile, another problem, although a minor one. I was looking up the phone number of a friend, and what do you think I found? There *is* a Josephine Malik in the Manhattan phone book. Funny coincidence ... but libel suits have been built on less. Wilson had better come up with another name for that character.

G. B. to J. C.:

Funny coincidence, indeed. ... The latest manuscript to arrive on my desk is by Josephine Malik. Honest to God! And, yes, she is a Women's Liberationist, but not associated with anything with a name as absurd as God's Lightning.

J. C. to G. B.:

Is it true that Wilson is an initiated witch, or is that just one of his publicity stunts? My sister tells me she was at a lecture by Josephine Malik last night, and it was at the Hotel Chelsea on Twenty-third Street. (Remember the 23 theme in *Illuminatus?*) See me for lunch tomorrow.

LOSERS IN THE SCARED RAW DOOMHAUNTS

The Copenhagen view promotes the impression that the collapse of the state vector, and even the state vector itself, is all in the mind.

—BRYCE DEWITT, *Physics Today*, SEPT. 1970

Joe Malik opens a book and falls in.

The cover slams.

He is pierced by a punctuation mark. Call his state the marked state. He reads:

Is God a "dope"? Are earthquakes, floods and famines part of His design, or is He just plain clumsy?

"You haven't had an orgasm until you've had OR-GASMOR."

A distinction is drawn:

Guilt. Money. Despair. Alien signals.

Count, if you can, the number of times Schrödinger's Cat jumps over the lazy Pavlov's Dog.

Jo escapes into another book.

A dangling "e" is left behind.

But first a word from the Bureau of Common Sense:

THIS IS HAGBARD CELINE SPEAKING. WHEN YOU REALIZE THAT YOU ARE BISEXUAL AND IMMORTAL YOU WILL BE FREE OF ALL FICTIONS. I REPEAT: YOU WILL BE FREE OF ALL FICTIONS.

qeerwtyuioplkjhggumc839,03,877777333pqpqpqy$%()3434#$
+trewwertyuiopoiuvic
ghghghghghghghghghghghghghgh
xcxcxcxc
jhjhjejejejekkkkkkkllll;;;;)&%
bbbbbbbb b&&&&&&&&&777777733333 # # # #

Joe Malik realized he had landed in one of the possible universes where form had never emerged from chaos.

He leaped to another *eigen*state.

THERE ARE NO
FNORDS
IN THE ADVERTISEMENTS

THE TRICK TOP HAT

by Robert A. Wilson

You forgot the one thing
missing from your act:
Backstage you left your trick top hat.

—*Luna Wilson*

LOCKET BOOKS
Philadelphia 1980

THE TIME MACHINE FROM RETICULI

The ironic truth is that our concept of reality is so
fragile that it collapses in a matter of days if we do
not have continual spot announcements reminding us
of who we are and that our reality is still there.

—LEARY AND WILSON, *Neuropolitics*

One of President Hubbard's first acts after assuming
power in 1981 was to abolish the F.B.I. "The American
people survived over a century without a Secret Police
agency," she said, "and they can learn to survive without it again."

Tobias Knight, after nearly fifty years in the service,
was heartbroken at what he regarded as vicious in-
gratitude. For almost half a century he had looked
over the American people, tapping their phones, opening their mail, prying into their bank accounts, pro-
tecting them from all subversive influences internal
and external—"and now," he mourned, "they turn me
out to pasture like a broken-down old war horse."

Eventually Knight pulled himself together and got a
job with the Goodman-Muldoon private detective
agency. When old Saul Goodman, president of the
agency, died of a heart attack, Barney Muldoon invited
Tobias to become his new partner. Muldoon and Knight
remained in business for nearly thirty years thereafter
—until the information explosion made all secrets impossible and rendered the profession of detective as obsolete as that of buggy-whip manufacturer. By then
rejuvenation drugs had made thousand-year life-spans
normal. Knight next became an engineer on a starship.
Two hundred years later he was reported as a governor

of one of the planets of the Zeta Reticuli system. It was Tobias Knight, in fact, who authorized the time-warp research which ultimately made Zeta Reticuli the most powerful scientific and political entity in the galaxy, since traveling widdershins in time allowed them to change the past and create any reality they wished. It had been Reticulan timedwarfs, indeed, who had contacted several Terrans in the decades 1950–1970, thereby helping to create the universe in which Hubbard became President of Unistat instead of Furbish Lousewart.

ALL HAIL DISCORDIA

Say the magic word and the duck will come down and pay you $100.

—MARX

TERRAN ARCHIVES 2803:

The Discordian Society was created in 1959 in a bowling alley in Yorba Linda, California, near the boyhood home of Richard Milhous Nixon, known as "Dangerous Dick," a celebrated football hero of the 1920s, who subsequently had a short career as a Congressman in the 1940s. The instigators of the Discordian Society were named Gregory Hill and Kerry Thornley, but they later changed their names to Malaclypse the Younger and Ho Chih Zen.

Malaclypse always claimed that the Discordian revelation was delivered to them by a miraculous talking chimpanzee. Ho Chih Zen said that that was a damned lie intended to make the movement appear supernatural and attract the gullible. Due to this dispute, Ho and Malaclypse subsequently excommunicated each other, Ho becoming the Pope of the Discordian Orthodoxy and Malaclypse the Pope of the Protestant Discordians and Lunatic Fringe.

ANOTHER EIGENSTATE

It is found, however, that any measuring instrument introduced to determine what is going on enters an undecided or "schizophrenic" state, for it, too, is a collection of probability amplitudes. For the same reason, the same thing happens with any chain of instruments brought in to monitor the first one. . . . The regression is terminated only with the introduction of an observer's consciousness.

—LAWRENCE BEYNAM, IN *Future Science*,
ED. BY WHITE AND KRIPPNER

Benny Benedict passed the corner of Lexington and Twenty-third and continued on his way home entirely unmolested. This was hardly remarkable, because in his universe the high percentage of all crime that was due to poverty had vanished after President Hubbard abolished poverty. People walked the streets of Manhattan, or even of Chicago, at three in the morning without fear. Some people didn't even bother to lock their doors anymore.

In 1984, the G.N.P. reached three hundred fifty trillion dollars and the population of Unistat (including colonists in the numerous L-5 space cities) was three hundred fifty million. Three hundred fifty million consumers who were all millionaires had a gargantuan demand (in the economic sense of ability to purchase) for new products of all sorts.

Since Earth alone could hardly provide the raw materials to feed this appetite, the space-cities were proliferating a hundred times faster than even the most enthusiastic space-nut of the 1970s had expected; cheap, non-polluting solar power was pouring back to Earth in megawatts per hour and the vast mineral wealth of Luna and the asteroid belt was arriving in megatons per day.

It was estimated that the G.N.P. would be over a quadrillion dollars within five years and each citizen's national dividend would be four million dollars per year.

All this was, ultimately, due to the shaping of American beliefs and behaviors by the timedwarfs from Zeta Reticuli circa 1950–1970. When Tobias Knight sent out the time-ship to Earth, he had drawn up a very specific program of "Close Encounters of the Third Kind." The encounters were designed to appear absurd to Establishment scientists and intelligence agents, thereby guaranteeing that they would be ignored. At the same time, the contacts were so frequent and so widespread that a vast yearning for space was planted in the collective psyche, thereby preparing the public for Hubbard's program of extraterrestrial industry, life extension and quest for Higher Intelligence.

The domesticated primates of Terra had solved the bio-survival problem; everybody had a decent living standard and longevity was taking them on the first steps toward immortality. They had solved the emotional-territorial problem; by escaping the closed system of Terra and entering the open system of Space, they had imprinted, as Blake Williams predicted, the neurological revolution first observed in the original astronauts. They had solved the semantic problem; the neurological revolution had taught them that each brain must take responsibility for the reality-tunnel it creates. They had solved the socio-sexual problem; post-domesticated life gave them all the space, all the time and all the intelligence they needed to achieve love, bliss and harmony.

They were ready for contact with Higher Intelligence.

And Higher Intelligence was ready for them, with some surprises.

ANOTHER EIGENSTATE

> The future exists first in Imagination, then in Will, then in Reality.
>
> —LYN BURWELL, 1979

Joe Malik decided he liked the new novel; Wilson was on the right track at last.

Joe settled down to enjoy living in *The Trick Top Hat*.

He crossed over and entered the form.

His adventures there were so remarkable it will take a whole book to describe them.

INTEROFFICE MEMOS

J. C. to G. B.:

See me at once. You may have missed the logical deduction at the end of Part Two, but I most certainly didn't. If *Josephine-Malik-as-author* is in our universe, then we are inside the novel, not outside it. In that case, how can we be reading the novel? Wilson is altogether too tricky to be trusted and I definitely resent being a character in his book when I thought I was just an editor reading it. I thought I was outside and really I'm inside. The worst part is that I'm not even a character but just an allegory on Bell's Theorem.

G. B. to J. C.:

Hold on, I'm way ahead of you. Since we're outside the novel in some sense (as editors judging it), then we stand as gods to the characters who are only inside it. The way I see it, the fact that we're also inside it only makes us incarnate (or imminent) gods. That seems fine with me. *Haven't you ever wanted to be a god, man?* As the Poet said, "I myself am Heaven and Hell."

GLOSSARY:

A GUIDE FOR THE PERPLEXED

BELL'S THEOREM: A mathematical demonstration by Dr. John S. Bell, which shows that if quantum mechanics is valid, any two particles once in contact will continue to influence each other, no matter how far apart they may subsequently move. This violates Special Relativity, unless the "influence" between the particles is not employing any known energy. This is the "form" in Spencer Brown's sense of *The Trick Top Hat*.

COPENHAGEN INTERPRETATION: The theory formulated by Niels Bohr, according to which the *state vector* (see below) should be regarded as a mathematical formalism. In other words—which some physicists will dispute— the equations of quantum mechanics do not describe what is happening in the sub-atomic world but what mathematical systems *we need to create* to think of that world.

EIGENSTATE: One of a finite number of states that a quantum system can be in. The Superposition Principle says that, before measurement, a system must be considered to be in all of its eigenstates; measurement selects one eigenstate.

COSMIC GLUE: A metaphor to describe the quantum interconnectedness that must exist if Bell's Theorem be valid. Coined by Dr. Nick Herbert.

EINSTEIN-ROSEN-PODOLSKY EFFECT: The quantum interconnectedness as described in a paper by Einstein, Rosen and Podolsky. The purpose of said paper was to prove that quantum mechanics cannot be valid, since it leads to such an outlandish conclusion. Since Bell's Theorem, some physicists have chosen to accept the interconnectedness, however outlandish it may seem. See QUIP.

EVERETT-WHEELER-GRAHAM MODEL: An alternative to Bell's Theorem and the Copenhagen Interpretation. According to Everett, Wheeler and Graham, everything that can happen to the state vector (see below) does happen to it. This is the Brownian "form" of *The Universe Next Door*.

FORM: In the sense of G. Spencer Brown, a mathematical or logical system necessary to systematic thought but having the inevitable consequence of imposing its own deep structures upon the experiences packaged and indexed by the form. See COPENHAGEN INTERPRETATION.

HIDDEN VARIABLE: An alternative to Bell, Copenhagen and Everett-Wheeler-Graham. As developed by Dr. David Bohm, the Hidden Variable theory assumes that quantum events are determined by a sub-quantum system acting outside or before the universe of space-time known to us. Dr. Evan Harris Walker and Dr. Nick Herbert have suggested that the Hidden Variable is consciousness; Dr. Jack Sarfatti suggests that it is *information*.

INFORMATION: A measure of the unpredictability of a message; that is, the more unpredictable a message is, the more information it contains. Since systems tend to disorder (according to the second law of thermodynamics), we can think of the degree of order in a system as the amount of information in it. Ordinarily information is transmitted as an ordering of energy (a signal), in which the energy and its ordering (the message) is transmitted from one place to another. Dr. Jack Sarfatti has suggested that the non-locality of the ERP effect and Bell's Theorem may entail the instantaneous transfer of order from one place to another *without any energy transfer*. Thus we can have both Bell's Theorem and Special Relativity, since Special Relativity only prohibits the instantaneous transfer of energy and does not say anything about instantaneous transfer of information.

NEURO-: A prefix denoting "known or mediated by the nervous system." Since all human knowledge is neurological in this sense, every science may be considered a neuro-science; e.g., we have no physics but neuro-physics, no psychology but neuro-psychology and, ultimately, no neurology but neuro-neurology. But neuro-neurology would itself be known by the nervous system, leading to neuro-neuro-neurology etc. in an infinite regress. See VON NEUMANN'S CATASTROPHE.

NON-LOCAL: Not dependent upon space and time. A non-local effect occurs instantaneously and with no attenuation due to distance. Special Relativity seems to forbid all such non-local effects, but Bell's Theorem seems to show that quantum mechanics demands them. The only solutions thus far offered to this contradiction are that non-local effects involve "consciousness" rather than energy (Walker, Herbert) or that they involve "information" rather than energy (Sarfatti.)

NON-OBJECTIVITY: One of the two alternatives to Bell's Theorem (the other being the Everett-Wheeler-Graham model). In order to avoid non-locality, some physicists such as Dr. John A. Wheeler prefer this option, which holds that the universe has no reality aside from observation. The extreme form of this view says *"Esse est percepi"* —to be is to be perceived. This is the "form" of *The Homing Pigeons.*

POTENTIA: The name given to the presumed sub-quantum world by Dr. Werner Heisenberg. Space and time do not exist in *potentia;* but all the phenomena of the space-time manifold emerge from *potentia.* Compare with HIDDEN VARIABLE and INFORMATION.

QUANTUM: An entity whose energies occur in discrete lumps; e.g., photons are the quanta of the electromagnetic field. Quanta have both wave and particle aspects, the wave aspect being the probability of detecting the particle at a certain place and time.

QUANTUM MECHANICS: The mathematical system for describing the atomic and subatomic realm. There is no dispute about how to *do* quantum mechanics, i.e., calculate the probabilities within this realm. All the controversy is about what the quantum mechanics equations imply about reality, which is known as the *interpretation* of quantum mechanics. The principle lines of interpretation are the Copenhagen Interpretation and/or Non-Objectivity and/or Bell's Theorem and/or Non-Locality and/or the Everett-Wheeler-Graham multi-worlds model.

QUIP: The quantum inseparability principle. An acronym coined by Dr. Nick Herbert to refer to the non-locality implicit in the Einstein-Rosen-Podolsky argument and explicit in Bell's Theorem.

STATE VECTOR: The mathematical expression describing one of *two or more* states that a quantum system can be in; for instance, an electron can be in either of two spin states, called "spin up" and "spin down." The amusing thing about quantum mechanics is that each state vector can be regarded as the superposition of other state vectors.

SYNCHRONICITY: A term introduced by psychologist Dr. Carl Jung and physicist Dr. Wolfgang Pauli to describe connections, or meaningful "coincidences," that do not make sense in terms of cause-and-effect. It is thought by some that such connections may indicate the Hidden Variable at work or some sort of non-local Information System.

VON NEUMANN'S CATASTROPHE: More fully, Von Neumann's catastrophe of the infinite regress. A demonstration by Dr. John Von Neumann that quantum mechanics entails an infinite regress of measurements before the quantum uncertainty can be removed. That is, any measuring device is itself a quantum system containing uncertainty; a second measuring device, used to monitor the first, contains its own quantum uncertainty; and so on, to infinity. Wigner and others have pointed out that this uncertainty is only terminated by the decision of the experimenter. Compare NEURO-.